#THROWBACK
for Murder

#THROWBACK
for
Murder

A TRENDING TOPIC MYSTERY

Sarah E. Burr

LEVEL BEST BOOKS

First published by Level Best Books 2025

This novel is entirely a work of fiction. The names, characters and incidents portrayed in it are the work of the author's imagination. Any resemblance to actual persons, living or dead, events or localities is entirely coincidental.

Author Photo Credit: Doug Walters Photography

First edition

ISBN: 978-1-68512-942-2

Cover art by Level Best Designs

This book was professionally typeset on Reedsy.
Find out more at reedsy.com

To our happily ever after, George.

Praise for the Trending Topic Mysteries

"In *#Throwback For Murder*, Sarah E. Burr crafts an elevated modern mystery. A diverse cast of characters, a sparkling setting, and a layered whodunit coalesce to give this story a timeless feel with forward-thinking flare. Has a murder mystery ever felt so on fleek? I think not!"—Leah Dobrinska, author of the Larkspur Library Mysteries

"If you are looking for a great mystery, you'll want this book to trend to the top of your to be read pile."—Carstairs Considers on *#TagMe for Murder*

"I love Coco Cline… She is like a breath of fresh air in the cozy world."—Dollycas Great Escapes

"Sleuth Coco Cline is confident, chic, and cool."—Lane Stone, author of the Buckingham Pet Palace Mysteries

"Ms. Burr has her finger right on the pulse."—J.C. Kenney, bestselling author of the Allie Cobb Mysteries and the Darcy Gaughan Mysteries

"Sarah Burr's *#FollowMe for Murder* is an accomplished, witty, and perfectly delightful mystery. The narrative unfolds with clear, precise details, and the heroine, Coco Cline, is indeed, someone we'd all want to follow."—Lori Robbins, award-winning author of the On Pointe Mysteries

Trigger Warning

The Trending Topic Mysteries are cozy in nature, yet I strive to depict the challenges we, as complex humans, face during our lifetime. While not explicitly detailed, please be aware that Coco and her friends discuss or encounter the following topics: anxiety, alcoholism, murder, domestic violence, and miscarriage.

Chapter One

SOS, Cokes. Can you come to my booth? I need backup.
Charlotte Whittaker's text popped up just as I snapped a photo of Chief Lloyd McInnis and the rest of the Central Shores Police Department taking the outdoor stage we'd cobbled together in front of their brand-new station. Despite the sweltering late June weather, my blood ran cold at the cryptic words on my phone. SOS? Backup? Charlotte wasn't one for the dramatics. She left that to me and my other bestie, Jasper Hastings. **Omw. Are you all right?** I realized my harried reply was a bit redundant. Of course, she wasn't all right.

Her response came quickly. **Please just get here ASAP.**

I scanned the crowded parking lot, trying to get my bearings. The newly paved blacktop was crawling with festivalgoers and vendor booths, a far cry from how quiet the site had been yesterday during event setup. The Central Shores Community Safety Center had officially opened its doors, and it seemed the greater Rehoboth Bay, Delaware, area was out in full force to commemorate the special occasion.

I spotted Charlotte's cheerful Brewed to Perfection logo splashed across a tent banner on the opposite side of the festival grounds, and I took off, my feet moving as quickly as the sweaty crowd would let me. Mumbling "Excuse me" and "Coming through" to the faces—familiar and new—that greeted me, I managed to close the distance between me and the café tent in less than two minutes.

The relief I felt upon seeing my friend standing behind the booth vanished when I took notice of her outward appearance. Charlotte commanded

1

attention wherever she went, with her stunningly gorgeous features and sunny personality, so it took me a beat to process the cowering woman before me. Charlotte stood in the shadows with her shoulders curled forward, her Brewed to Perfection hat covering her face. I'd never seen her looking so defeated and...scared? What sketchiness had I just barged into?

Eager to figure out this mystery, my attention slid to the unfamiliar customer leaning against the coffee counter. With a tall, tan, muscular physique, he gave Jasper a run for his money in the bodybuilder department. His back was to me, but I could see from his stance that he held his beefy arms in a pleading gesture. Whatever conversation he was having with Charlotte wasn't going well.

"Hey!" I burst onto the scene, coming around to the side of the booth Charlotte occupied. My hand went protectively to the small of her back. "How can I help?" Not yet understanding what exactly was going on, I didn't want to embarrass Charlotte in front of a customer.

From my new position, I could now see the guy's face. He had a jaw square enough for the perfect Instagram pic with photogenic features to match. Piercing blue eyes and shaggy, sandy blond hair completed his handsome appearance. On top of that, he oozed confidence, knowing just how good he looked.

Charlotte's fingers gripped my wrist. "Please just stay with me," she whispered, her entire body trembling.

Red flags sprang up, and I squeezed her hand in return before narrowing my gaze at the hulking customer who'd put her on edge.

"Come on, Char, I said I was sorry," Big, Tall, and Beefy whined in a Southern drawl as if he didn't even see me. "I'm six months sober now. I'm not that guy anymore, I swear."

Charlotte's grey gaze stared down at her workstation, where a half-made iced coffee drink stood sweating. "I'm glad you got the help you needed, Kiefer, but who you are now doesn't concern me."

Kiefer? I choked back an audible gasp as my confusion morphed into full-blown rage. What in the name of Sabrina Carpenter was Kiefer "Monster" Marsh doing here?

Charlotte shot me a sidelong glance, her eyes wide with restrained panic. I put an arm around her with a reassuring look of my own. *I got you.*

To Kiefer, I did my best to keep my cold words level. "Kindly take your leave, or I'll have to call the police. And since we're at a police department event, I'm sure it won't take them long to get here." I smiled as sweetly as I could so as not to draw attention from the happy crowd milling around the CSC grand opening.

Kiefer cocked an eyebrow at me. "Jeez, calm down, girlie. There's no need to get the cops involved."

Dude, when has telling a woman to calm down ever worked in your favor? At twenty-nine years old, I was hardly a "girlie." I was an entrepreneur and popular social media influencer with three successful murder investigations under my belt. Girlie, no. Total Girl Boss, yes.

"Oh, I think there is," I clapped back. Especially since Deacon Lait, Charlotte's boyfriend, was the team supervisor of the CSC forensic analysis department. But the less Kiefer knew about my bestie's personal life, the better.

The lethal delivery of my threat must have resonated with Kiefer as his plastered-on smile went slack. "Fine. Can't say I didn't try." He held his hands up in defeat. "I'll just take my iced latte and go." He folded his arms and turned away, casually leaning against the sturdy tent pole.

I was about to tell him he could scram without his coffee when Charlotte touched my forearm. "Of course. I'll have it ready in a minute," she mumbled softly as she put her head down to focus on the drink in front of her.

I wanted to scoop her into a hug and whisk her away from Monster Marsh's odious presence, but I respected her professionalism. Gosh, I hated, hated, *hated* what this man had done to my beloved friend years ago, and I hated what he was doing to her now. Charlotte, who usually sparkled so brightly that she lived life in a different stratosphere than us mere mortals, seemed to wilt in the shadow of this goon.

"Coco," she murmured out of the side of her mouth, "can you ask the Sweet Resolutions crew if they have any extra cocoa powder I can use? I'm almost out."

While I loathed the thought of leaving her side, our town's new chocolate shop was only two tents down from Charlotte, so I wouldn't be more than a few yards away. "Sure thing."

"Make sure it's nut-free, please," she added, her wary gaze darting to Kiefer.

Although he didn't glance her way, I saw the corner of Kiefer's lip curl with slight satisfaction. *What was* that *about?* I made a note to ask Charlotte later.

With my glare still trained on Kiefer, I side-shuffled over to where Sweet Resolutions had set up for the festival.

"Hiya, Coco!" Rosie Miller, who'd moved to Central Shores this past November, greeted me with a wide grin and tapped the brim of her University of North Carolina Tar Heels baseball cap. I rarely saw her without it—a proud token from her hometown. Her warm smile, though, quickly turned to confusion as soon as she comprehended my tense posture. "Uh oh. What's going on?" she asked as she boxed an order for a customer.

Regrettably, I was forced to take my eyes entirely off Kiefer and address the pretty thirty-something-year-old head-on. "Hey, Rosie. Big favor to ask. Do you guys have any nut-free cocoa powder Charlotte can use for an order?"

"Nut-free? You bet!" she answered brightly as she motioned to the mouth-watering spread of handmade chocolates decorating the booth. "Nut-free is the only type we stock, and we've got plenty. Not many folks are ordering Thomas's hot chocolate with the weather being what it is." She dusted off her latex-gloved hands on her apron, then reached for a container sitting to the side.

"It's an affront, I tell you." The man himself appeared from behind Rosie with a ball of molding chocolate in his hands. German-born Thomas Neumann seemed to be gearing up for a chocolate-making demonstration.

His husband and Sweet Resolutions co-owner, Tom Kingsley, chuckled as he held out a sample tray for passersby at the other end of the booth. Yes, you read that right—Tom and Thomas. "They don't know what they're missing," the forty-something trained chocolatier said in a sing-song voice.

At the mention of the deliciously luscious and silky treat I'd consumed more than my fair share of in recent months, I smiled. "Agreed. Their loss." I gratefully accepted the plastic shaker Rosie handed me. "Sorry to dash, but Char is dealing with a rude customer at the moment." I gave a covert nod in Kiefer's direction. Even though we were a few tents down, his imposing size made him stand out. The scowl on his face as Kiefer assessed the Central Shores festival made him appear all the more intimidating. "Be back soon."

Rosie's eyes widened as she caught sight of Kiefer. "O-of course. No rush." The nervousness that splashed across her face seemed to indicate that she knew a thing or two about dealing with prickly patrons. "He looks like bad news."

"Yeah, I doubt those muscles are just for show." Tom gave a low whistle. "Let us know if you need backup."

Thomas snorted. "Don't be afraid to put him in his place."

"Thanks." With a haphazard wave, I hurried back to Charlotte's side with the cocoa powder.

"Nut-free?" she confirmed, and once I nodded, Charlotte took the container and sprinkled some on the iced latte she'd finished preparing.

As she reached for a cover, Kiefer caught her by the wrist. "I don't do straws, remember? Bad for the environment and all." He smirked like it was some private joke.

Charlotte ripped her arm from his grasp, and sagged against me for support. "Here," she said, pushing the coffee across the counter toward him.

He picked up the paisley-pattern plastic cup with Brewed to Perfection's branding. "How much do I owe you?" He licked his lips, a slimy grin remaining.

I shuddered at how gross he made me feel.

"Four twenty-five." Charlotte tapped expeditiously on the tablet serving as her register.

Kiefer whistled and raised a condescending eyebrow. "Do you think you're some fancy New York barista or something?"

"Charlotte makes the best coffees in Delaware." I stuck my chin out defiantly.

She nudged my side with her elbow. "It's fine, Cokes."

It was not fine, but I held my tongue. I didn't want to give this beast a reason to stick around any longer.

Charlotte rang him up, and he tapped his phone to pay. "Well, it was good to see you, Lottie." He raised his cup as if in a toast.

She flinched at the nickname.

"Good*bye*." I scowled at him.

Kiefer finally took the hint and sauntered off into the crowd.

Once his muscular frame was no longer visible, Charlotte lost her composure and sank to the grass, hiding behind the booth.

I knelt at her side, wrapping her in a bone-crushing hug. "I'm so sorry, sweetie."

She clung to me like she never had before, and even among the din of the joyous crowd and Chief McInnis's voice over the loudspeakers, her soft, terrified whimpers met my ears.

Chapter Two

A few minutes passed before Charlotte pulled away from our tight embrace. "T-thanks for coming, Cokes." She wiped her tear-stained cheeks. "Seeing him, I-I just completely panicked."

I quickly found a stack of napkins on her table and grabbed one for her. "I'm glad you texted me." I studied her as she dabbed her eyes. "Should we go find Deacon?"

Charlotte shook her head and pointed over her shoulder. "He'll be onstage with Chief McInnis and the team. I don't want to ruin his moment in the spotlight."

"He would *want* you to." I adjusted the brim of her B2P baseball cap that had come askew.

She took a deep, steeling breath and peeked out from behind the booth. "It's all good. Kiefer's gone."

"What the fu-fudge is that jackwad doing here? At *our* festival?" Beyond wondering whether Charlotte was okay, that was my most burning question. Even though I knew who Kiefer Marsh was, I'd never met him. He'd been a part of Charlotte's life before she'd uprooted herself from South Carolina and moved to my hometown of Central Shores, Delaware. A very, very *bad* part. Charlotte told most folks who asked that she'd left South Carolina to open her dream coffee shop in a more affordable area when, in fact, she'd felt compelled to escape her terrible relationship with Kiefer.

"I guess one of his college pals bought a house in Ocean Hollow a few years ago." Charlotte's chin quivered. "He said he's here helping him with some overdue home renovations."

Even though I had a million more questions, I could see that talking about the brute was taking a significant toll on Charlotte. "Here, let's get you something to drink." I swallowed my curiosity and helped her to her feet. The oblivious people milling by B2P's booth probably thought we'd been stocking coffee ingredients under the table or something. Charlotte's red face was more indicative of the summer heat than the fact that she'd been crying.

I assessed the ingredients she'd brought for her stall and whipped up a cold glass of ginger peach lemonade. Since everything was pre-mixed in plastic pitchers, it didn't take much effort other than scooping fresh ice from a cooler.

Charlotte accepted the cup and took a draining sip. "Thanks." She removed her baseball cap and fanned herself. "I needed that."

She still looked a little peaked. "Want me to help you break down the tent?" I suggested. "We can skip out a few hours early and hit the beach?" The festival was scheduled to go until six this evening, so we still had a ways to go.

Charlotte glanced at her watch. "No. I committed to staying here until the end. Besides, aren't you supposed to be live-tweeting or live-X-ing this whole thing for the PD's socials?"

I batted away the notion. "I'm already done with my shift. Bernie's on deck for the afternoon."

Bernice "Bernie" Carter was the CSC's new community liaison and worked closely with me in my role as the PD's social media consultant. In the five months since she'd been hired to assist both the police and fire departments, we'd become fast friends. She'd also been the driving force behind this festival, and from the looks of the happy, engaged crowd, it was panning out to be a roaring success.

Charlotte still shook her head. "I'm fine now. I promise. Seeing Kiefer right there in front of me was just… a shock."

"Well," I offered after a beat, "I won't force you to leave, but let me stick around and help, okay?"

She released a tired giggle. "Adding café bouncer to your growing skillset, are we?"

"You know me." I grinned. "Always looking for my next big career move."

This time, a heartier laugh escaped her. "Makes sense. It's been pretty quiet on the amateur investigator front, after all."

"Go figure." I swept my arm toward the expansive, two-story building perched at the opposite end of the parking lot. "We spend all this time and money on the Community Safety Center, only to have crime dry up," I grumbled with feigned exasperation. In reality, I was thrilled that whatever bad juju had besieged Central Shores last year was finally kaput. Over the past nine months, life had returned to its idyllic, normal nature. Or as normal as life can be when you have over ten million people on the Internet following your every online move.

But I pushed thoughts about Instagram, Facebook, and the like from my mind and focused on my bestie in front of me. "How can I help?"

Charlotte assessed her workstation. "Well, I'm going to pop by my truck real quick and grab an extra container of cocoa powder. I left it in my backseat cooler." She pointed to the shaker Rosie had lent me. "I'll also return this to Sweet Resolutions."

I glanced over my shoulder at Charlotte's neighbor, both at the CSC festival and on the Central Shores strip. Rosie's head was down, boxing up another order, but I ended up catching Tom's eye as he handed out his last free sample. He waved the empty tray like a victory flag, and I smiled at his goofy behavior. The specialty chocolate shop had launched in December, and it was a welcome addition to Central Shores's beachside boardwalk. I'd been fortunate enough to work alongside Tom and Thomas to help the dynamic duo develop their brand and bring their shop from concept to life as part of my social media marketing business, Center of Attention Consulting.

"Why don't I go?" I scanned the area, searching for Kiefer at any of the nearby booths. I feared Charlotte might have another run-in with him as she navigated the crowd.

She shook her head. "I appreciate the concern, but it'll be easier for me to do it. Don't worry, I'll go the back way." She'd obviously read my mind and indicated she'd walk behind the tents rather than through the festival grounds.

"What if someone asks me for a drink?" I shot a nervous look at all the fixings on the large folding table that doubled as her coffee counter.

Charlotte grinned. "Tell them the 'resident beverage artist' will be back in five."

I laughed at the boujee title and saluted my understanding. "Okay, that I can do."

She gave me two thumbs up and took off toward the freshly mowed field where all attendees and vendor cars were parked, dropping the borrowed cocoa powder at Sweet Resolutions' booth on her way. Once she was out of sight, I skimmed my surroundings again. The tension in my shoulders relaxed slightly when I didn't spot Kiefer in the nearby crowd. Chief McInnis's muffled voice no longer floated over the PA system, either. Instead, it sounded like Mayor Sullivan had stepped up to the mic for a few words, but from where Charlotte's booth was positioned toward the back edge of the parking lot, I was too far out of earshot to make sense of the mumbles being piped through the second-rate outdoor speakers. I could see a group gathered onstage, though, so the speeches must still be underway. That meant Jasper had to be up there, too. His media company, *Divulge,* was being honored for its generous donation to the CSC project. "Just a bit of good PR," he'd said at the time when he'd pledged two hundred fifty thousand dollars to the fund. I still thought he'd done so out of secret concern for our hometown.

I waved at folks I recognized as they passed by the booth, and although they returned the friendly greeting, people skillfully re-routed themselves away from Brewed to Perfection, inherently understanding that it was safer to place an order when Charlotte was back behind the makeshift counter. The perk—or downside—of living in a small town, depending on the way you looked at it. Locals saw me manning the B2P tent and knew it was safer to ask me about Instagram filters rather than coffee filters due to my somewhat notable work in the social media sphere. Although, my most viral posts, like the live-streamed takedown of a murderer, had been wholly unintentional.

I seized the unexpected break in my schedule to take a few calming breaths. The adrenaline spike from our tense encounter with Kiefer still had my nerves on edge. It didn't help that I was running on fumes, either. I'd been on site since five AM this morning, spearheading last-minute festival logistics until Bernie had relieved me from official CSC duty at eleven. I'd only stuck around to grab some extra photos for the PD's socials, eat my way through the vendor tents, and watch Jasper be honored. *Sigh.* So much for best-laid plans.

"Hi there. I thought I'd introduce myself." A chipper voice pulled me from my thoughts.

I turned and found a beaming, dark-haired woman dressed in a blue sari waving at me from the booth directly next to B2P.

"Sangeetha Kagan." She held out her hand. "My husband, Dimitri, and I own The Foam Apothecary over in Ocean Hollow."

As we shook, I did a quick sweep of her well-stocked table. Sangeetha had every color and scent imaginable on display in the form of oval-shaped soaps. "So nice to meet you. I'm—"

"Coco Cline." Her smile grew even wider. "Sorry, I know. I've seen you on TV. And online, obvi. I love your content. Big fan." The brown skin on her cheeks tinged with pink. "And now I'm babbling. Sorry."

I placed a gentle hand on her shoulder. "No need to apologize. You're fine." I hoped my light chuckle would put her more at ease. "Thank you for your enthusiasm." Even after all my time in the low-watt spotlight, I still got nervous meeting fans in person. Online, I could hide behind my keyboard or phone, editing the content I delivered until it was just right. In real life, though, I didn't have those handy-dandy edit features. I had to be perfect—on top of my game—or risk shattering people's expectations of me. "Did you make all of these?" I motioned to her soaps.

Sangeetha nodded proudly. "Everything in the shop is handmade and organic. I use goat and oat milk as my bases."

"They smell divine." I stepped closer and inhaled. The cacophony of therapeutic scents was just the balm to soothe my lingering nerves. "Could I buy one of those bundles from you?" I pointed to the soap sets she had on display.

"Oh, you don't need to buy it, Ms. Cline." Sangeetha selected a bundle and placed it reverently in my hands. "But, if you like it, feel free to tag us on Insta at @thefoamapothecary. I make custom orders, too."

Sangeetha certainly knew the art of the hustle. I had to give her props. "Sure thing. Thanks. This is very kind of you." I nodded toward the soap set.

Before she could respond, three chattering women swooped in, smelling soaps left and right, ruining her carefully curated display in the process. Sangeetha mouthed, "Sorry," before turning her attention to assist them.

Since I had no customers to deal with, I took a few moments to check out the fragrances in the bundle Sangeetha had gifted me: Lemon Green Tea, Elderberry Sunset, and Tea Tree Thyme. Each smelled incredible, and their pastel aesthetic begged to be Instagrammed, too. Sangeetha knew what she was doing. *I wonder if she'd consider working with CoA?* I made a note to check out her @thefoamapothecary handle and see what kind of engagement she was getting online.

"And here I was, worrying I wouldn't have anything novel to post tomorrow." I smiled as I put the set off to the side and resumed my booth-watching duties. After being in the social media game for several years, the biggest challenge I faced these days was coming up with new and engaging content to share with my followers. Once in a blue moon, I'd hit the innovative jackpot. Like a few weeks ago, when I'd made a Reel replacing popular curse words and phrases with the word "Hashtag." Inspiration for the video had come from a desperate need to express frustration around my five-year-old nieces and nephew without sullying their young ears. Thank goodness sheer genius had struck when it did. Now, Auntie Coco could drop "What the hashtag" bombs whenever the triplets destroyed my home while visiting. And the Reel had been a home run when it came to fun content. I'd even gotten #whatthehashtag to trend. But viral moments like that had grown fewer and farther between the longer I stayed in this industry. Unlike most of my contemporaries, I didn't have a pet or 'grammable hobby to rely on when the creative well ran dry. When I wasn't working with my CoA clients, I was bingeing true crime podcasts or TV shows. Murder and mayhem didn't exactly vibe with the *Trending Topic* lifestyle brand I'd built throughout my twenties. At least Sangeetha's soaps would be something cute and practical to share on my socials tomorrow.

As time stretched on, I glanced at my watch, wondering where Charlotte was. Way more than five minutes had passed. She couldn't have been parked *that* far away, could she?

I frowned at the time. Two o'clock. We still had four more hours of the festival to get through. As smoothly as everything had been going—other than Kiefer's appearance—between the heat, running around snapping photos, and recording attendee testimonials for the CSC website, I was beat.

Over the garbled speakers—ugh, I wished our tech budget had been a *little* higher for the event—I faintly heard Chief McInnis's gruff voice reclaim the soundwaves. Yikes, Mayor Sullivan must've had a lot to say to the crowd if the chief was just getting the mic back.

I strained to catch what the chief was saying. Was he thanking the CSC donors? I cringed, knowing Jasper would be furious that I was missing his big moment up on stage. But my larger-than-life best friend since second grade would immediately forgive me once he learned what had gone down between Charlotte and Kiefer. Jasper might have been a demanding diva, but he was loyal to the end when it came to his friends.

"—none of this…possible without…substantial…Hastings and *Deluge*—I mean, *Divulge* media enterprises."

I nearly choked on my laughter at Chief McInnis's nervous misspeak. Oh boy, Jasper would be *fuuuuming* at that one. But my giggles died in my throat as the crowd before me parted, and a familiar hulking figure stumbled toward the B2P booth.

I swelled with anger, ready to tear Kiefer Marsh into metaphorical pieces for daring to return to this area, but his terrified expression made me swallow my rant.

"Puh-lease…h-help me!" His labored breathing stilted his words as he staggered forward, clutching his chest and desperately pulling at his collar.

On instinct, I reached for my cell before realizing help was much closer than a phone call away. I shouted to the bewildered onlookers around me,

"Get the chief! Alert the paramedics!" Bernie and I had organized for an EMT crew to be onsite at the CSC grand opening in case someone needed medical assistance. At the time, we'd imagined scenarios involving heat stroke, not…whatever this was.

My cries for aid seemed to snap people from their mesmerized stupor, and the nearby crowd sprang into action. I focused my attention on Kiefer, darting out from under the tent to assist him.

Sangeetha abandoned her soaps, and Tom dropped a box of chocolates before dashing forward. They did their best to clear the crowd to give Kiefer some space.

But as I studied his face, slowly turning the color of a red grape, I realized this guy needed more than just breathing room.

Chapter Three

"Please...my...pen..." Kiefer collapsed to his knees, and I barely managed to prevent his heavy body mass from hitting the pavement at full speed. My muscles burned as I eased him onto the blacktop as gently as I could.

My stomach churned with dread as his gasping intensified but somehow became even more strangled. What did he mean by pen? *Pen, pen, pen...* Omigosh, did he mean an EpiPen? Was Kiefer having an allergic reaction to something?

Frantically, I began to search the pockets of his cargo shorts, hoping my hunch was right. But to my growing dismay, I found nothing.

Scaring the daylight out of me with his sudden movement, Kiefer violently gripped my right wrist, almost twisting it all the way around as he pulled me closer. "M-my...pen."

"Where is it? It's not in your pockets!" I inspected the nearby pavement. Had he dropped it? Had he left it in a bag somewhere?

I realized I was crying, both in frustration and with pain. He clenched my wrist so hard I thought he might snap it. But just as quickly, his hand dropped to his side, and he went eerily quiet.

"Kiefer? Kiefer!" I screamed, lightly smacking his cheeks in the hopes I'd get a response. But none came.

"Oh goodness, is he...?"

"What the heck happened?"

"He just came charging outta nowhere!"

The concerned murmurings of the crowd began to register in my ears as the panicked ringing faded into abject horror. I backed away from Kiefer's massive form, wiping tears as they streamed down my cheeks.

I felt comforting arms encircle me. "Shhh, Coco. Help is here." The smell of rich, deep chocolate washed over me as Tom guided me to my feet. "You've done all you can for now."

It was then I understood why he'd pulled me away from Kiefer. The paramedics had arrived and dove into immediate action. Chief McInnis's face emerged from within my blurry fog, as did his nephew, Gavin. Deacon and Adrian Riley were there, too, their gazes darting from me to the fallen form on the ground. I felt as though I was watching the chaotic scene from above.

"Coco?" The worry in Gavin McInnis's hazel eyes brought me back to my body with a vengeance. He jostled me a little as he gripped my shoulders. "Are you okay?"

I stared at him, open-mouthed, for a moment before shaking my head to rid myself of this stunned fog. "I-I'm fine. But is he...?" I nodded in Kiefer's direction.

The two paramedics had now hooked him up to some portable machine while Chief McInnis issued orders into his cell phone.

Deacon wrapped an arm around me. "Come on, Cokes. Let's get you out of here." He shot an instructive look at Adrian, who immediately began asking for people to move back and let us pass.

Deacon and Gavin guided me through the wide-eyed crowd that had circled around us like a flock of vultures. Luckily, their attention was too focused on the drama unfolding on the pavement rather than me. In my stupor, I caught sight of folks holding up their phones, recording the harrowing events on camera. I winced. *Great. Another viral moment for the books.* I hushed my self-centered notion before thinking how tacky it was that people were filming Kiefer's struggle. Social media had messed us up so much as a human race.

Out of nowhere, my best friend Jasper Hastings appeared, looking very out-of-place from the festival crowd in a three-piece, pink-striped suit.

"Is she hurt?" His porcelain skin turned even more pale as he looked me up and down.

Why not ask me directly? I grumbled inwardly. But more importantly, why didn't I answer myself?

"I don't think she's physically hurt," Deacon assured him, "but she's definitely in shock."

His expression pinched, Jasper surveyed the area. "Hey, Lacie? Can we borrow this for a few minutes?" He pointed to a vacant folding chair stationed by the vendor booth closest to us. The tent belonged to Lacie Burbank and her juice business, Squeezed.

Lacie nodded, her brown skin creased with worry. "Of course. Have at it. Coco, you look like you need something to drink." She went to work pouring fresh ingredients into a blender.

Jasper and Deacon eased me into the seat, my entire body giving way to quivering spasms. I gave them each a weary smile of gratitude, but from their uneasy expressions, they didn't seem appeased by my efforts.

Gavin knelt in front of me so he was at eye level. "Take some deep breaths, or you'll pass out."

At his light command, I tried focusing on myself rather than the world around me. I was startled to discover I had succumbed to some strange emotional mix of sobbing and dry heaving. My cries rang foreign to my ears, like I couldn't quite process what was going on. No wonder Jasper had been worried about me. But I did as Gavin instructed, and by the time Lacie handed me a glass of thick, orangey-red liquid, I'd gotten myself more under control.

"Can you tell us what happened?" Gavin asked in a gentle voice.

I took a fortifying sip of the juice Lacie had whipped up. Bright bursts of strawberry, carrot, and ginger danced across my tastebuds, and the sharp flavor brought everything into clearer focus. "I'm not sure. I was watching Charlotte's booth when Kiefer came staggering through the crowd, looking like he was choking or something. He then fell to the ground and…shortly after, the cavalry arrived." Absently, I pressed the cold paper cup against my right wrist and winced at the flash of pain. Gavin and I both assessed the origin of my reaction, and I was stunned to find massive purple bruises peppered around my skin like a morbid bracelet cuff.

Jasper and Deacon noticed my injury, too. "Yeesh, Cokes. Where did that come from?" Jasper studied me warily with his icy blue eyes.

"Kiefer grabbed me, asking for help." I pressed the cold cup against my skin again, bracing myself for the sting. I wanted to try to keep the swelling to a minimum. "H-he told me to get his pen. I assumed he meant an EpiPen, but I couldn't find one."

"So, he believed he was having an allergic reaction." Gavin's frown deepened. "Who's this Kiefer guy anyway? From the quick glance I got, the guy didn't look like a local."

"He's, uh," I paused and shot a guilty look at Deacon. Had Charlotte shared her traumatic past with him? It didn't seem fair or right for me to throw such a bombshell into the mix, so I simply said, "He's someone Charlotte knows from her South Carolina days."

I saw the metaphorical lightbulb flash above Jasper's head of expertly coifed dark hair. "Holy sh—Shakira. *That* Kiefer?"

Deacon raised an astute eyebrow. "What do you mean '*that* Kiefer'?"

Way to go, Jasper. I resisted the urge to roll my eyes.

But before my bestie could dig us into an even deeper hole, our attention was drawn to the shriek of an ambulance approaching. Whether it was the shrill sirens or the vehicle's sheer size that warded people away, the crowd parted much faster for the ambulance than it had for the festival paramedics.

We watched in eerie silence as the ambulance EMTs jumped out and, with the assistance of the onsite team, loaded Kiefer onto a stretcher and into the vehicle. The whole thing took mere minutes, and before long, the ambulance left, wailing, confusion in its wake.

"Goodness, that was scary." Tom darted toward our little group gathered at Lacie's vendor tent. He wrung his hands, surveying the agitated crowd, and waved down two figures. His husband, Thomas, soon joined us, along with Sangeetha.

"Are you okay, Coco?" Sangeetha cooed.

Thomas removed his chocolate-speckled latex gloves as he eyed me up and down. "You look white as a ghost."

Gavin opened his mouth to speak when his phone buzzed at his hip. He answered with a curt, "Detective McInnis."

His use of his new title brought a loopy smile to my face, but I quickly sobered due to the strained atmosphere.

Deacon, Jasper, and I observed him intently as he listened to the other end of the line. He nodded and covered the mouthpiece. "Deacon, it's Chief. You're with me. Coco, can you hang tight for a few?"

I bobbed my head before I remembered the post I'd abandoned. "I'll be at Charlotte's tent, though. I left it unmanned." I pointed several booths down from where we were all assembled now.

Gavin dipped his chin in acknowledgment before he and Deacon hurried in the direction the chocolatiers and Sangeetha had just come from.

"I wonder what that's about?" Thomas nibbled on his lower lip, his German accent noticeably less thick when he wasn't putting on a show for customers.

Sangeetha twisted the end of one of her braided pigtails. "Damage control, most likely."

"Yeah." Jasper stroked his clean-shaven chin. "Not exactly the best look to have someone pass out in front of the safety center."

I jumped up from the plastic folding chair and elbowed him in the side. "Read the room, please. Not appropriate."

"I kid. I kid." Jasper rubbed his side in feigned pain. "You know I use humor to cover my deep emotional scars."

I rolled my eyes. "Yeah, you sound torn up."

His growling rebuttal was low enough for my ears only. "Come on, Cokes. After what Kiefer did to our girl, you actually feel sorry for him? That toxic throwback deserves to pay the cost of an emergency room visit one hundred times over."

The memory of Kiefer's limp hand falling to the ground vaulted through my mind. Call it my amateur sleuth intuition, but I had a sick feeling that the emergency room wouldn't be Kiefer's final destination. "I'm heading back over to B2P. What do I owe you, Lace?" I turned to our gracious hostess and held up the already-empty smoothie cup.

A sympathetic smile curled on her lips. "On the house."

19

Bowing my head in thanks, I gave a weak wave toward Lacie, Sangeetha, and the Sweet Resolutions duo before scurrying toward Charlotte's empty tent.

"So," Jasper, my newfound shadow, whispered as we arrived, "you gonna tell me what Monster Marsh was doing here?"

I held my hands up defensively. "I really have no clue. I got a text from Charlotte saying she needed backup, and when I came by her tent, Kiefer was there." I motioned to the customer side of the coffee counter. "He was whining about how he'd changed, but Charlotte wasn't having any of it. He eventually threw in the towel and left her alone."

Jasper's gaze traveled to the thinning crowd that was being forced to disperse from the immediate area where Kiefer had collapsed. Chief McInnis and some junior officers were setting up a yellow tape perimeter while Gavin, Deacon, and Adrian, Central Shores's other newly minted detective, crouched near the ground in deep discussion.

Jasper and I watched as the dreary scene unfolded only a dozen or so meters away from B2P's booth. My friend then glanced at his honking silver Rolex. "Where the heck is Charlotte anyway?"

I turned around to the field of parked cars, shading my eyes as I scanned the sprawling area. "I don't know. Maybe she got to talking with someone?" *Or maybe she needed some time alone to decompress from her run-in with Kiefer.*

"Wait 'til she hears that Monster Marsh had to go to the hospital." Jasper gestured with a chef's kiss. "Karma tastes so sweet."

Although my bestie wasn't the fuzziest teddy bear around, he mustn't have understood the seriousness of the situation if he was making such crass jokes. "Knock it off, will you? Kiefer was in *really* bad shape."

He immediately noticed the emotional catch in my voice. "How bad are we talking?"

I didn't want to share my thoughts out loud.

"Hey, was that an ambulance I saw pulling away?" Charlotte's confusion was written all over her face as she jogged up from behind the long row of tents.

Relieved to be spared from answering Jasper's question, I waited until

Charlotte placed a small plastic tote full of ingredients on the makeshift counter. "Thought I'd stock up while I could," she explained as she unloaded a bag of coffee beans, two shakers of cocoa powder, one of sugar, and more stacks of B2P-branded cups. "So, what happened? Did someone faint?"

"That's what I was just wondering." Jasper folded his arms and stared at me expectantly.

I chewed on my lower lip. "Well, uh, someone collapsed. An allergic reaction of some sort, I think." I couldn't quite meet Charlotte's startled gaze. "It…it was Kiefer."

"Kiefer?" She choked out the name. "Omigosh. His peanut allergy!" She ran a hand through her long ponytail. "It's really severe. But he's usually so careful about it."

I eyed the jar of peanut butter situated among Charlotte's beverage ingredients. "He didn't mention it here."

"Well, because he knows I know about it," Charlotte replied, like that should have been obvious. "Remember? I asked you to borrow nut-free cocoa powder. Wait—it *was* nut-free, right?"

"Yes!" I hurriedly reassured her. "Rosie said it's the only kind they keep in stock."

"Thank goodness." Charlotte blew out a sigh of relief. "Every date we went on, Kiefer had to make sure his meal or drink hadn't come into contact with peanuts. But I still don't understand. Did his EpiPen not do the trick or something?"

"I couldn't find it." I swallowed the sudden surge of guilt. "He kept asking me about it, but then he lost consciousness."

Charlotte did a double-take. "Wait, what do you mean *you* couldn't find it?"

"He came staggering through the crowd, heading for your booth." I hugged myself. "He…kinda collapsed on top of me."

"Dang, I'm sorry, Cokes." Jasper patted my shoulder, and I could see regret etched in his countenance over the tasteless jokes he'd made.

Charlotte began wringing her hands as she stood on her tiptoes to survey the scene. "Why are the police sectioning off the area, then? I mean, this was just a terrible accident, right?"

Hashtags. I inwardly cursed at her lingering question. I feared we weren't going to like the answer.

Chapter Four

Charlotte, Jasper, and I stood in a tight huddle as the Central Shores PD swarmed the area. In the center of all the activity, Chief McInnis took a phone call, and his expression grew stormier by the second. After a few terse words with Gavin and Adrian, he barreled toward the opposite end of the parking lot, near the front entrance of the CSC.

Taking control of the situation, our two new detectives seemingly briefed their officers, and together, with the forensic team led by Deacon, they all began sweeping the area and cordoning off larger sections of the pavement.

Chief McInnis's voice came over the loudspeaker, the subdued atmosphere of the festival making it slightly easier to hear his words. "Folks, looks like…have to shut this down early. I'm sorry…inconvenience, but there's…an incident that the police need to look into. Please make… to your cars through the south side…festival grounds." The directions he gave had the crowd moving further and further away from what looked increasingly like a crime scene.

"So much for needing more ingredients." With hands on her hips, Charlotte gave a laborious sigh. "Sorry." She grimaced. "That was insensitive."

"Join the club." Jasper tapped the brim of her baseball cap. "I'm the president."

Their barbed banter brought a slim smile to my face, but it quickly vanished when a shout came from one of the guys clad in a forensic tech uniform. From our position, it looked like he had found something on the ground. What it was, I had no clue.

"Coco!"

Bernie Carter jogged toward me through the thinning crowd, her lips set in a thin line.

"I'll be right back," I told my friends before meeting up with Bernie and pulling her off to the side.

"What's going on? I just heard over the loudspeaker that Chief wants to close us down." Bernie's ebony skin wasn't prone to wrinkles, but her forehead was creased with obvious worry.

I motioned to the taped-off area. "A festivalgoer collapsed. I really don't know anything more at the moment." Speculation, yes, but that wouldn't be helpful.

"Ending the festival because of a medical emergency?" Bernie stomped her foot, folding her toned arms in a huff. "This is not a good PR look. It makes it seem like the CSC can't handle more than one issue at once."

I knew it was her job to think the way she did, so I didn't remind her that someone's life was in jeopardy.

She rubbed her temples, the sun glittering against the tight coils of her dark hair. "But then again, the chief puts concern for community members first and foremost, so it makes sense to conclude the celebration." Bernie seemed to be working through her public address about the incident.

As I raised my hand to comfort her, she jolted back. "What the heck happened to your wrist?" She pointed, her jaw going slack.

I dropped my gaze, and my stomach flipped at the eggplant-colored bruising. Was I still in shock? Because my arm didn't hurt a fraction as bad as it looked. "I got grabbed during the shuffle." I didn't want to replay Kiefer's collapse again.

"You should get that checked ASAP, my friend." Bernie's concern sounded more like a command. "I can handle things from here. I was already scheduled to work takedown. It's just getting moved up a few hours." She turned on her heel but paused halfway. "Hold off on posting pics from the event, will you? Let's see how this all plays out." With her finger, she drew an air circle around the focused group of officers. "I need to speak with the chief about our messaging."

"Sure thing." Even if she hadn't directed me to do so, there was no way I'd be posting anything else to the PD's socials today—not until we learned more.

I wished Bernie good luck and returned to help Charlotte and Jasper pack up the B2P booth.

"Bernie say anything?" Jasper asked when I joined them.

I shook my head. "She's more in the dark than we are."

"After all the hard work she put in to make this event happen, it must suck for Bernie to have it end on such a sour note," Charlotte murmured before palming herself on the forehead. "Sorry. I-I don't know what's gotten into me."

Jasper pulled her hand away before she could whack herself again. "Hey. As someone who's always been empathetic to a fault, you're fine."

We continued to stock Charlotte's Rubbermaid coolers with milk, cream, and liquids before moving on to the dry ingredients. By the time we were preparing to box up the coffee grinder, Gavin strode toward us, his expression grim and full of authority.

I steeled myself, assuming he wanted to speak with me again. I was not looking forward to rehashing Kiefer's terrible struggle before his collapse.

"Hey, Charlotte? Got a minute?"

Wait—Charlotte? Why her and not me? She hadn't even been around when Kiefer had his episode.

The three of us all stopped what we were doing as Gavin leaned against the booth's countertop.

My bestie chewed on her lower lip, shooting Jasper and me a nervous glance. "Um, sure. Fire away."

Gavin cleared his throat. "What can you tell me about Kiefer Marsh? Coco said you knew him."

My heart jumped into my throat. "Hold up, Gav." I reached for his arm. "What do you mean by *knew* him?"

The detective uttered a curse under his breath. "Nothing gets past you, does it?" He then issued a long sigh. "I'm sorry to inform you guys, but

Mr. Marsh didn't make it. We got notification from the paramedics a few minutes ago. He was pronounced DOA at the hospital."

Jasper's jaw dropped as Charlotte stifled a muted gasp. I, on the other hand, sagged with defeat. I usually liked being right. This time, not so much.

"Omigosh…" Charlotte's gaze took on a faraway look, and I couldn't help but note relief mingled among the shock in her ethereal grey eyes. "That's terrible."

"I know this is distressing news," Gavin pushed onward, "but it would be really helpful to our investigation if you could tell me how you were acquainted with Mr. Marsh."

Jasper cocked an eyebrow. "What do you mean, investigation?"

Gavin gave him a brusque *not-now* look. "Charlotte, if you will?" He took out a small recording device and pressed a button. His professional demeanor made it hard to reconcile that he was the same guy I'd gone to junior prom with during high school.

"Um, well," she stuttered as she stared at the recorder, "I met Kiefer back when I lived in South Carolina. We attended the same university for a time. His fraternity and my sorority did a lot of events together."

"So, he was a college friend?" Gavin was clearly encouraging her to divulge more.

Charlotte bobbed her head as she tugged and twisted the hem of her B2P polo.

I studied her intently, trying to mask my confusion. She and Kiefer had definitely been *more* than friends. Why was she being so cagey about their relationship?

It was then I saw Deacon approaching the booth from behind Gavin. Ah, now it made sense. Charlotte probably wasn't comfortable sharing her traumatic past in front of her current romantic partner.

Gavin's frown deepened as he assessed her behavior. "How close would you say you two were?" His tone was thinly layered with suspicion.

"I haven't spoken to him in years," Charlotte admitted more freely. "Not since I moved to Central Shores."

"I see." The detective paused to consider his next words. "But in college, you two were close?"

She shrugged. "I suppose you could say that."

"Close enough to be aware of any medical issues, like life-threatening allergies?"

Deacon nudged Gavin's arm. "Where are you going with this, boss?"

Realizing Deacon had joined the group, Gavin's expression grew even more stormy. *Becoming more like his uncle by the day,* I thought sardonically.

"Your guy Iko found something," he explained to Deacon, and I remembered one of the forensics guys sending up the alarm. Gavin then turned his focus back to Charlotte. "Again, were you aware of Mr. Marsh's peanut allergy?"

She shrank slightly at his sharp question. "Yes, I was."

"So, you would've known not to make a drink containing peanuts?"

At her barista skills being called into question, Charlotte's nose wrinkled with indignance. "Well, of course. But even then, not many of my drinks contain anything peanut-related, anyway." She pointed to the Skippy jar we'd yet to pack up. "Just my Peanut Butter Mocha Blitz."

Gavin's gaze followed hers, and at the sight of the jar, he appeared to relax a little.

Deacon folded his arms. "What exactly did Iko find, Gav?"

The detective's gaze darted over his shoulder toward the roped-off scene. Whatever he saw caused him to lean forward and lower his voice, "Nothing good, guys. We found a drink cup on the ground a few meters from where Marsh collapsed. It had bits of peanuts caked at the bottom."

A low whistle sailed across Jasper's lips.

"Of course, we won't know if it was his until we conduct fingerprint and DNA analysis, but *if* it turns out to be his cup..." Gavin's foreboding words trailed off.

"Then it's quite possible someone purposely triggered the vic's allergy," Deacon said aloud what we were all likely thinking.

"But why?" Charlotte's chin trembled. "Who in Central Shores would have it out for Kiefer? Who even knew he had a peanut allergy?"

Jasper's anxious gaze latched onto mine. *Other than you, Charlotte? That's an excellent question.*

Gavin sucked in a raspy breath. "Char, I hate to ask this, but were you telling the truth earlier about your relationship with Marsh?"

She bristled. "Why would you even think that?"

After a quick swivel of his head, Gavin murmured even softer, "Because the cup we found the peanuts in had your Brewed to Perfection logo on it."

If the situation hadn't been so dire, it might have been comical how rapidly Jasper, Charlotte, Deacon, and I all glanced down at a stack of B2P cups sitting atop the makeshift coffee counter.

"That's impossible!" Charlotte squeaked. "I made him a regular iced latte. Coco was standing right beside me when I made it. I even used nut-free cocoa powder to dust it with."

I nodded so hurriedly that my vision went a bit blurry. "No peanut bits were in sight." I kept to myself that a portion of the latte had already been mixed when I arrived *and* that I had to step away to visit Sweet Resolutions. Since Charlotte was one hundred percent innocent, there was no need to muddy the waters.

The newbie detective, who was only a year younger than me, reached for the back of his neck to massage the stress away. "You still haven't answered my question about your relationship with Marsh, Char."

This sounds bad. I caught Charlotte's pinched gaze and willed her to come clean. *Tell Gav the truth, and we'll go from there. We've got your back.*

She must have realized this for herself. "Fine. You're right, Gavin. I wasn't sharing our full history. But not for the reason you're probably thinking," she hurriedly added. "You see, we met freshmen year of college, but then I dropped out to pursue a degree online and save money…" Her voice warbled with a sudden swell of emotion. "We reconnected at a mutual friend's party a few years later and started dating. We were together for two years before…I decided to leave."

Instinctively, I reached for her hand and squeezed.

Gavin's expression was one of concern. "I take this breakup wasn't amicable?"

"No."

It was a one-word response, but it contained so much emotional weight. I saw Deacon's desperate desire to wrap his girlfriend in his arms, but he stood stoic at Gavin's side, ever the professional.

The detective muttered another low curse, stroking his chin with a heavy hand. "Can you think of anyone else in town who might've known this guy?"

My heart clenched. I could clearly hear the pain in Gavin's question. As our friend, he didn't like the optics of the situation any more than the rest of us. It was also clear, due to his "colorful" language, that he hadn't taken my viral "What the Hashtag" Reel to heart like I had.

Charlotte started shaking her head but stopped short. "Actually, Kiefer mentioned he was staying with a college buddy in Ocean Hollow, but he didn't use a name." She tucked a loose strand of hair behind her ear. "Since I was only enrolled for a few semesters, he probably assumed I wouldn't know the guy."

"Ocean Hollow, huh?" Gavin then turned to me. "Kiefer didn't mention anyone while you were with him, did he?"

I winced as the memory entered my mind. "No. He just kept asking for his EpiPen."

"Kiefer may have been many things, but he was careful about managing his allergy." Charlotte's frown grew. "The times that he slipped up when we were dating...well, thank goodness for his EpiPen. He knew the extreme consequences if he didn't. Why did he not have it on him?"

Gavin studied her for a long minute. "That's a very good question."

"He seemed to think it was in his pocket," I recalled. "But...it wasn't."

"Maybe it fell out when he initially began to struggle," Deacon suggested. "Or while he was just walking around the festival." His dark brown eyes glimmered with determination. "We'll do a sweep of the whole lot and see what we can find."

Gavin nodded. "I'll see what info I can collect from his cell phone. The paramedics left it with us."

"What can we do?" The words were out of my mouth before I had time to rein them in.

To my surprise, Gavin actually smiled instead of immediately putting me in my place. I suppose having a hand in solving three murder investigations had earned me a bit of goodwill with the Central Shores police. "Hang tight for now. I may have some more questions about Marsh's contacts in the area. The phone stuff shouldn't take me too long. I was able to unlock it using his FaceID before Marsh was loaded into the ambulance. Also disabled FaceID, too." He gave a slight *no big deal* shrug.

"Look at you, thinking fast on your feet, Mr. Detective." I gave him a thumbs-up as he excused himself from our group.

"I better check in, too." Deacon kissed Charlotte's cheek and held her worried gaze a moment before following in Gavin's wake.

Once it was just the three of us, Charlotte dropped her face into her palms. Jasper and I quickly wrapped her trembling figure in a tight hug. "It will be okay, Char," I reiterated for what felt like the millionth time.

"How can you say that, Cokes?" Her quiet cries grew more panicked. She pulled away from us, her eyes wide with fear. "You're all about optics, aren't you? Peanuts in a Brewed to Perfection cup? There might as well be a sign over my head saying *I killed Kiefer*."

Jasper folded his muscular arms. "Well, that sign would be wrong." He paused and arched an eyebrow. "Right?"

"Of course!" Charlotte tossed her arms up in frustration.

He held his hands palms-out in surrender. "Hey, just checking to make sure I don't have to book us a flight to Switzerland or something. First-class, of course."

I shot him a silencing look. Now was not the time to be making jokes about fleeing to places without extradition treaties.

"How on earth did peanuts get in the drink I made?" Charlotte rubbed at her red, teary eyes. "You guys don't know what it's like to live with a severe allergy like Kiefer's. He was always so, so careful wherever we went. He may have changed since we were together, but I doubt he's changed so much that he would knowingly let someone put peanuts in his drink."

I placed a hand on each of her arms, trying to calm her down. "I know you're freaked out right now, and you have every right to be. Your monster ex shows up out of the blue, and now he's dead..." I realized I was only exacerbating the problem by stating the facts. "Listen, I saw Kiefer strut away from your booth without a lid on his cup. All someone would need to do is distract him *juuuust* enough to drop in a few small peanut bits. They'd have plenty of options to choose from." I motioned to the plethora of vendor tents running along the festival's perimeter. Within twenty feet of Brewed to Perfection alone, several booths boasted various forms of snackable peanuts on their posted menus.

"Maybe…" Charlotte scanned the area as she considered my theory. "His allergy *was* so acute that just drinking the liquid the peanuts were in would trigger it." She rubbed her eyes. "But then why—Oh, gosh. He must've thought I was the one who put the peanuts in his coffee." Her words grew shrill. "That's probably why he came staggering back toward my tent. To confront me!"

"We don't know that, Char." I rubbed her back, trying to alleviate her escalating fears. "Besides, if his allergy were as extreme as you say it was, if you put peanuts in his drink right from the start, Kiefer would have reacted sooner than he did, right?"

Jasper cleared his throat. "I hate to play devil's advocate, but the police could very well say there's a chance he didn't drink the latte right away. And they also know Charlotte stepped away from her booth," he countered. "What's stopping them from suggesting that she snagged some peanuts, found Kiefer in the crowd, and dropped them into his cup while he wasn't looking?"

Not helpful! I scowled at him, but I couldn't deny he'd made some good points. There were a lot of people here. Someone could very well swipe a handful of peanuts from a distracted food vendor. While I knew Charlotte would never do such a thing, the scenario in itself was plausible enough. "Let's just finish breaking down your booth." I motioned to the other vendors around us, who were doing the same thing.

Over at the Sweet Resolution's tent, Tom must have thought my gesture was a wave because he bounced right over. "I saw Detective McInnis chatting you guys up. Is he already consulting his best investigator?" He winked at me.

My cheeks burned from a mixture of pure embarrassment and slight pride that my crime-solving reputation preceded me. "He just had some questions for me about the incident." I chose not to bring up Charlotte's connection to Kiefer. She was right about one thing. The optics surrounding the whole situation did not look good for her.

Tom nodded, and Rosie and Thomas appeared behind him. "You all right, Coco?" Rosie's worried gaze darted to my wrist as she asked.

I glanced down and flinched at the nasty bruise that had already developed. "Looks worse than it feels. Trust me." I'd completely forgotten how intense Kiefer's grip had been before...before...

"Why all the police activity, do you know?" Thomas surveyed the bustling site with curiosity. "The chief said over the loudspeaker that the young man collapsed from a medical incident. Seems strange to have so many officers on scene."

Jasper, Charlotte, and I shared a wary look, and I could tell we were all thinking the same thing. We could keep our mouths shut—which was hands down the wisest decision—or we could control the narrative with a selective retelling of what we knew.

Luckily, Lacie Burbank joined our little gathering, sparing us from making the wrong choice. "Gosh, this is wild, right?" She rubbed her arms, her skin rippled with goosebumps. "I just got asked to step away from my booth so Deacon and his team could take some photos."

"Photos?" Tom flashed an alarmed look at his husband. "But our workstation is a mess!"

Thomas hurriedly reassured him, "I'm sure they're not photos for the health department, hon."

Tom's eyes widened. "Oh my, you mean *crime scene* photos?" His head whipped toward Lacie.

She shrugged. "I think they're just making a record of what happened."

"So, what *did* happen?" Rosie asked as she adjusted the brim of her worn UNC cap. "These two haven't made a lick of sense since I returned from my break." She thumbed a finger toward her employers. "Did someone pass out? Why are the police involved?"

I felt all attention land on me. When you had a habit of solving mysteries, people came to you for answers. "I don't know more than you guys do right now."

Before the Sweet Resolutions team could pepper me further, Deacon arrived at their booth with two uniformed techs in tow. "Hey, guys?" He flagged the chocolate trio down. "Mind if we take some shots?"

While everyone else was distracted, I pulled Charlotte and Jasper close. "Do you think Deacon's cataloging all the vendors to see who had immediate access to peanuts?"

Jasper shrugged. "I'd imagine so." He scanned the area. "Looks like other booths are getting photographed." He pointed to the row of tents on the opposite side of the parking lot. We could make out some similarly dressed people with cameras.

Charlotte's summer tan lost its dewy glow. "I guess we should probably stop packing things away. Otherwise, they'll think I'm disposing of evidence."

My stomach flipped. "Yeah. Good call."

Chapter Five

"Wow. It really is all hands on deck." Jasper assessed the whirlwind of police activity around us. "It's good to know my *Divulge* donation was put to good use."

I sighed in agitated agreement. Over the past nine months, the Central Shores PD had tripled in size to properly maintain the Community Safety Center. While that kind of growth might sound far-fetched, it'd been necessary. More than five hundred new homes, built by various development groups, were sold during the same time frame. Our local woodlands had been razed and turned into posh neighborhoods oozing with beachy charm. With all the new development, Central Shores's population had more than doubled. Despite a troubling recent trend in crime, people were eager to call our little slice of American paradise home.

"I can't believe this is happening." Charlotte pressed her palm against her forehead. "I-I can't believe he's *dead*." Her last word was a mere whisper as a haunted look eclipsed her face.

I moved to put my arm around her shoulder when my cell phone buzzed in my romper pocket. A text from my fiancé, Hudson Caruthers.

Millie says something's going down at the CSC festival. She's sending a news crew. Everything OK?

I smiled at his digital concern. He was filming a segment for his true crime show *Crime Sweet Home* up in Wilmington today.

All good now. Will fill you in when you get home <3

As I sent the message, I imagined Hudson's producer, Millie Stabler, running around WMTG studios over in Milton, giving orders left and right.

I cringed at the thought of news crews swarming the parking lot. The last thing I wanted right now was for my face to wind up on TV.

Again.

Most social media influencers would love the chance to be in the spotlight, but I'd learned the lesson that there *was* such a thing as bad publicity, and with one of my best friends being so closely connected to the victim, it would be better for everyone involved if I remained on the sidelines. At least in the eyes of the Internet.

"Was that Dad checking in?" Jasper asked, referencing Hudson by the nickname he'd given him years ago when we'd first started dating.

I nodded. "Millie got wind of something going on down here and is sending a news crew."

A pout graced his lips. "I'm surprised she hasn't reached out to—oh, speak of *The Devil Wears Prada*." He held up his phone to reveal Millie's contact info, filling his screen. Jasper was also a part of the WMTG family. He hosted *Divulge Direct,* a local afternoon talk show that was then uploaded as a podcast for worldwide consumption. He'd gained a lot of traction in recent months and had a healthy subscriber base, meaning he was a golden goose for Millie, and therefore, she worshipped the ground he walked on. It had been *sooo* great for Jasper's ego.

"Hi, Mills," Jasper answered. "Yep, I'm there now."

I mimed zipping my lips at him. My bestie tended to let his ambition do most of his decision-making, and I feared he'd spill the beans about Kiefer without thinking through the ramifications for Charlotte.

Jasper batted me away like I was a buzzing gnat. "Nah, the police are just taking pics. Not sure what's going on. But if I find out, you'll be the first to know." He gave his phone an air kiss and ended the call.

He must have seen the surprise in my face. "Like I'd throw Char to the wolves in favor of breaking a big story," he muttered.

I pinched his pale cheek. "Aww. You really are a softie."

Charlotte stood only a few feet away from us. With her arms crossed and brow furrowed, she looked like she was off in another world. Although, perhaps she was watching her boyfriend take pictures of Sangeetha's soap display. He and his team were moving down the line of vendors. Which meant Brewed to Perfection was next.

"Hey, guys." Deacon waved cautiously as he approached. "Mind if we take some pics? We're just getting some reference shots."

"Get my good side." Jasper pressed his hand against his right cheek in a dramatic pose.

Deacon chuckled. "Of the vendor booths."

"Is it a problem we already started packing up?" Charlotte twisted her ponytail. "I'm so sorry. I just assumed since Chief McInnis called off—"

"It's fine, babe." Deacon gave her a reassuring smile. "We'll snap some shots of your containers and such. No biggie."

Her shoulders sagged. "Okay, phew. Yeah, go nuts." The words were barely out of her mouth before she gasped. "Omigosh. That's not…not what I meant."

"Hey." I felt for her, having uttered the wrong turn of phrase many a time in my twenty-nine years. "Deep breaths, okay?" I reminded her as I cupped her elbow.

Charlotte let me escort her a few yards away from the tent, allowing Deacon and his two team members to do their thing.

Jasper tapped his foot on the pavement as we watched them work efficiently. "Should you be coordinating with Bernie or something?" he mumbled out of the side of his mouth.

"This is her wheelhouse now." Bernie's role as community liaison made her the official spokesperson for the CSC and its departments. "She'll let me know what to share on socials once the chief gives her the all-clear." My consulting work with the PD these days involved managing their online presence. Everything else publicity-related fell to Bernie.

At her mention, I searched the crowd for the bubbly thirty-six-year-old, but I didn't spot her petite silhouette anywhere.

"All right, guys. Let's hit the next tent." Deacon gave us a thumbs up. But because his gaze was on his team rather than the ground in front of him, he stumbled into the little covered trashcan Charlotte had behind her booth. As it tumbled to the asphalt, its cover popped off, and the discarded contents spewed across the ground.

Deacon grimaced at his faux pas. "Dang. Sorry, Char. What a—" All emotion evaporated from his face, and his dark brown skin lost its usual luster.

"What's wrong?" Charlotte, Jasper, and I rushed forward to clean up the mess before the wind blew paper towels and coffee-stained napkins away.

Deacon held up his palm, halting us mid-step. "Stay there." His typically warm tone was ice cold. He continued to stare at the ground a heartbeat longer before a string of expletives whispered across his lips. Apparently, he hadn't seen my "What the Hashtag" Reel, either.

"Get Detective Riley or McInnis, will you?" he snapped at one of his underlings.

Curious over what had drastically changed his demeanor, I cleared my throat, but Deacon's silencing glare had me swallowing any questions. *Uh oh.*

Adrian appeared without needing to be summoned. "Hey, Charlotte. Got a few more questions for you..." His request trailed off as he took stock of the tense scene. "What's going on?" he asked Deacon.

Our friend rubbed his temples with evident frustration. "You're going to want to take a look at this," he said, pointing to the pile of trash.

As he stepped back to make room for Adrian, Deacon's pinched gaze found Charlotte, and the unease radiating from him clawed at my throat.

"Take a look at what?" Jasper asked, adjusting his tall frame to see if he could get a better vantage point.

Adrian knelt beside the trashcan's contents and, with gloved hands, extracted a small, bright yellow tube from the pile of used paper products.

"What is that?" Jasper nudged my side. "An archaic tampon or something?"

I couldn't summon the energy to humor him.

Adrian studied the tube, his features grim. He motioned for one of Deacon's guys to take some pictures before he dropped the tube into a plastic evidence bag.

I gulped. *Evidence bag?*

As he rose, Adrian gave a curt nod to Deacon. "You know what this means, right, bro?"

Deacon's hand raked over his face before he bowed his head in agreement. "I do."

Adrian then shifted his focus to Charlotte, his warm brown eyes tight with anxiety. "Please tell me there's a perfectly innocent explanation for why Kiefer Marsh's EpiPen is in your trashcan."

Chapter Six

"W-what? That can't be right." The question stunned Charlotte so much that she stumbled backward. "It's not possible."

Jasper and I closed ranks around her, lending her our silent support.

Adrian approached and held the clear baggie for us to examine. "I'm afraid it is."

I squinted as I read the condemning information on the prescription sticker. *Marsh, Kiefer.* My heart plummeted to my butt. How in the name of Travis Kelce had Kiefer's EpiPen ended up in the trash? *Charlotte's* trash, no less.

"Adrian, I swear, I don't know how it got there." Her eyes welled with tears.

The detective sighed. "I'll need more than your word, Char, as good as it is." He studied her intently. "We have a Brewed to Perfection cup laced with peanuts, and the victim's EpiPen found near your booth. A victim *you* have a history with. You've got to see that this looks bad. Very bad."

"Charlotte doesn't even *have* peanut bits here at her booth," I snapped, my anger getting the better of me. "Besides, anyone could've used her trashcan, Adrian. You can't seriously believe—"

"It's not about what I *believe*, Coco," he cut me off in a gentle but stern tone, "but what the evidence suggests."

Tears streamed down Charlotte's sun-kissed cheeks as she swayed unsteadily on her feet.

Deacon wrapped his strong arms around her and pulled her into his chest.

"Unless you're arresting her now, I'm going to take her home." His gaze narrowed in the detective's direction.

Adrian rolled his eyes. "Of course, we're not arresting her, D. Don't make this harder than it needs to be."

"What *I* need to do is take care of my girlfriend." Deacon's tone grew steely. "The lab hasn't even confirmed the B2P cup was Marsh's. To say nothing that you haven't tested for prints or touch DNA on his EpiPen." Through gritted teeth, he added, "I know we're all under pressure with this being the CSC's opening day, but if you start tossing around accusations before the dust settles—"

"I wasn't accusing her of anything." Adrian stepped forward, folding his arms. "I was merely saying it would be in Charlotte's best interest to help us understand the situation so we can move forward and figure out what *really* happened. Come on, man, we're all friends here." He motioned to our small group.

Deacon quickly countered, "You said so yourself, the evidence right now is pointing at her. And the DA will want to move fast. So, you do your job, and I'll do mine."

Adrian winced. "You know you can't work this case with your girlfriend being so intricately involved."

"What?" Charlotte stilled in Deacon's arms, gazing up at him with alarm.

"I meant my job as her partner." Deacon glowered at the man he'd just been bro-ing out with on the makeshift stage not fifty minutes ago.

Gavin appeared at Adrian's side with a triumphant grin on his face. "Got a few leads from the phone." He paused and noticed the cool expressions surrounding him. "Uh, something the matter?"

Adrian handed the evidence bag to his cohort. "This was in Charlotte's trashcan."

Gavin's victorious demeanor quickly wilted as he scanned the contents. "Please tell me I heard that wrong."

"Gav, I swear, I didn't know it was there." Charlotte tried to hold her head up high, but her chin quivered uncontrollably.

He gave her a sympathetic nod before turning to Adrian. "Let's get everything to the lab for testing, yeah?"

Adrian bowed his head in acknowledgment and bid us a curt goodbye, his hasty strides taking him toward the CSC building.

"And you guys…" Gavin sucked in a fortifying breath as he directed his attention to our group. "…should pack up and head home. We'll be in touch."

I reached for his forearm. "Charlotte had nothing to do with whatever happened to Kiefer."

"Come on, Coco." He brushed off my hand, his expression one of annoyance and hurt. "If Adrian or I thought she did, she'd already be christening our new jail cells."

Jasper raised an eyebrow. "Why do I feel a big *but* coming on?"

Gavin sighed. "Because you guys know how this works. The optics aren't great right now, but we're just getting started. I'm sure our tests will put Charlotte in the clear." He reached into the small satchel hanging from his shoulder and extracted a device that looked like a portable label maker. "This here is a digital fingerprint reader. If I can just get your prints for elimination, Char, you're free to go."

She gulped. "Um, all right."

Deacon held out his arm to stop her. "You sure you want to do this without a lawyer present?"

"I've got nothing to hide." She held his gaze momentarily, and the hair stood on the back of my neck at their wordless communication.

Deacon finally relaxed his arm. "Okay."

Gavin murmured the simple instructions Charlotte needed to follow to capture her prints, and the effortless process was over in mere seconds. I wrinkled my nose, remembering the first time I'd had my fingerprints taken. Getting the awful ink off my hands had required industrial-strength cleaner. Oh, the wonders of technological advances and a bigger department budget.

"All set." Gavin slipped the device back into his bag. "We'll be in touch once we've had some time to review our initial findings."

I swallowed. I didn't think it possible; his guarantee that he and Adrian would be reaching out to Charlotte left me even more unnerved.

Gavin patted Deacon on the shoulder. "I'll let Maven know he's lead on this case for now." Maven Gunderson was Deacon's most senior subordinate and an all-around good guy. He was a valued member of the forensic crew, and I had faith he'd do a good job in Deacon's stead.

Deacon answered with only a stiff nod.

"I can't believe I'm affecting your job." Charlotte pressed her head against his chest. "I'm so sorry."

He began stroking her hair. "Don't worry. This isn't your fault," Deacon calmly reassured her. "It's just part of the process." While he spoke with confidence, his gaze seemed haunted.

Gavin studied the couple before turning to me. "Now, Coco—"

"You're outta your mind if you think I'm sitting on the sidelines for this one." Hands on my hips, I stared him down.

He snorted. "What I was *going* to say is: we could use your eyes on the vic's socials, like you did for the LaTàge case. Let me or Adrian know if you come across anything noteworthy, okay?" His brow furrowed. "But be careful. Just because you're on the department's payroll as a consultant, it doesn't mean you have diplomatic immunity if you get in the way of the *official* investigation."

Note to self: stay in my lane. I held my hand up in pledge, grateful that after three successful cases, Gavin trusted my ability to dig up social media intel that people tried to keep buried. "You got it, boss."

With a sardonic chuckle, he marched off to confer with his fellow officers.

Jasper released a low whistle. "Dang, Char. It's a good thing you're a beautiful white lady, or this could've gone a whole heck of a lot differently."

While Jasper's social commentary about the American justice system had its unfortunate merits, I hoped Gavin and Adrian believed in Charlotte's innocence for other reasons.

"No. This reeks of a setup to me," Deacon grumbled. "And I'm sure Gav and Adrian see it, too."

"A setup?" Charlotte stepped away from his protective embrace, her eyes going wide. "You mean, like someone is trying to frame me?"

"Or just throwing suspicion off themselves in a horrible coincidence," I countered. "I mean, if you were going to off Kiefer, would you really be so foolish as to use a B2P cup *and* toss his EpiPen into your trashcan?"

Charlotte recoiled at the troubling scenario. "When you put it like that..."

"Who in Central Shores knows about your history with Kiefer?" Deacon threaded his fingers through Charlotte's trembling hand.

She gnawed on her lower lip. "No one beyond Coco and Jasper. It's not a part of my life I normally share."

"And we would *never* share her personal story with anyone." Jasper folded his arms. "Right, Cokes?"

"Of course not." I nodded. "But we're forgetting about who *Kiefer* may have told."

Deacon frowned. "You're right. And it could be that someone from his circle thinks they can pin the crime on Charlotte."

"But who's even *in* his circle?" Jasper scoffed. "Wasn't this dude from South Carolina?"

I pointed over my shoulder to where Gavin stood with his officers. "Didn't you hear what the good detective said when he came over here? He found a lead on Kiefer's phone. Someone else in the area obviously has ties to him."

"And possibly a reason to want the guy dead," Deacon murmured.

Charlotte dropped his hand and began organizing the remaining items scattered around the booth. "I wish I'd asked Kiefer who he was staying with."

We all jumped in to pack up the rest of her things. "No. That would've required you interacting with the scumbag for longer than necessary." Yes, I knew it was uncouth to speak ill of the dead, but Kiefer's untimely demise didn't erase how horrible he'd been to Charlotte.

A clattering *crash* made Jasper, Charlotte, and me jump back from the table, only to find that Deacon had knocked over a tub of coffee stirrers.

"Sorry." He winced, but he didn't quite meet our concerned gazes. His skin was drawn tight around his mouth, and I realized the poor guy was grinding his teeth together in anger.

Charlotte placed a gentle palm on his forearm, and he covered her hand with his. "You don't have to tell me about your history with Marsh if you don't want to," he began, his voice hoarse, "but just know I'm here if you ever want to talk about it."

She squeezed him tightly, conveying her wordless appreciation.

I had to give Deacon major props for keeping his cool. When I'd found out Hudson had been sexually harassed by a coworker, I hadn't been as graceful.

"So, what's the plan?" Deacon glanced at Jasper and me.

Jasper smirked. "Are you formally applying to be a member of the Central Shores Sleuth Squad?"

"Won't you get in trouble with the PD?" Charlotte's brow wrinkled with worry.

Deacon shrugged. "What Chief McInnis doesn't know can't hurt him."

"The more the merrier." In our previous investigations, we'd had to ice Deacon out for fear of getting in trouble with the chief and the team. It would be nice this time around to have him working with us. "I say we start by figuring out who Kiefer knew in the area. Why don't we all meet at my place for a social media deep dive? Between the four of us, it won't take us long to track down what profiles Kiefer had online."

With a plan ready to execute, we helped Charlotte carry all her coffee equipment to her truck before going our separate ways. The CSC was located only a few miles from the Sunny Shores development where we all lived, so it wasn't long before I pulled my British racing green MINI Cooper into my two-car garage. Noting Hudson's empty spot, I sent him a quick text message.

The gang will probs be here when you get home.

His reply came as soon as I crossed the threshold into our two-story condo. **For fun or because of what happened at the CSC?**

His investigative journalist instincts were good. **The latter. When will you be home?**

Wrapping up in 20. Want me to pick up dinner from The Pearl?

I smiled at his thoughtful offer. The Pearl was a favorite spot where we often went for dinner with Charlotte, Deacon, Jasper, and, more recently, Eli Holt. While Jasper "wasn't into labels," he'd been casually seeing the handsome fitness instructor for a few months now. **Sounds perfect. Thanks, babe.**

See you soon.

I tossed my phone and bag onto the kitchen island, taking stock of the living area to make sure the home we'd shared for more than two years was in acceptable shape for visitors. Not that my friends expected too much from me when it came to my domestic skills.

I was busy preparing a pitcher of strawberry-peach iced tea when Jasper waltzed in through the front door with an airy, "I have arrived."

I offered him a drink, which he readily accepted.

He glanced at his watch as he took a seat on a kitchen barstool. "I'm surprised I beat Power Couple Number Two here. Do you think Charlotte's filling Deacon in about her history with Kiefer?"

"She might just need a moment to decompress." I went about pouring a bowl of water for Deacon's labrador mix, Maisie. Since moving in with Charlotte, he'd had an open invitation to bring the sweet girl along whenever they visited. "I know I would."

Jasper dipped his head in conciliation. "It's a good thing Deacon didn't know about Kiefer before this all went down, or both of them might be viable suspects."

"The same could be said for me." I stilled at the notion, and my focus dropped to the bruising around my right wrist. "I saw the guy right before he died, after all."

Jasper clasped his hand over my mouth. "Why would you even put that idea out there? As if you need the Internet thinking you're a killer, *again*."

I licked his palm, and he ripped his hand away in disgust. "Gross."

I chuckled at our sibling-esque behavior. "Like Gavin said, I'm sure once the PD do their testing in their new fancy crime lab, this will all blow over."

"I don't know, Cokes. Testing takes time, and time lets rumors fester." Jasper stared at me, his icy blue eyes pinched with worry. "And since when do things involving you and murder simply blow over?"

Chapter Seven

I shivered at Jasper's ominous remark. "I can't believe Kiefer is dead. Char and I were literally just talking to him, and then..." I closed my eyes, trying to wish away the terrible memory of Kiefer's panicked face as he stumbled toward me. I also couldn't wrap my head around another nefarious murder in my hometown. One that seemingly targeted a dear friend, no less.

Jasper gingerly patted me on the back, the extent of our less-than-touchy-feely nature. "Is Hudson in the loop?"

"He knows something went down, but we can fill him in when he gets home." I checked the wall clock. "He'll be on his way in a bit. He's bringing dinner."

"Nice." A wary look enveloped Jasper's face. "What about Amanda? Are you going to tell her about what went down?"

My chest tightened at the mention of our friend and my CoA coworker. "I imagine so, but I won't bother her with it on a weekend. Perhaps during our Monday sync." Amanda Highgrove had enough heartache in her life right now. I didn't want to add worry for Charlotte to the mix.

"Yikes. I didn't realize she was back to work already." Jasper swirled his drink, the ice cubes clinking. "She didn't take much time off, did she?"

I shook my head. "I tried to convince her to take another month, but she said she needed the distraction."

He propped his elbow on the counter and let loose a long sigh. "I feel so terrible for her and Arthur. I don't know how to help them, either."

"Same." Emotion pricked at my eyes as I thought about the grieving couple.

46

Amanda and her husband, Arthur, had suffered a devastating loss eight months into her pregnancy, a mere week after Charlotte and I hosted a baby shower for them. Since losing their little boy, we'd been trying to support our friends as best as we could, but I worried letting Amanda come back to CoA so soon hadn't been the right call as her boss. But as my therapist repeatedly reminded me, everybody grieved differently, and all I could do was be there for her.

A weighty silence settled over us as I finished prepping drinks. Anxiety for our loved ones rattled at the base of my skull. Charlotte, Deacon. Amanda, Arthur. Why did bad things happen to good people?

I swiped away a few stray tears before Jasper saw them fall and turned my attention to clearing the dining table to make room for everyone. It was currently covered in various brands of bath bombs I'd been reviewing and rating for *Trending Topic.* The blog post was set to go live next Saturday, a week from today, and I was still trying to find the right background to photograph the bath bombs against. Usually, the white paneling I had in my office studio space worked fine, but since many of the bath bombs were pale or pastel-colored, the pics looked washed out. Hence, I'd moved my work to our new espresso-wood dining table for optimal pop.

Jasper offered to help carry an armload of bath bombs into my office. "How many brands do you have here?"

"Thirty-two." I assessed the heaping pile. "It was a *lot* of baths."

"First-world problems, huh?" He eyed all the samples. "That's gotta be a new record. Good news for your bottom line, right?"

I nodded, not quite meeting his gaze.

"But not good enough to rethink giving it all up?" Jasper raised a searching eyebrow.

I gritted my teeth together. "When did you get to be so perceptive?"

"I mean, it's hard *not* to notice." He snorted. "Any time *Trending Topic* is mentioned these days, you look like you just found out that we have to wait for *Wicked: Part Two.*"

I winced. "Am I that obvious?" I thought I'd been doing a good job at going through the motions, posting features about things like bath bombs, makeup, and soaps. Did my followers sense that my heart wasn't in such happy-go-lucky lifestyle content anymore? I yearned to make a difference with my work, and as much as I promoted environmentally friendly brands that had charitable mission statements, I felt like I had the obligation and the drive to do more. But what could I do as a lifestyle blogger that would *actually* make a real impact on the world? The question had been plaguing me for nearly a year.

As we headed back into the kitchen, I sighed, wondering if my next words could solve this ongoing inner battle. "I got an offer," I muttered, half-hoping Jasper wouldn't hear me.

"An offer? For what?"

No such luck. "For *Trending Topic*. Rae Livingston wants to purchase it from me. The site, the copyright, the subscriber list…everything."

Jasper sucked in a harsh breath. "Hold up, Rae Livingston? As in *Raeliana* Livingston, Dirk Livingston's nepo baby?"

I snorted at his crude snark. Photographer Dirk Livingston was a huge name in the fashion industry, and his twenty-year-old daughter Rae was a regular on the catwalks of Milan and Paris.

"Why does she want to buy *Trending Topic*?" Jasper pressed for more details. "No offense, but your millennial mindset doesn't exactly jive with Gen Z."

I folded my arms, remembering the initial introductory email she'd sent me two weeks ago. "She wants to retire from modeling and go into lifestyle services. And she'd rather make an established brand her own than start from the ground up."

Jasper rolled his eyes so hard that he must have seen the back of his head. "Translation: she wants to use Daddy's money to buy her way to success."

"You said it, not me."

He leaned his hands against a chairback, making us more eye-level. "So, what's she willing to pay? You gonna take the offer?"

I opened my mouth, feeling unsure of my answer, when a perfunctory knock came from the front door, announcing the arrival of Charlotte, Deacon, and Maisie.

"An offer for what?" Charlotte tilted her head as she, her beau, and their dog joined us at the kitchen counter. "You're not selling the condo, are you?"

"No way." I didn't want to go into the details about Rae's lucrative offer right now. Not when we had much more pressing issues to address. "Nothing could take me away from our happy little commune." In an attempt to avoid further questioning, I bent down to greet Maisie. "Hello, my little sweet pea." The not-so-little lab mix nuzzled my side as I stroked her soft brindle fur. I never considered myself to have any maternal instinct, but something about Maisie had awakened it within me.

For dogs, mind you.

"How's my precious puppy doing today?" I made kissy noises as I rubbed under her chin. Deacon was waiting on a doggie DNA test to tell him what breed Maisie was mixed with, but we all thought she had to have Australian Shepherd in her due to her pretty coloring. "Any updates for us?" I glanced hopefully at her owner.

He smirked. "In the twenty minutes we've been apart? No, I'm afraid not."

My cheeks heated at his light teasing. I should've known better than to ask such a naïve question. Good police work was a slow and often painful process. Nothing like the *CSI* effect we all saw on TV. Of course, the testing Gavin mentioned wouldn't have been done yet. We'd be lucky if it took only a few days. I shuddered at the notion as Jasper's cautious words echoed in my mind. A few days was a lifetime within the Central Shores gossip circles. My anxious gaze fell on Charlotte. Once word got out about who Kiefer was and how he died—and no doubt, it would—public suspicion would inevitably fall on my bestie. I didn't want her to take that hit. Both Jasper and I had been there before, and it was no picnic.

Charlotte rubbed her palms together as Maisie eagerly lapped from the water bowl I'd prepared. "Okay, Sleuth Squad, where do we start?"

"How about you walk us through your entire interaction with Kiefer?" Deacon recommended softly. "At any point, did you leave his drink unattended while making it?" He sounded like he hated asking his girlfriend to relive her experience, but such questions were necessary.

"Of course." Charlotte's grin looked forced. "As soon as I saw him heading for my booth, I texted Coco. He sticks—stuck out in a crowd, given his size. Once he arrived at my booth, he told me how good it was to see me." Her gaze dropped to Maisie sitting patiently at her feet. "I was kinda like a deer in the headlights, though, so when I didn't immediately tell him to pack sand, he started saying how he was sober and that he'd gotten his anger issues under control. Coco arrived around that point in the conversation." She shot a grateful look my way. "I-I don't think I took my eyes off the latte for more than a few seconds."

"Did Kiefer watch you make the drink?" Deacon pressed.

Charlotte chewed on her lower lip. "N-not really. He turned away in a huff because I told him to get lost." Tears welled in her eyes. "He trusted me not to trigger his allergy, even after everything that happened between us."

A moment of strained silence passed before any of us spoke. "Okay, so based on what you've told us, we think we can safely assume the peanuts ended up in Kiefer's cup *after* he walked away from your booth." Deacon stroked his chin. "Although, how someone managed to drop them in, we don't yet know."

"He obviously trusted Charlotte—an ex—to make him a peanut-free drink. Maybe he trusted the wrong person to leave it with. A friend who turned out to be a foe." I motioned for everyone to join me at the dining table. My laptop and tablet now occupied the spots where the bath bombs had been. "We gotta find out who else in the area Kiefer knew. Everyone's phones charged?"

"Yep. Can I get your WiFi password?" Deacon stood ready with his device.

I quickly shared it and got him connected. "I think the best place to begin is on Kiefer's socials. See who he was hanging out with and what he's been up to in the area. It shouldn't take us that long to find him since his name isn't exactly mainstream." I shot Charlotte a sidelong glance. "Unless you happen to remember his handles?"

Her tanned skin paled slightly. "I-I know he definitely had an Instagram account. Try @thebigkief."

As Deacon placed a comforting hand over hers, I chided myself for my own stupidity. *Duh, Coco.* Charlotte would obviously remember the profile that had hounded her online until she eventually blocked him.

Jasper frowned as he typed rapidly on his phone. "Um, I'm not finding that handle on Instagram." He shrugged. "Maybe he rebranded himself? The Big Kief? I sure would." He added an extra judgy sniff for emphasis.

Charlotte managed a light giggle, and I appreciated Jasper's uncanny ability to lighten the mood. Maisie sat beside Charlotte and placed her head on Char's lap for added support, too. The perceptive pup was such a great addition to our team.

Shelving Instagram for now, I typed Kiefer Marsh into my Facebook search bar and waited for the results to load.

I squinted at the profiles staring back at me. "That can't be right," I murmured as I retyped Kiefer's name and searched again.

"What's wrong?" Deacon asked.

"You're not going to believe this, but there isn't a single Kiefer Marsh coming back in my results." I held my phone screen so they could see for themselves. "There are a few Keefs and a ton of Marshes, but not one profile with the name Kiefer Marsh."

Charlotte chewed on her lower lip. "I mean, he wasn't big into social media when we dated. Instagram was the only one I remember him using. He liked the pictures. Facebook was 'too wordy' for his taste."

Jasper looked like he was desperately trying to swallow an off-color comment.

"Okay, so let's dig more into Instagram." Doing my best to stay positive, I tapped open the app and decided to ignore the annoying fact that both Kiefer and I preferred this platform over others.

I selected the magnifying glass and typed Kiefer's name once more. "What the hashtag? What's going on here?" I studied the extensive list in front of me. Yes, Instagram had returned more results than Facebook, but the closest items matching Kiefer were profiles with the name "Marshall."

Charlotte and the guys tapped away on their phones, their faces reflecting the same discouragement I was feeling.

"Does this mean Marsh deleted the account he was using back in the day?" Deacon asked. Out of the four of us, he was the least social media savvy. The guy could parse out multiple DNA profiles from a single sample, but still struggled to share a public Reel to a private DM. In the Sleuth Squad, we all had our strengths.

Charlotte's mouth popped open. "Hold on. I think I can check."

We listened to the sound of her fingernails clicking against her onscreen keyboard, each of us sitting on the edge of our seats with anticipation.

"I'm checking the accounts I've blocked in my settings," she explained as she maneuvered through the app. A moment later, she positioned her phone on the table so we all could see. Even though Charlotte had a private Instagram profile, she still had a laundry list of blocked accounts.

"Are these all profiles he tried contacting you through?" Jasper sounded alarmed.

She shook her head. "Most are just random pervs who've tried to chat me up. But maybe Kiefer was masquerading behind one of these?"

I understood her theory and agreed. People—especially creepers—could create shell accounts on social media to limit their traceable activity. "Let's divvy up their profiles and check them out. Here, Char, you can use my *Trending Topic* account." I slid my tablet across the table, which was logged into my blog's Instagram page. Since Charlotte had blocked the handles on her profile, she wouldn't be able to search them under her own account.

Even though there were a lot of blocked users, it didn't take us long to wade through the list. Many were private profiles, but seeing the minuscule number of posts and followers on their page confirmed these were shell accounts. Shell accounts often had little to no identifying info tied to them for fear of the user behind the digital curtain getting caught by a prying spouse or partner.

One thing was clear about the blocked handles: Kiefer Marsh wasn't readily among them.

"Okay, so no dice on Facebook or Insta. Luckily, we've got plenty of places to check." I summoned my earlier positivity and instructed my friends to focus on the myriad of social media platforms jockeying for our attention.

An hour and several platforms later, we still had nothing.

"A millennial with no social media footprint?" Jasper held a hand to his throat, looking truly aghast. "Makes sense that the guy turned out to be a psychopath."

Chapter Eight

Jasper's insensitive comment earned a swift kick from me in his shin. "Ow!"

But before he could launch into an extensive hissy fit, Hudson lumbered into the condo, carrying a hefty bag of takeout with him.

"Uh oh, gang. Why so glum?" my fiancé asked before swooping in to kiss my cheek and greet Maisie with an ear scratch. As he straightened and noticed all our tech, he arched a dark eyebrow. "What exactly happened at the CSC festival?"

Surprise washed over Jasper's face. "You really haven't heard?"

Hudson shook his head. "I was on a work call while driving home, so I couldn't listen to the news." He caught my eye and winked.

His covert reaction made my heart skip a beat, both with flirtatious desire and excitement. No doubt, Hudson would catch me up on *Crime Sweet Home* once our friends had left. He was in the middle of a cold case featuring a missing seventeen-year-old, presumed dead, and through our combined efforts of scouring the young man's inner circle via social media, we'd uncovered a potential new source. I was willing to bet this "work call" had been with said source.

While we helped Hudson unpack containers of garden salad, roasted chicken, garlic parm mashed potatoes, and sautéed squash, we updated him on Kiefer's suspicious death. By the time we finished recounting events, we were gathered around the outdoor table on the back deck, eating the yummy meal.

Hudson released a low whistle. "Wow. I'm sorry you're going through this, Charlotte." He gave her shoulder a brotherly squeeze. His compassion for her situation brought tears to my eyes. Even though their experiences had been different, he knew firsthand how terrible it was to deal with an abuser who lorded their power over him.

Hudson took a bite of mashed potato, and once he swallowed, his concerned gaze turned to my bruised wrist. He wasn't happy I'd been injured, but what was done was done. "So, now that I'm up to speed, I gotta say, guys…aren't we jumping the gun on this one? I mean, Gavin and Adrian know Charlotte wouldn't purposely trigger someone into having an allergic reaction, no matter the reason. To say nothing of *stealing* the guy's EpiPen and tossing it in the trash."

My nostrils flared at his lackluster response to our fledgling investigation. "You're really going to try and convince us not to get involved?"

"Well, of course not." He held up his palms in mock surrender. "But now, at least I can truthfully tell your parents that I attempted to make you see reason."

Charlotte and Deacon chuckled at his sheepish grin. Jasper, however, did not look amused. "Detective Buddies One and Two may believe in Charlotte's innocence, but they're not the only players involved here. With all the recent development and population growth, Central Shores is now on a much grander stage, and the district attorney's office is going to have its eye on the CSC's activities. The mayor, too." He shot Charlotte an apologetic look. "I'm sorry to rain on everyone's parade, but what *if* Char's prints are the only ones found on the cup? Not to mention, there's simply her word that she didn't slip peanut bits into his cup unnoticed. In the eyes of the official investigation, she has means, motive, and opportunity. What prosecutor wouldn't want to take that to trial?"

His heavy words settled over us, and the roasted chicken turned to rocks in my stomach.

Emotion shimmered in Charlotte's eyes as fear radiated from her.

Jasper continued, "I know our previous cases have been like glamorous scenes out of *The Devil Wears Prada*—with me being Meryl Streep, obviously, but Charlotte's in serious jeopardy, guys. More so than anything we've ever dealt with before."

I felt incredibly foolish being lectured by Jasper, of all people. But he was right. The only reason Charlotte hadn't been led away from the festival in handcuffs today was because Gavin and Adrian believed she wasn't a cold-blooded killer. If her prints *were* the only ones on the murder weapon, our detective pals would have a really hard time explaining away their reasoning, given her turbulent history with Kiefer.

"Then we need to find credible suspects who had even more means, motive, and opportunity than Char." I punctuated each word with a wave of my fork.

Deacon nodded. "Means and opportunity are the easiest. There were a ton of booths selling nuts in various forms. Anyone at the festival could have distracted him and dropped peanut bits into his cup as he was wandering the grounds."

"Motive is where we come up short." Charlotte ran a frustrated hand through her long hair. "I mean, I *clearly* had a reason to want Kiefer out of my life for good."

Deacon looped an arm around her. "If the sweetest gal on the planet wanted Marsh gone, I'm sure the guy's got a list of enemies a mile long."

"And since we can't determine who he's been staying with from his online profiles," I added, "we're going to have to ask around. Boots-on-the-ground style." I lightly pounded my right fist into my left palm for emphasis, but ended up sending a nasty jolt through my bruised wrist. Swallowing the pain, I continued, "I have a few clients in Ocean Hollow. I can arrange to check in on them and sniff out whether anyone knew what Kiefer was doing in town."

"Going old-school Miss Marple, huh?" Jasper grinned. "How retro."

Hudson didn't look as confident. "Ocean Hollow may be a small community, but your clients don't strike me as the type who'd associate with a guy like Kiefer."

I was just about to comment about making assumptions when Deacon's phone buzzed. His eyes widened momentarily as he read the screen before answering. "Hey, Gav. What's up?"

The rest of us stilled, not even daring to set down our silverware for fear of making noise.

"Yep." Deacon's jaw tightened. "I'm with her at Coco and Hudson's place."

I reached for Hudson's hand underneath the table. Was Gavin calling to find out where Charlotte was so they could arrest her?

"Sure thing, man." Deacon pulled the phone away from his ear and laid it in the center of the table before hitting the speakerphone button. "Okay, we're all here."

"Great," Gavin warbled from the phone. The background noise cut off an instant later, and he lowered his voice. "First things first, this call never happened, all right?"

Even though he couldn't see us, we all bobbed our heads in solemn promise. "What call?" Jasper quipped.

Evidently satisfied, Gavin continued, "Charlotte, I need you to think back to your chat with Marsh earlier today. Did he mention the name Eric Brady at all?"

She wrinkled her nose. "Eric Brady? No..." Charlotte drummed her fingers on the table. "No, he didn't," she responded more assuredly. "But then again, he didn't mention anything other than he was staying with a friend in Ocean Hollow."

"Hmm, I see. Well, I appreciate your time. Thanks, guys." Gavin hung up before we could ask anything further.

Jasper stared at Deacon's phone. "That was odd...right? Who the heck is Eric Brady?"

"And why is Gavin asking Charlotte about him?" Deacon slid his phone into his shorts' pocket.

I nearly choked on a bite of squash. "Hashtags. That sneaky little..." I grappled for my own phone and typed **Eric Brady** into Facebook. As anticipated, I got a slew of results, but some quick filtering had me narrowing down the list in a speedy manner.

Eric Brady, Owner of Gold Score sports memorabilia shop, Ocean Hollow, DE.

I tapped the entry, and Eric's profile filled my screen. While I didn't recognize the brown-haired, blue-eyed white dude holding a huge gold trophy in the profile pic, I definitely knew the muscular, blond guy posing next to him. He'd collapsed to the ground right in front of me only a few hours ago.

I held my phone for my companions to see. "Guys, I think Gavin just gave us our first suspect."

Chapter Nine

"Eric Brady, huh?" Jasper stroked his chin. "Does he look familiar to you, Char?"

She squinted at the profile picture on my phone. "No. Not really." She pointed to the logo on Eric's polo. "But he's got my college shirt on. He must've been someone Kiefer met after I left."

Hudson took a turn assessing the picture. "Looks like they're holding a golfing trophy. Teammates, perhaps?"

Charlotte's eyes widened in recognition. "That could be it. Kiefer played all four years."

I reached behind my lounge chair to grab the tablet I'd brought outside. A few finger swipes later, I had Eric's Facebook profile loaded on a larger screen. "This is good. His privacy settings are fairly low." Even though I wasn't Facebook friends with Eric, I could still see plenty of personal info, posts, and pictures he'd shared on the platform. According to the data dump in his Overview section, he'd been born in Ocean Hollow and went to college in South Carolina, ultimately graduating with a master's in business administration before moving back to the area. "Check this out. Just a few hours ago, Eric uploaded a promo photo for an upcoming sale at Gold Score next weekend." I checked the timestamp. One PM. The announcement had gone live roughly an hour before Kiefer died. "I wish I could tell whether it was a scheduled post or one he'd uploaded manually."

"I've heard of Gold Score before." Hudson leaned back in his chair, having cleaned his plate. "Arthur bought an autographed Ray Lewis jersey from there a few weeks ago."

"Are we supposed to know who that is?" Jasper raised an eyebrow.

Hudson chuckled. "Sorry, forgot what audience I was speaking to."

"Baltimore Ravens player," Deacon clarified, proving his mettle to Hudson. "One of the best defensive players of all time."

Before Jasper could jump in with a tragic Kanye West impression of "But Beyonce is one of the best defensive players of all time," I waved the topic aside. "Gavin dropped Eric's name for a reason. He *has* to be the person Kiefer was visiting."

Deacon's expression grew solemn. "Gavin's gotta be rattled by the evidence if he's feeding us information through unofficial channels." He glanced worriedly at Charlotte.

"Gavin has access to Kiefer's phone," I pointed out. "He's probably already realized that Kiefer has a next-to-zero social media footprint for us to investigate and decided to do us a solid." Considering the number of times I'd helped the Central Shores police department uncover something useful in a case, it seemed the least our friendly neighborhood detective could do.

"Yeah, but if anyone finds out Gav let Eric's name slip, we're all in big trouble." Deacon's stern gaze traveled around the table.

Jasper mimed zipping his lips as we all nodded agreement.

I continued skimming Eric's Facebook page. Most everything was Gold Score related. I tapped on the Contact and Basic Info tab, and my breath hitched in my throat. He had an Instagram account linked. One click later, a new page loaded on my laptop, and Eric's Insta profile appeared.

While the same Gold Score images were displayed on his profile grid, there were also a ton of personal pictures scattered in between. My heart drummed against my chest as I selected an eye-catching photo featuring a group of people lined up with arms linked, smiling at the camera.

"I've got something, guys." I ushered everyone's focus toward the tablet screen.

Leaving their dinner plates, my friends huddled behind me, and Hudson leaned against my left arm.

I double-checked the timestamp and caption: "This was uploaded five days ago. Does anyone look familiar?" I positioned the tablet for optimal viewing, ensuring the fading sunlight didn't cause a glare.

"Well, there's Kiefer." Charlotte pointed to her hulking ex.

Jasper tapped the guy next to him. "And that's Eric Brady. Wait a second... isn't that Rand Windham on the end?"

A triumphant grin spread across my lips. "It is indeed." Born and raised in Central Shores, Rand Windham worked over in Ocean Hollow selling luxury yachts. He'd been a few years ahead of Jasper and me in school and had been involved in one of our previous cases.

Hudson narrowed his dark brown gaze at the photo. "Isn't that Sid Jr. next to him?"

I beamed at Hudson, impressed he remembered. Sid Jr.—more commonly known as Sy—helped manage Central Shores's pizza joint, Saucy Sid's. Although "helped" might have been too generous a word. Every time Hudson and I visited the pizza parlor, Sid Sr. complained about his son's lack of commitment toward taking over the family business.

"So, beyond Eric, we've got two other guys with close ties to Central Shores who knew Kiefer in some capacity." Deacon snapped a reference picture of the Instagram post with his phone. "It's a good start."

"I wonder where this shot was taken." Jasper edged closer to the screen.

I scrolled to see if I could find a geo-tag, but nothing popped up. "Looks like a bar?" Behind Sy and Rand, I could make out a few bar stools.

Charlotte pointed to a silver, blurry blob in the background. "That reminds me of a beer tank."

"Think it could be Sand Bar Brewing?" Hudson cocked an eyebrow. "They had a big tasting event last weekend, remember? I tried to get Arthur to go." At the mention of our grieving friend, his enthusiasm dimmed.

"That's right." I'd seen a sponsored post in my newsfeed about the Ocean Hollow brewery. I quickly grabbed a notepad I'd set aside and began scribbling down what we'd uncovered: *Sy Ramone, Rand Windham, Eric Brady, Sand Bar Brewing.* "Any idea who this woman is?" I gestured toward the pretty, petite brunette sandwiched between Eric and Kiefer.

Charlotte shook her head. "Haven't seen her before."

I hovered my mouse over the picture, hoping Eric had tagged the people in the photo. No such luck. We'd have to figure out who she was the old-fashioned way. "Okay, so in a span of ten minutes, we went from having no clue about who Kiefer knew in the area to having a whole crew." I smiled at our findings, however limited they may be.

"Should we let Gavin know?" Deacon arched an eyebrow.

I considered the best way to play this. "If he gave us Eric's name, I'm sure he and Adrian will be looking into Eric's socials. If they haven't already." In the past, I hadn't given Gavin enough credit when it came to utilizing social media in his cases, and I wasn't about to insult his intelligence after he'd so generously given us a lead. With that in mind, an idea for our next move formed. "I say we have a casual, off-the-record chat with Sy and Rand, see what they have to say about Kiefer and Eric, then go from there."

Charlotte frowned. "Why not just go right to Eric?"

"Yeah. In all likelihood, he's suspect number one," Deacon agreed. "The person with the closest ties to Kiefer."

Jasper snorted. "Best friend-turned-backstabber?"

"Hey, I'm totally with you guys." I held up my hands in feigned surrender. "But since we don't know Eric socially, it would be totally sus if we showed up on his doorstep asking about Kiefer out of the blue." I paused as my reasoning settled in. "At least, if we get Sy and Rand to mention him by name, we have a connection, tenuous as it might be."

Charlotte nodded. "So, Sy and Rand are stepping stones to Eric?"

"For now." I grabbed a screenshot of the Instagram photo and saved it to my cloud storage.

"Wish I hadn't grabbed food." Hudson surveyed our empty plates. "We could've gone out for pizza."

I gave him a reassuring pat on the shoulder. "I doubt we'd find Sy working at his dad's place anyway." I glanced at my smartwatch. "Not on a Saturday night."

"Think he's hitting the bottle at Harper's?" Jasper asked, referring to Sy's well-known party-hard ways.

Charlotte smirked. "Not unless Shanice lifted his lifetime ban."

For the past two years, Shanice Richards had managed Harper's Pub for the Harper family. She ran a tight ship and tolerated no nonsense at the local dive bar. "Sy got kicked out?"

Charlotte nodded. "A few weeks ago. She told me all about it the next morning when she came by for coffee." As the owner of one of Central Shores's most popular establishments, Charlotte had her finger on the town's pulse more often than I did. "Shanice said he would never again be allowed to set foot into a business run by her."

"Yikes." I balked at the harsh sentence. "What'd he do?"

"Something involving the women's bathroom, a fire extinguisher, and way too many Rum & Cokes."

"Charming." Jasper scoffed. "So, if Harper's is off his list, where's Sy going to go for his booze? I doubt Beaufort's would tolerate his fashion-forward dress code."

I chuckled at the mental image of Sy, in his signature tank top and basketball shorts, sitting at one of Beaufort's fancy, chic tables. "I'd say the same for Andre's wine bar." Vine cultivated a sophisticated aesthetic and was more popular with the Central Shores elites than our working-class folks.

"We could try The Beach Pit," Hudson suggested. "Seems like the place to be these days."

I'd totally blanked on our town's newest late-night hotspot. "Worth a shot. And if it's a bust, we can always enjoy a round of drinks." Having opened its "doors" in April, The Beach Pit was an outdoor social club located near the strip. Catering to locals and visitors alike, The Beach Pit hosted DJs and bands and was a club-type place to vibe out. Since Central Shores wasn't home to a plethora of nightlife, The Beach Pit had been a big hit with the under-forty crowd, of which Sy was definitely a part.

"I'm getting a cocktail either way." Charlotte gave a half-hearted laugh. "Since it's been a day."

Jasper eyed her warily. "You think it's a good idea to go out on the town? It might be a better idea for you to hole up at home. You know, outta sight, outta mind?"

"I understand your concern, but I want to help." She frowned at his suggestion to remain on the bench. "Sy's a frequent B2P customer, so I have a better rapport with him than any of you."

She made a good point. "What are the chances Rand will be hanging out with him?" From previous experience, we knew Rand got together with a bunch of pals at Harper's on Fridays. What he did Saturday nights was anyone's guess.

"We can always track Rand down at the marina while he's on the job." Hudson rose from his seat and began gathering the dishes to take inside. "It might be better to speak with these guys separately, anyway. See if their stories align."

"We've got to be careful about how we approach it," Deacon warned as we all joined in the effort to clean up dinner. "The PD has yet to formally announce Kiefer's passing, so we can't reveal too much."

His comment prompted me to check my email for any work-related messages from Bernie, but I found nothing. She'd send me a statement for social media once the police were ready to go public. "I'm surprised an initial announcement hasn't already been made. I'd think Chief McInnis would want to reassure the public that the CSC team was all over the case."

Deacon glanced at his watch. "It's only been a few hours. Perhaps it's taking a while to track down Kiefer's next of kin."

But just as the words were out of his mouth, Bernie's contact info lit up my screen.

"Hey, B, what's up?" I answered as everyone paused loading the dishwasher to listen.

A jostling of papers preceded Bernie's harried sigh. "Hi, Coco. I hope I'm not catching you at a bad time?"

"Nope. Can I help with something?"

"I wanted to give you a heads up that the chief and I will be doing a press conference for the six-thirty local news about the man who died at the CSC festival. Gavin and Adrian told me you're already in the loop." More sounds of shuffling came through on Bernie's end. It sounded like a madhouse at the station. "I'm sending over a brief statement for you to upload to our socials. But can you hold off until six forty-five to post it? We want the formal press announcement to hit airwaves first."

I did some mental math. That meant I had an hour to get everything prepped. Plenty of time. "Of course. No problem." I could schedule the posts from my desktop and then head down to The Beach Pit with the Sleuth Squad to see if Sy was in residence.

"Thanks a mill. As for all the promo shots you took for socials, we're going to have to shelf them for now. I hope we can use them in the future." Her disappointment radiated through the phone line, and I felt for her. All her hard work to make the festival a PR success had been completely overshadowed by this tragedy.

"Maybe we can incorporate them into the community page on our website," she suggested on a hopeful note. "Oh, and sorry in advance for the vague media statement. We don't have much to share currently." Bernie paused and lowered her voice. "Keep an eye out for sus comments if you can, too. Anything to help us understand this vic and why someone would want to off him."

I tried to tamp down the giddy smile that threatened to spread across my lips. It felt good that Bernie and the PD valued my skills enough to help them in this somewhat official manner. "You got it," I said.

I wished her luck with the press conference and signed off. I recapped the call for my friends, noticing Charlotte grow increasingly fidgety.

"Everyone will know about Kiefer soon." She chewed on her lower lip as she tugged a strand of her hair.

Deacon pulled her close. "Chief McInnis will keep it short and to the point."

I agreed. "Yeah, if you're worried about being called out—"

"It's not that." Charlotte cut me off. "It's just...I'm sure people saw Kiefer bothering me at my booth. They might not have thought much about it then, but they're bound to remember if his picture pops up on the news."

I hated that she was right. Charlotte was going to be dragged into the suspect spotlight even faster than we anticipated. "Let me get the PD's posts scheduled, and then we can hit up The Beach Pit. They've got TVs all around the covered bar. We can gauge reactions to the news while we're there."

Hudson nodded. "Good call. Whoever laced Kiefer's cup with peanuts could be operating under the assumption that his death would be ruled an accidental medical event. When they learn it's being investigated as a homicide, they may show their cards."

"Well, that only works for us if his killer is *at* The Beach Pit," Deacon countered, "but still, it's worth keeping an eye out."

"Give me ten minutes to get the uploads situated." I darted into my first-floor office and fired up my iMac. By the time my Internet browser burst to life, Bernie had emailed me the statements she wanted shared.

"Yeesh, she wasn't kidding when she said the deets were vague," I murmured as I scanned the text intended for Facebook.

> **The Central Shores Police Department regrets to confirm that an individual died at the Community Safety Center grand opening festival. Thirty-one-year-old Kiefer Marsh of Seabrook Island, South Carolina, suffered an extreme medical event while on CSC grounds. Due to the sudden nature of his passing, the police are investigating his death. Anyone with information about Mr. Marsh and his activities while visiting the area is encouraged to contact the CSC hotline.**

The good news was that the brief statement didn't allude to Charlotte remotely in any way. But I knew how Central Shores operated. People would begin to talk about Kiefer, and someone was bound to remember spotting him at Charlotte's booth. Hashtags, the Sweet Resolutions crew practically had a front-row seat to the drama. I'd even told the trio that Kiefer had been giving Charlotte a hard time when I asked to borrow their cocoa powder. What's more, while Rosie and Tom weren't ones to gossip, Thomas *thrived* when it came to spreading juicy rumors. He spent most of our library reading group contributing to the grapevine and not what was between the book's spine.

Shaking worries about chatty Thomas away, I pasted Bernie's statement into my all-in-one social media management application to schedule posts for Facebook, Threads, and Instagram. I then attached the "official Central Shores PD statement" graphic I'd designed for such instances, hoping the arresting image would capture the attention of folks aimlessly scrolling through their feeds. I did the same for the PD's X account, rolling my eyes at the fact that we now had to line Elon Musk's pockets in order to access this scheduling feature. How I missed good ol' Twitter being free to use and not pay-to-play.

With the statements situated, I joined my friends in the living room.

"Sounds like a plan." Hudson gave Jasper a thumbs-up.

I perched on the arm of the sectional next to my fiancé. "What plan?"

Charlotte smiled sadly. "We were just brainstorming ways to show Amanda and Arthur some love. Get them out of town and give them a change of scenery, perhaps?"

"I've been invited to a dinner cruise up and down the coast in mid-July. Some charity event," Jasper explained with a shrug. "*Divulge* was given a table, so I thought it might be fun if we all went together."

"Sounds like a nice night out." I hoped we could convince the Highgrove-Bushmans to join—anything to help bring some light and joy into their lives. But since this charity cruise was several weeks away, I wondered if we could come up with some other activity in the meantime that allowed us to surround them with love and support. Maybe a beach day where we could all relax and unwind.

Hudson glanced my way. "All ready to go?"

I nodded. "Should we Uber?" I asked as everyone rose from our sectional.

"I'll run Maisie home real quick." Deacon whistled, and a slumbering Maisie jumped into action. She'd been sleeping in a barely-there sunspot by the door leading out onto the deck.

Jasper did the car summoning honors. "You've got fifteen minutes until Ethan arrives in his Honda Pilot," he called as Deacon disappeared out the front. While the rideshare service had cars idling up and down the Delaware coastline, we were still far enough out in suburbia to warrant modest wait times.

Charlotte and Deacon's condo was only a few hundred feet up the road, so Deacon didn't take long. Our driver pulled up three minutes ahead of schedule, and we all crawled into the SUV.

"Been taking a lot of groups down to The Beach Pit tonight," Ethan commented as he did a U-turn in my driveway and navigated toward the strip. "Place must be doing good business."

The Beach Pit had opened its doors at the first signs of warm weather and was managed by the same development group that ran Cyprus, a swanky, glam club located over in Cherry Springs. With all the new growth in Central Shores, it was a smart business move. We needed more variety in our nightlife, and The Beach Pit currently had dibs on that corner of the market.

Twelve minutes later, Ethan pulled the SUV up to The Beach Pit's drop-off point. The whole idea of the place was outdoor entertainment, with a stage, a bar, and a dance floor. There was only one all-weather structure on the property, which housed the kitchen, admin offices, and restrooms.

"Good thing it isn't raining." Hudson slid an arm around my waist as we got out of the Uber. The strobe lights pulsing from the DJ booth flashed across his bronze skin, making him look like a glowing god.

I kissed his cheek, happy he could join us for this sleuthing adventure. *Crime Sweet Home* was prepping for its second season, and work had kept him busy of late, leaving little time for us to spend together, let alone try to get a handle on our wedding planning.

As we all gathered outside the roped-off entrance, I asked Jasper, "Why don't you invite Eli to join us?" I wiggled my eyebrows, egging him on.

He swatted the idea aside. "I'm not ready to expose his unblemished soul to the seedy underbelly of our investigations."

Charlotte giggled. "You make us sound like *Bosch.*"

"Yeah, I'd say our vibe is more millennial *Murder She Wrote.*" At the rate we were going, Central Shores would be a worthy rival to Cabot Cove's body count. The sad thought made the laughter die in my throat. "All right, everyone. Keep an eye out for Sy and Rand. Heck, anyone in Eric's photo." I held up my phone to flash the Instagram pic at my companions and jog their memories. "And keep an ear to the ground about what people are saying about the CSC festival."

We all bumped fists and headed toward the bouncer standing guard at the archway entrance.

Chapter Ten

Music thumped on the light breeze, and it made sense why the developers had been forced to set up shop a mile north of the strip. I doubted the local family establishments like Jewel's Ice Cream and Beaufort's wanted club beats shattering their quiet, picturesque atmosphere.

After paying the twenty-dollar entrance fee, we were ushered down a red-carpeted pathway toward the main area of the club, known as "the pit." Even though the place was perched right on the beach, the recently poured cement floor was surprisingly free of sand.

A DJ's beats raged all around us, the hammering pulse already beginning to give me a headache. "Maybe this isn't the best place to chat up people." I leaned into Hudson's tall frame. "I can barely hear anything."

"What?"

It took me a moment to realize he was teasing me.

"Let's start with drinks," he suggested and made a circular motion with his finger, signaling he was going to grab them for everyone.

I nodded. The covered bar, with TVs scattered about, would be a good place to begin our search. Most screens showed a sports game, but I spotted the news on one or two.

Jasper scanned the area as he was the tallest of us all. "I'm going to do a lap and see what I can find. I'll meet you guys at the bar." With a wave, he began pushing his way deeper into the crowd of dancing, happy people.

The rest of us squeezed through the throng of sweaty bodies—gross—toward the flashy, industrial-looking bar. Instead of leaning into a beachy aesthetic, The Beach Pit had gone full futuristic with grays and metallics.

I checked my phone, noting we had about twenty minutes before the PD's press conference kicked off. We had to play it safe with our questions until then or risk raising eyebrows.

Hudson managed to wedge into an open spot and grab the nearest bartender's attention, and I did a double-take when I recognized her. "Hey, Noelle!" I yelled over the music, waving to the Central Shores Public Library director as she poured a round of shots for the group next to us. She must've been working here part-time.

Her tight grin brightened into a genuine smile once she noticed me. "Hi, Coco! Hey, guys." She wiped her hands on a towel and flung it over her shoulder. "Don't normally see you all here."

I tried to disguise my wince with a smile. "We're celebrating." I didn't want to raise her suspicions about why we were out on the town when our friend group much preferred spending the night in, playing games, and goofing off.

"Ooo, celebrating what?" She glanced at my engagement ring. "You two finally pick a date?"

Here we go again. I didn't realize that you needed to have every single detail about your wedding day already planned out the moment you got engaged. I'd lost count of the number of times Hudson and I were asked, "When's the wedding?" within the first hour of our engagement. But, after being engaged for nine months, I'd mastered my canned response. "We're still looking at our options."

Yes, truly brilliant stuff.

In all honesty, we weren't really looking at options at all. Hudson and I were committed to each other and had been for years. In our eyes, we were already married. Yes, a big party to celebrate our union would be fun *in theory,* but then the reality of making that party happen set in. As someone with high anxiety and a bit of control freak baked in, the thought of planning a wedding on top of everything we already had going on in our lives had me seriously considering elopement.

"I see. So, what's the special occasion?" Noelle asked as she perched her elbows atop the bar, the strobe lights shimmering on her dark skin.

I summoned the white lie. "Making it through the CSC grand opening relatively unscathed. Glad to have all that planning behind me."

Noelle nodded sagely and asked us for our drink orders. As she began making a round of Dark and Stormies, she said, "I hear you. I'll be glad when the library lit drive is over." She flashed a guilty smile. "I can't thank you enough for the promo posts you made."

My cheeks heated. "Happy I could help." As part of Center of Attention's efforts for community outreach, I volunteered our services to help the library zhuzh up its social media presence with a few pro-bono campaigns. "Hey, uh, any chance you've seen Sy Ramone around here tonight?" I wracked my brain for a plausible excuse. "I've...got a question about a CoA request his dad sent me."

Noelle didn't seem to notice the remorse I felt over lying to her, but I reassured myself that sometimes our investigations warranted fibbing to good people. "You just missed him, actually." Her friendly expression faltered. "I don't think he was in the headspace for answering work-related questions, though."

"What do you mean?" Charlotte asked, her forehead wrinkled with worry.

Noelle leaned across the bar so she could speak at a more normal level. "He somehow got overserved. Could barely sit on his barstool by the time I realized he'd been rotating bartenders." She pointed over her slender shoulders to the landline phone on the wall. "I had to call him a cab."

I shared a curious look with Hudson, Charlotte, and Deacon. Sy's tendency to overindulge was well-known around town, but he was also a highly functioning alcoholic.

My mind began to race. For him to be hitting the bottle so hard, he couldn't sit up straight...Had he already heard about Kiefer's death and was drinking away his woes? Or his guilt?

Whatever the case, our plans to speak with him dissolved on the spot. Hashtags. We'd have to find another way to chat with him about his ties to Kiefer.

Noelle set our drinks in front of us. "Anything else I can get you?" she asked as Hudson gave her his card to open a tab.

"All set." We thanked her, and she hurried down the length of the bar to assist the next people vying for her attention.

"I wonder what has Sy so worked up?" I raised an eyebrow at my companions as we sipped our—*ahem*—very strong drinks.

Hudson snorted. "I can think of one major thing."

"Char said Kiefer's only been in the area a few weeks." Deacon swirled his glass, the ice clinking. "Could he and Sy really have gotten *that* close in such a short amount of time? We're basing all our assumptions off of *one* picture."

I tugged my phone from the little clutch I'd brought and navigated to Eric Brady's Instagram profile. In my excitement at seeing Kiefer in a post, I hadn't given the rest of his account as much attention. "Lucky for us, there's way more than just one pic." I motioned for my friends to huddle around me. "Look here. Photos of Kiefer started showing up on Eric's profile Memorial Day weekend."

"Gives us a better sense of how long he's been in the area." Hudson squeezed my waist appreciatively.

Charlotte leaned in, her hair falling forward and obscuring my phone screen. "Wow, Eric sure posts a lot." She pushed her hair out of the way. "And look!" She pointed to several thumbnail images. "There are at least six other times that Kiefer, Rand, and Sy were all together."

"That brunette woman from the first pic shows up even more." I tapped to see if her handle had been tagged in any recent posts. No dice. "I wonder who she is. Eric's girlfriend?" If that were the case, though, why was she clinging to Kiefer in photos like her life depended on it?

"Okay. Okay." Deacon held his palms up, admitting defeat. "Clearly, Kiefer embedded himself quite deeply into this friend circle while he was here."

"They've got to know something." I studied Eric's profile grid one more time. "But since Sy might be dealing with a hangover tomorrow, how about we track down Rand Windham first? Maybe he'll be in better shape to talk."

Charlotte nodded. "We should start at Ocean Hollow Marine. Rand mentioned the last time he was in for coffee that he's working most weekends this summer."

I used my phone to check their business hours on Google. Sundays, they were open from nine to six. "Sounds like a good plan of attack." I was about to suggest that we go find Jasper and get out of this sweaty, bass-thumping nightmare when a familiar figure on one of the TVs caught my attention.

Chapter Eleven

"The press conference!" I tugged Hudson's arm, pulling his gaze in the TV's direction. While we obviously couldn't hear what was being said, the screen showed subtitles capturing Chief McInnis's speech.

Good evening. Regretfully, my office is here to confirm that an individual passed away due to an extreme medical event during the opening of our Community Safety Center. The man, identified as thirty-one-year-old Kiefer Marsh, was visiting the area from out of state. At this time, we are investigating the incident, and anyone believing to have information about the victim is encouraged to reach out to our CSC hotline at 302-555-8734.

I felt conflicted as the closed captioning text flickered across the screen. While I was glad Chief McInnis remained vague about Kiefer's manner of death for Charlotte's sake, his statement would undoubtedly cause a field day for the local rumor mill.

"So," Jasper's voice from behind jolted me from my thoughts, "the news is out." He stared grimly at the TV.

I handed him the cocktail we'd ordered for him. "See anything noteworthy out on the dance floor?"

He shook his head. "Nope. No sign of anyone from Eric's friend group."

We updated him on what Noelle had told us about Sy having to be asked to leave and the additional pictures we'd checked out on Eric's profile.

Jasper took a thoughtful sip of his drink before responding. "So, something had Sy feeling out of sorts. You think it's news of Kiefer's death?"

I shrugged. "It's possible, but I guess we won't know until we're able to track him down."

"Which may be hard to do if he's sleeping off a bender." Jasper stroked his chin. "Chatting up Rand sounds like the best next move."

"What's the right way to approach him?" Charlotte drummed her fingers on the bar top. "Think he's forgotten about the last time we tried to get intel from him?"

I thought back to a rather tense incident at Harper's Pub during our investigation the previous September. "Yeah…Rand may not be too happy to see us. Especially me."

Jasper snapped his fingers. "What if he thinks there's a sale involved?" A devious grin spread across his face. "This dinner cruise *Divulge* has been invited to could've sparked the desire for me to become a yacht bro."

Hudson chuckled at the notion, and I raised an eyebrow.

"What?" Jasper turned up his nose. "It could happen."

Deacon folded his arms. "It's better than showing up, guns blazing. Although, speaking of guns," he added, his shoulders slumping, "I should probably sit this one out. I could write off running into Sy and questioning him as a fortuitous circumstance during a night out on the town, but showing up at a potential suspect's place of work might be harder for me to explain to the chief if it gets back to him."

Charlotte rested a reassuring palm on her boyfriend's back. "The same goes for me, too, actually. I'm working the café all day tomorrow since Maria held the fort down by herself today. It's probably for the best, though. I have no idea if Kiefer told his friends about our shared history, and if he did, Rand would definitely be on high alert if I showed up at his workplace, asking questions."

I was grateful Charlotte came to this conclusion on her own. I hated the thought of having to ask her to stay behind because I shared her concerns. "If you've got some downtime tomorrow, why don't you guys team up and dig into Eric's, Rand's, and Sy's social media accounts? We'll swing by B2P once we're back from Ocean Hollow and compare notes."

The couple nodded.

Hudson tugged at my elbow. "I can't join, either. I have an interview scheduled with Jermaine Norris's former girlfriend tomorrow." A guilty wince enveloped his handsome face.

"She finally agreed to speak on the record?" I nearly choked on my drink with excitement. This must have been the big *CSH* development Hudson had alluded to earlier this afternoon.

"Halfheartedly. But we're in." Hudson's face glowed with hope.

Jermaine Norris was the featured victim in Hudson's latest *Crime Sweet Home* project. He was a seventeen-year-old star basketball player who mysteriously disappeared one night after a playoff game. Authorities in the neighboring county had written him off as a runaway, but Jermaine's family insisted their son had been a victim of foul play. It'd been over ten years since Jermaine vanished, and Hudson was determined to jumpstart the case by raising public awareness.

"That's amazing, babe." I squeezed his hand and pressed my lips closer to Hudson's ear, so only he could hear me. "I'm glad Ivy's cooperating with you." Hudson had asked for my help in wooing Ivy Chu. For years, she'd been unwilling to speak about her high school boyfriend's case, even to the police. But a few encouraging emails from Coco Cline, lifestyle blogger and social media influencer, had piqued her interest in talking to Hudson. I was proud to serve as a secret weapon when Hudson needed help getting victims' reluctant families and friends to go on the record. My stardom, limited as it might be, loosened the tongues of *Trending Topic* fans, and Ivy Chu was *definitely* a fan. Her Insta handle could be found frequently in my Likes notifications. A major, valuable benefit to the fame I'd gained.

"Jasper and I will tag team Rand." I reassured my companions that their absence on our next sleuthing adventure was completely understandable. "He'll be less likely to suspect something is up with fewer people there."

With a plan in place, we all cheers-ed with our drinks and hurriedly gulped down their remaining contents. From the cringing expressions on the Sleuth Squad's faces every time the DJ dropped an even louder beat, I could tell we were all ready to vacate The Beach Pit. The place was way too loud with too little food being served to really be our scene. "Shall we jet?"

* * *

As we waited for our return Uber in the designated pick-up location outside the club, I noticed Dionne Burbank standing nearby with a group of her friends.

"Omigosh, it's Coco!" Lacie's younger sister squealed as she tugged on the arms of her two closest gal pals within reach.

Despite Dionne always being very friendly, I could tell from her overhyped reaction that she was probably a bit drunk. Watching her and her group stumble toward us all but confirmed this. "Hi, Dionne. Having a fun night out?"

"Just getting started!" she giggled. "We're heading up to Cyprus now."

Jasper sighed. "Ah, the vigor of youth."

The group of young twentysomethings laughed. "Come on, Mr. Hastings. You're not *that* old."

Jasper, who'd recently hit the big three-oh, looked like he might combust on the spot.

Charlotte, who was nearing thirty-one but could easily pass for twenty, patted him on the shoulder with a teasing *tsk*. "Yeah, you're not *that* old."

"Where are you guys heading?" Dionne asked as she swayed back and forth on her high heels, her enviable long legs on display in a silver miniskirt.

I sheepishly grinned. "To bed." Online, I may have cultivated a cool and sophisticated lifestyle, filled with fun fashion, décor, and makeup, but there was no hiding that I was a relative homebody from the folks who'd grown up in Central Shores, knowing me my whole life. Even the younger ones who followed me on socials.

"I get it." Dionne propped an arm on my shoulder. "Lacie told me you guys had a wild day at the CSC festival. Something about a guy dying right in front of your booth?" Her last remark was directed at Charlotte.

My friend grimaced. "Y-yeah. I wasn't there at the time, though."

One of the other young women gasped. Dionne's gaze slid back to me. "But you were, right, Coco? Lacie said the guy hurt you."

I glanced down at my bruised wrist. "I'm sure he didn't mean to." The memory came unbidden, and I tried to push Kiefer's desperate expression from my mind.

"Totally crazy." Dionne shook her head. "Dead bodies seem to love you, don't they?"

In her inebriated state, I tried not to take her slurred words to heart, but being associated with death wasn't a great feeling.

"Oh, look, our ride's here!" Jasper's needlessly loud interjection cut Dionne and her crew off from making further comments. With a wave goodbye, he herded us further down the sidewalk.

Since our car hadn't *actually* arrived, I expected a moment of awkwardness, but Dionne and her friends began carrying on as if we hadn't been chatting seconds ago, completely oblivious to our continued presence.

Charlotte reached for my hand. "I'm so sorry you're tangled up in this, Cokes. As if you need word getting out about being involved in *another* murder." She sighed. "If only I hadn't texted for you to come by my booth."

"Hey, don't say that." I shushed her. "I'm glad I was there." And it was the truth. As a somewhat public figure, I probably should've been more concerned about how this might affect my livelihood, especially with Rae Livingston's generous offer to buy *Trending Topic* on the table. But I was honestly relieved Dionne associated me more with Kiefer's death than Charlotte. If my taking the brunt of public scrutiny kept the heat off her, I'd do it in an instant. I'd weathered such scandals more than once and emerged relatively unscathed. I'd willingly do it again if it meant keeping my friends safe.

Our Uber arrived five minutes later. The drive back home to our condo development was spent in contemplative silence, and once the Sleuth Squad tumbled out of our rideshare, we bid each other goodnight.

"I hope this all gets resolved soon," Hudson murmured as we ambled up the pathway leading to our front door. "Poor Char seems wracked with guilt."

I nodded in agreement. Not only was she stressed about Kiefer's death, but I could tell Charlotte was worried about my rep taking a hit and whether Deacon's position at the CSC might be compromised. While forensic testing on the B2P cup and EpiPen couldn't come soon enough, I knew better than to put all my hopes in one basket. As of now, I really had no clue who Kiefer Marsh was or what he'd been up to while visiting Ocean Hollow and the surrounding area. "Let's hope Rand is willing to cooperate with us this time around."

Hudson pulled me close as we stepped inside the kitchen. "Let's just hope *he's* not the killer."

Chapter Twelve

"Are you sure you don't want me to come?" I asked Hudson the next morning as I handed him an egg bagel smeared with copious amounts of cream cheese. "Jasper and I can hit Ocean Hollow Marine later in the day."

Hudson took a bite of his breakfast and shook his head. "I appreciate the offer," he mumbled through a mouthful of yummy carbs, "but I think Ivy might be more genuine if it's just me. Not trying to impress the great crime-solving cyber sleuth, Coco Cline, and all."

I rolled my eyes at his teasing. With his hit TV show, Hudson's star shone just as brightly as mine these days, if not more. "Sure, Jan." I referenced our favorite *Brady Bunch* meme. "You just want to be able to smooth-talk her into spilling what she knows without your fiancée in tow." I ran a finger over the bronze skin of his cheek. Hudson knew how to weaponize his Regé-Jean Page good looks to get people to talk. It was one of the things that made him such a savvy and successful investigative reporter.

He playfully grabbed my wandering fingers and kissed them. "We're going to have to set aside some time soon and figure out how we turn my fiancée into my *wife*."

A battalion of butterflies went wild in my stomach at the thought. But anxiety won out over excitement. I wanted to be Hudson's wife, truly, I did, but the task of planning a wedding seemed so insurmountable. Who were we going to invite? How would we make sure everyone was happy? What would we feed them? What would I wear? Who would be in my bridal party beyond Jasper, Charlotte, and Amanda? Hudson had so many more close friends than I did. I didn't want him cutting out people just because I'd reached my friend quota.

"Hey." Hudson gripped my shoulders and gave me a little shake. Clearly, he could see me spiraling. "You know I'd be happy to marry you any time, anywhere, in front of anyone, right? Even if it's just us?"

I robotically moved my head up and down, even if I didn't really mean it. I'd been conditioned by the world around me that a big, fabulous wedding day was the ultimate symbol of a couple's love. If we didn't do the grand, traditional wedding, what would that really say about our relationship?

Your wedding should be what you and Hudson want, Coco. Not what you think the world expects.

See? A reasonable, rational side did exist within me. She just didn't show herself very often.

I took a deep breath as I pushed my wayward wedding anxieties into the dark corners of my mind. I would table this to work on with Dr. Ashawari during our weekly therapy sessions. "What time do you think you'll be done with your interview?" I changed the subject.

"I should be out by noon." Hudson finished off his bagel and began stuffing his messenger bag with his things. "Want me to ask Diamond if she can run a background check on Kiefer for me, and then I'll send the data dump to you?"

I smiled as I pictured the newest member of Hudson's production team, Diamond Hendricks. A Yale graduate, Diamond had worked for the Delaware FBI office as a data analyst for seven years before leaving her job to go into the private sector. During the past year, not only had she decided to change careers, but she'd realized her desire to live authentically as a proud trans woman. Four months ago, she was hired by Millie and Hudson to consult on law enforcement procedure, as well as help gather intel on potential sources and suspects using her Bureau connections. With her background in research and profiling, she'd been a great asset to *Crime Sweet Home*.

"Is that okay to do since you guys aren't reporting on Kiefer's case?"

Hudson gave me a deadpan stare, and my heart dropped.

"I got an email from Millie this morning." He rubbed his temples. "She wants me to cover the story for the nightly news while it's in progress and then do a *CSH* feature on it once we have enough."

I opened my mouth, but he cut me off. "Don't worry. I'll keep coverage off Charlotte as long as I can. The only problem is…" He handed me his phone so I could read the email in question.

> **Hudson,**
>
> **I'm told that Coco, YOUR fiancée, is the one who found the body. We're going to need to get her in front of the camera, ASAP. Is she working with the police on this one? Can we get her to interview the new detectives on the case? I want her exploits to be front-and-center; people love her. It's like Nancy Drew reality TV or something. Get her on board.**

My jaw nearly hit the countertop by the time I finished reading her unhinged request. Get me on board? With what, painting a target on my back that said, "Hey, Kiefer's killer! I'm looking into his murder, so feel free to shut me up permanently."

"Rest assured, I'm going to put my foot down on this one." Hudson's lips pressed against my dyed strawberry-champagne-colored hair. "Millie's obviously got no clue how dangerous it would be to advertise your involvement in this case."

"What will you say?" I appreciated him taking a stand, but I didn't envy anyone who had to tell the formidable Millicent Stabler, "No."

He shrugged. "That you are letting the police do their jobs for once."

I hesitated. "You're going to lie to her?"

"To protect you? Of course." He cupped my chin. "Then I'll feed you to the media wolves once you solve the whole dang thing."

I blushed at his teasing praise. "You're giving me a lot of credit."

"I believe in you. Especially when it's Charlotte's freedom on the line."

His words were a sobering reminder of what was at stake here. "Let me know if Diamond finds anything useful. And good luck interviewing Ivy."

With one final kiss goodbye, Hudson headed out the door. I stood in the entryway, watching long after he'd disappeared into our two-door garage. Millie's email demands continued to roll around in my head. I hadn't exactly "found" Kiefer's body, and he'd very much been alive when I'd come across him. The dark purple bruises on my wrist were proof of that. But her version of events made me wonder just what was being said online about this case.

"Guess it's now or never." I took a fortifying breath and headed into my office to check my socials. I'd been doing my best to ignore the notifications on my phone while Hudson and I enjoyed some couple time this morning, but now, duty called.

My anxiety spiked as I loaded my X homepage. *Might as well get my least favorite platform over with first.* What once had been Twitter, a fun, engaging community for *Trending Topic* followers, had devolved into a cesspool of conspiracy theorists, disinformation, and doomposting. For months, I'd been trying to get up the courage to deactivate my account and leave the platform entirely like so many others had, but then I'd think of my loyal followers who still commented about how much they appreciated my happy, upbeat content amongst the sea of negativity. I couldn't leave them out to dry.

Isn't that what you'd be doing if you sold your brand to Rae? The nagging thought poked at the back of my brain. Rae's overly generous offer to purchase *Trending Topic* certainly was tempting. But could I really just hand over everything I'd built since graduating college and leave it all behind? Heck, twenty-five-year-old me hadn't been able to do it when Mark Zuckerberg was the one offering to buy the IP, back when Meta acquired LiveIt, the social media app I'd had a hand in developing.

But I wasn't that happy-go-lucky twenty-five-year-old girl anymore. After solving three murders in my beloved hometown, my rose-colored glasses view of the world had definitely shattered. Evil was out there. Ignoring it was just as bad as championing it. I tried shining a light on suffering by featuring charitable organizations and sustainable businesses, hoping to make a difference. But I needed to do more. *I* wanted to make a positive impact. Yet, you'd never know that from my somewhat vapid content. How was sharing beauty tips and décor ideas helping homelessness and child hunger if all I was doing was linking out to nonprofit organizations in my posts?

With the money Rae Livingston was offering, I'd be in a better financial position to help. I could start a small foundation or something. But without *Trending Topic*, I'd lose my voice. I reached millions of people through my social channels, and I had the power to inspire them into action—if only I could figure out how. If I sold everything to Rae, I'd have to start from scratch, and there was no guarantee my fans would follow me down this new path if they believed I was turning my back on them for a paycheck.

As the X notifications page began to load, I realized Rae's offer was a problem for another time. I had a more immediate issue at hand. Mainly, my name trending alongside my hometown.

#CocoClineStrikesAgain

#CentralShoresCrimeHub

#DeathbyCocoCline

"What in Zendaya is going on here?" I yipped out loud, clicking on the last unflattering hashtag.

A video loaded underneath the first tweet on the list. "Oh no." I watched in horror as the scene from yesterday unfolded again before my eyes. Someone had filmed Kiefer staggering toward me. From the angle of the video, you couldn't see Kiefer's face, but you sure could see mine. At first, I looked murderous, which, to be fair, I was at seeing Kiefer's monstrous mug again. But then confusion quickly took over, and as Kiefer lunged forward and grabbed my wrist, all the camera caught was my panicked, pained expression. Video me reached out and tried prying Kiefer's hand away. He dropped to the ground a heartbeat later, and the video cut.

Through blurry vision, I read some of the comments attached to the video.

All she does is touch him and he dies?

First LaTàge, now this dude. Lock her up!

Can this poor girl get a break? Dead bodies for days!

Come on, people. Coco did nothing but help this man. #Coco-

ClineisaHero

What is up with this chick? Is she cursed?

Who is this poor guy? What did he do to deserve this?

I had to tear myself away, or I risked going down a dangerous rabbit hole. I rubbed my temples, feeling a headache swirling beneath my skull. I didn't bother asking how this had spiraled so quickly. Someone had uploaded the clip to social media, and the damage was done. I may not have been an A-list celebrity, but I was a notable enough figure to warrant public attention, especially when something dramatic was involved.

What bugged me the most was that LaTàge's name had been dragged into this mess. LaTàge, a waaaaay more famous influencer than I could ever hope to be, had been killed while she'd been staying in Central Shores, and I'd been at the top of the Internet's suspect list. The fact that her killer had been apprehended, yet faceless people on X still believed *I* had murdered her, was unsettling, to say the least. It boggled my mind how out of touch some people were with the truth simply because they believed everything they read.

A buzzing noise pulled me from my pity party, and I realized I'd left my phone on the kitchen counter. I made a mad dash from my office to grab it and saw several texts from Jasper. Despite my aversion to talking on the phone, I called him.

"I take it you've seen your newsfeed?" he answered in grave greeting.

I sighed as I sat back down in front of my computer. "Yup. Just saw a video someone snapped."

"They got your good side, at least," Jasper offered in conciliation.

His teasing only made me feel minutely better. "I can't believe people think a *touch* from me killed Kiefer."

"Remember that half the world is below average intelligence, Cokes. This is just another blip."

I stared at the comment, **Come on, people. Coco did nothing but help this man.** So, at least one person on this thread was coming to my defense. Why couldn't their **#CocoClineisaHero** hashtag go viral rather than the less-than-flattering others?

"At least the heat is on me and not Charlotte." I willed myself to be happy about this tarnished silver lining.

"Yeah, but with the Internet trending hate toward you, it makes it a bit harder to fly incognito while investigating what Kiefer was up to." Worry wedged itself into Jasper's remarks. "Now, I'm not crazy enough to suggest we drop our busy-bodying scheme entirely, but do you want me to chat with Rand solo?"

I bolted upright in my chair. "No way! Even though you could beat him into a pulp with one hand, I'm not letting you go alone." I paused and considered a plan of attack. "This actually works to our advantage a bit. If Rand gets suspicious, I can complain about the Internet's assumptions, which opens the door to ask him about Kiefer."

"Hmm." Jasper didn't sound very confident.

"Rand is pretty active on social media." I reminded him. "He probably already knows I'm being blamed." Although, if I recalled correctly, Instagram was Rand's preferred digital playground, and, based on the usual amount of IG notifications I had, it didn't look like the Kiefer story had been picked up there...yet.

A burst of air radiated from my phone's speaker. "Fine. But promise me you'll play it cool."

"Since when am I not cool?"

He scoffed. "You don't want the answer. I'll pick you up in forty, okay?"

I checked the time. That would put us in neighboring Ocean Hollow right when Rand's work opened its doors. "Sounds good."

With an eye on the time, I did my best to do some damage control with my online accounts. And by damage control, I meant to try and ignore all the X comments and replies condemning my "murderous" actions. Instead, I turned my attention to my blog, a platform I had a modicum of control over moderating. Thank goodness trolls hadn't descended on yesterday's featured post about animal yoga experiences. I'd highlighted and interviewed a collection of different yogis who all relied on animals being a part of their workouts. From goats to bunnies to kittens to puppies, these enhanced sessions were popping up all over the country. I'd even participated in a few classes myself. Despite being hopelessly inflexible, I'd had a fantastic time, especially once I got to cuddle with the cute fur babies at the end of the workout.

I imagined the lack of nasty trolls commenting on the latest *Trending Topic* article had to do with the new security measures I'd put into place. Given three very public crime-solving exploits, traffic on my website had become somewhat unruly, what with random commenters hassling my long-time followers. Now, people had to be verified subscribers of my blog rather than just being able to enter a name and comment to post. It had cut down a *lot* on the negativity besieging my online world, which was a bonus.

Satisfied that the hate trending my way was limited mainly to X—go figure—I did a quick check of Instagram, Facebook, and my most recent social media addition, Bluesky. Would it become the next "OG Twitter?" Only time could tell, but as a social media personality, I couldn't afford to be out of the loop.

To my relief, there were no problematic comments surrounding the latest death to hit Central Shores on these platforms. Sure, there were mentions from creepers asking me to send them anything from locks of my hair to pictures of my feet, but that stuff was par for the course on any given day. Lifestyles of the moderately famous, right?

A shrill *beep* from outside sent me flying back in my desk chair, and I realized my forty minutes before Jasper's arrival were up. Luckily, I'd already showered and dressed before Hudson left for work, so I did a quick check of the condo to ensure no faucets were dripping or gas stove burners were leaking before grabbing my bag and hurrying outside to meet my impatient chauffeur.

Jasper eyed me up and down as I slid into the buttery interior of his sporty Porsche. "Everything okay? Not like you to be un-punctual."

I winced as I spotted the time on the dashboard. I was a minute late. Which, to my perfectionist psyche, meant the end of the world. "Sorry. I got hung up on some blog stuff."

"People aren't attacking you on *Trending Topic,* are they?" His frown grew as he put the car into drive and zipped out of our small coastal development.

I shook my head. "Thankfully, all the conspiracy theories are limited to Twit—*X* at the moment."

"Eli sent me a link to the video on someone's profile, asking me if you were okay." Jasper tried to casually play off his words, but I easily spotted the telltale blush flourishing on his pale cheeks.

I grinned. "That's very thoughtful of him. It's a good sign he's interested in the well-being of your friends."

"Or he's just fishing for gossip to spread at the gym."

I scowled at Jasper's cynical attitude. "Don't do that."

"Do what?" His gaze momentarily flicked from the road to me.

"Undermine your..." I searched for the right word since Jasper and Eli hadn't made things official. "...*situationship* with such negative thoughts." I folded my arms as I stared him down. "You guys are adorable together. He challenges you in the best ways and keeps you on your toes. He's also done nothing to deserve such suspicion."

Jasper's brow furrowed. "The worst heartbreakers never do until it's too late."

I was about to reply with a snarky remark when I noticed his chin quivering slightly. "You really like him, don't you?"

"Yeah." He gave a half-hearted shrug. "Which is why I'm bound to mess it up at some point."

As someone who'd been in Jasper's life since second grade, I knew all the skeletons he had in his walk-in closet. He had a terrible habit of sabotaging his happiness whenever things were "too good." Whether it was by being too clingy, too aloof, too jealous, or too noncommittal, all his prior relationships that had shown promise ultimately fizzled because Jasper had gotten scared. However, as his best friend, it wasn't my place to judge. Only to help him pick up the pieces in the hopes he'd finally learn the error of his ways.

"Have a little faith in yourself, please." I patted him awkwardly on the shoulder as he drove.

He snorted. "Well, maybe all the healthy relationships around me will finally rub off. You, Hudson, Amanda, Arthur, Deacon, Charlotte..." His voice trailed off.

I knew where his mind was going. "Deacon and Charlotte are going to be fine," I said, reassuring myself just as much as Jasper.

"But what if she gets arrested for Kiefer's death, Cokes?" It was rare to hear Jasper sounding so scared. "You and I have watched enough *Dateline* to know people have been convicted with less circumstantial evidence. If Char's prints are the only ones on that cup—"

"Hey, what did I say?" This time, I grabbed and shook his right wrist for effect. "No negativity. No sabotaging ourselves. We'll dig up the truth. We always do. Secrets don't stay buried in Central Shores."

He shot me a pointed glance. "But we're not on our home turf this time around. We're dealing with the Ocean Hollow crowd. An *unfamiliar* Ocean Hollow crowd."

I didn't need reminding. "Rand isn't Ocean Hollow, through and through. We grew up with him. We can take him. And besides, I've got loads of clients who can give us the inside scoop." Loads might have been a stretch, but I definitely had some. I immediately thought of Drew Wilson, the owner of The Twisted Candle Bookshop. Drew was a frequent CoA flyer who used our services to help manage her website and promotional campaigns. She rented a small storefront in Ocean Hollow's shopping district, situated right near the southern Central Shores town line. "If Kiefer was in the area for as long as we think he was, people will surely have had run-ins with him and Eric." Eric Brady's sports memorabilia store was located along the same strip as Drew's bookshop, so she was bound to have something useful for us. Tourist season wasn't in full swing yet, so out-of-towners were more likely to stand out among year-round residents.

We listened to a true crime podcast for the rest of the fifteen-minute drive. I paid careful attention to the recorded tapes of detectives interrogating their suspects, hoping to pick up some tips. But since we didn't have surveillance video or DNA evidence at our disposal, I came up short.

"Hold up!" I snapped my fingers just as Jasper pulled into a parking spot in front of Ocean Hollow Marine. "We *do* have surveillance video."

Chapter Thirteen

"Come again?" Jasper raised an eyebrow as he cut the engine. "I doubt Gavin and Adrian will give you access to the CSC parking lot cameras."

"I wish, but that's not what I'm talking about." I palmed myself on the forehead. "I can't believe I didn't think of this sooner. Bernie and I put up a ton of posters and signs at the festival, asking people to share posts with the hashtag #CelebratetheCSC."

"Clever."

I gave him a look letting him know that I, too, didn't think it was the most original phrasing, but Chief McInnis wanted it to be straightforward. I then turned my attention to my phone, tapping away at the screen until I reached Instagram's search feature. I typed in the custom hashtag and waited for the results to load.

With the car safely in park, Jasper's eyes widened as my screen filled with images. "Wow. Town pride for the win."

My grin grew as I scrolled through all the posts that had used the #CelebratetheCSC in their captions or comments. "We can basically chronicle the movements of everyone in the crowd at ground level. Even the security cameras around the CSC won't be able to get this up close and personal." No sooner were the words out of my mouth than I pulled up the group text message I shared with Deacon, Adrian, and Gavin. My "colleagues."

Hey guys. Just had a thought. If you want to get a better idea of people's movement throughout the festival, check out the uploads

with the #CelebratetheCSC hashtag. **Might give insight.**

Deacon's reply came first. **I'll pretend I'm not here.**

Oops. I'd completely spaced that he'd been benched for the time being. But another message from Deacon came in, this one on a different text chain also shared with Hudson, Jasper, and Charlotte. **Good thinking about the CSC hashtag, Coco. Char and I will expand our social media search and report back.**

Yeah, Charlotte added immediately. **We're just beginning to dive into Rand's Insta right now.**

We're parked outside OH Marine, I informed them. **If you come across something fishy, let us know, and we can work it into our questioning.**

Charlotte sent a thumbs-up emoji. **Will do. Be careful!**

I second that! Hudson chimed in on the conversation from wherever he was.

I reassured the missing members of the Sleuth Squad we'd be cautious with our approach, and I was just about to pocket my phone when a text from Gavin pinged.

Thanks for the tip about the hashtag. That's a good approach. Going over security cam footage now, but it's a slog and still grainy to boot. So much for a "state of the art" set up.

I shuddered, recalling how much of the CSC building budget had been spent on security cameras. **Glad I could help.** And I was. In this instance, the more eyes we had on footage from the day, the better. I knew I could count on Gavin and Adrian to do their best to lead a thorough investigation, but if all the evidence they collected pointed Charlotte's way... I shook my head free of the treacherous thought. It was time to question our first real lead.

Hudson's cautious words from the night before echoed in my mind. *Or suspect.*

"Ready?" I nodded toward Ocean Hollow Marine's regal entrance. Known for servicing yachts and sailboats, the store catered to a wealthy clientele, and its outdoor aesthetic reflected such.

Jasper climbed out of the car and tugged at his blue-and-white striped blazer. Once I joined him, I smiled at his chinos and Sperry boat shoes, which had to be right out of the box. "You look the part."

He smoothed back his dark brown hair. "Fab-u-*laws*." His fake posh accent reminded me of Moira Rose from *Schitt's Creek*.

I nudged his side as we walked up the white stone pathway to the sleek, glass front doors. "Rand knows what you sound like already. No need to go overboard."

"Fine. Correcting course." Jasper sighed as he held the door open and ushered me in.

The sharp smell of expensive plastic and salt air hit my nostrils with a wallop, and I sputtered through a coughing fit as my eyes adjusted to my surroundings. Mahogany walls polished within an inch of their life greeted me, and I realized we were in a small, dark reception room. Through a window, I could see the sales floor with several small models on display, as well as numerous items of boating gear that I had no idea of their use.

Jasper cleared his throat as he got his bearings. "Charming." He reached for a gold customer service bell atop a stately desk and gently tapped it, the ring sending shrill notes that made us jump.

The door behind the counter clicked open a second later.

"Hello, welcome to Ocean Hollow Marine." A peppy voice preceded the arrival of a petite Asian woman dressed in a skirt, collared shirt, and vest. Her outfit reminded me of Julie McCoy from *Love Boat* reruns I'd seen on *TV Land*. "Do you have an appointment with one of our brokers?" she asked Jasper as she flipped through a fancy-looking leather ledger.

Hashtags, I winced internally, keeping my language clean even within my own mind. Was this place so exclusive that we couldn't just drop in?

"Good morning." Jasper held his head high and drew back his shoulders, giving himself a good foot or more on the receptionist. "I don't, but I was hoping to speak with Rand Windham if he's in. I'm Jasper Hastings. We went to school together, so I'd feel most comfortable doing business with him."

"Oh, how wonderful." The receptionist gave him a friendly smile, and I hoped Jasper had won her over with his intent to "do business." She flipped through her book once more. "I believe he has an opening. If you don't mind waiting for a few minutes, I'll let him know you're here."

"Thank you." Jasper flashed her a dapper grin, using his chiseled jaw and piercing blue eyes to his advantage.

"Can I get you and your wife anything to drink while you wait?"

She finally glanced my way, and I did my best to keep a straight face. More so to avoid her noticing how deeply Jasper struggled to keep his composure.

"Oh," he said, tears of laughter and horror threatening to leak from the corners of his eyes, "this is my dear friend and trend guide, Coco Cline. She'll be assisting me with my choices today. She has better vision than I do for things like this." He waved his hand with a flourish as if I was well-versed in all things yacht.

"Oh my gosh, Ms. Cline. I'm so sorry I didn't recognize you right away." She reached for my hand and shook it in vigorous apology. My bruises ached underneath the fake gold bracelet cuff I wore to hide them.

"A personal trend guide?" Oblivious to my pain, the receptionist's expression grew starry-eyed, and I realized she was taking Jasper's introduction very seriously. "Wow. It's so nice to meet you. I must say, I'm a big fan. I've followed you for years. I just love your...style." She motioned offhandedly at my basic navy sundress, her giddiness slightly fading.

I gritted my teeth in sudden regret. *We're not in Central Shores anymore.* I should have put more thought into my appearance today, especially since we were going outside of my safe hometown bubble, where everyone knew me as Coco Cline, nosy busybody, instead of Coco Cline, influencer.

Jasper, a fashion icon in his own right, quickly came to my rescue. "Ah, yes. She left the most gorgeous Brunello Cucinelli blazer in the car just now. You should see it. It's a work of art."

I bobbed my head, hoping this nice young woman wouldn't ask anything further. Brunello Cucinelli pieces retailed in the thousands, and I definitely didn't have any of that in my T.J. Maxx-supplied wardrobe. Sometimes, I got a free item here and there from an upcoming designer to showcase on *Trending Topic,* but Brunello Cucinelli? Yeah, he didn't need little old me to shill his wares.

The receptionist's jaw dropped at Jasper's fib, and I could tell he'd hit the mark. "Amazing." She shook her head, snapping back into customer service mode. "I'm sorry. How unprofessional of me. Could I offer you something to drink? We have sparkling water, tea, and coffee."

We both accepted sparkling waters and claimed two leather chairs in the lobby while we waited for her to return from OH Marine's inner sanctum.

But a very different figure burst through the doorway. "Jasper, my man." Rand Windham rubbed his hands together, looking eager. "I hear you're looking to buy a boat, dude."

Out of the corner of my eye, Jasper visibly cringed at the bro-y greeting but quickly plastered on a smile as he rose to meet the salesman. "Hey, Rand. Yeah, I'm looking to explore my options."

They shook hands, and Rand clapped him on the back. "What made you decide to take the plunge?"

Seems as though women are a bit invisible in this establishment. I guessed I would have to wait a bit longer for him to acknowledge me, sitting just a few feet away.

Jasper casually shrugged. "The Kindred Spirits Coalition is hosting a dinner cruise aboard *The Good Life* for its donors. I saw some pictures and got curious."

"Dang, *The Good Life?*" Rand gave an impressed whistle. "That's Marty Nicolson's boat. No wonder it got you interested. It's a gem." As he ran a hand through his sun-streaked hair, Rand's gaze finally landed on me, and his smile evaporated. Clearly, the last time we'd had a run-in was still very much cemented into his memory. Was the jig already up? Would he guess we were here to question him about Kiefer's death?

Yikes. I had to do major damage control, and quickly. "Hi, Rand. I'm tagging along for moral support. Can't wait to see what you've got." I summoned my most perky smile. Maybe if we didn't mention Kiefer right away, he wouldn't grow suspicious.

Rand eyed me warily before reluctantly holding out his hand in greeting.

As we shook, I turned to Jasper. "We should grab some pics for the 'gram today. The backdrop will be incredible." I wanted Rand to think we were purely here for a fun, glamorous outing and that *he* wasn't the subject of our focus.

"Some shots of me at the helm of a yacht would def spruce up my *Divulge Direct* promos," Jasper mused as he stroked his chin.

Rand seemed to relax as Jasper and I blabbered on about what filter would be best.

Good. We didn't need to raise his hackles just yet.

The receptionist soon returned with bottles of Perrier, and after we thanked her, Jasper pointed outside toward the calm marina waters. "Do you keep the big ones out there?"

"Big ones?" Rand threw his head back in laughter. "My dude, there's an art to this process. We have a few clients mooring with us now that you can look at for ideas, and then we can talk wish-list." He checked the massive watch on his wrist. "I've got a few boat shows coming up, so I'll take your wish list with me and scope out our options." He motioned us through the doorway onto the main sales floor, where smaller motorboats and sailing crafts were on display. "Now, you're sure you wanna go big right out of the gate?"

Jasper shot me a nervous look, and I could tell he was having second thoughts about wasting Rand's time with the false promise of a sale.

"Maybe you should wait until you actually *go* on this dinner cruise?" I suggested to him, giving my bestie the perfect opening to bail. "You don't even know if you have sea legs." I hoped that was the right way to use the phrase.

"On the 'big ones,' it's harder to get seasick." Rand grinned mischievously.

Jasper rubbed the back of his neck, looking guilty. "Maybe I am putting the cart before the horse."

"Why don't we go walk around the deck of *Heaven's Gate?*" Rand draped a friendly arm around him. "It's our largest craft in residence and most comparable to Marty's behemoth. You can get a sense of what it will be like."

"Thanks." Jasper's sheepish smile conveyed his appreciation of Rand's understanding. The guy had every right to ask us to leave, but clearly, Rand was in this sale to win it.

He led us outside to the marina and pointed to a massive yacht anchored a few hundred yards off the coast in deeper water. "Lil' Betty will take us there."

Lil' Betty turned out to be a sleek, twenty-foot Riva Aquarama—according to Rand—docked right outside OH Marine. She was the "taxi" they used to reach the yachts moored away from the docks. The term didn't do her justice. With her shiny wood hull and plush cushions, Betty looked more like a James Bond getaway boat than a taxi.

While Rand piloted Lil' Betty slowly through the marina, Jasper and I lounged on the comfy seats, admiring the pristine view. Ocean Hollow was more harbor than beach town, much different than the vibe we were used to in Central Shores. Hundreds of boats occupied slips in the calm marina, and there were even more anchored away from the coastline. *Heaven's Gate* was just one of six yachts peppering the shimmering Atlantic.

But before I let the beautiful scenery completely sidetrack me, I considered how we were going to broach the subject of Kiefer's death, especially now that our investigation had taken us out onto open waters. As Ocean Hollow Marine grew smaller on the shore behind us, a sudden shiver ran down my spine at how alone we now were. We'd come to Rand looking for information, but Hudson's eerie words reverberated in my mind. Could he be Kiefer's killer?

Pretending to admire the harbor, I studied Rand from behind my sunglasses. He didn't seem like the type of guy who'd practically poison someone to death, but I'd once suspected him of being a murderer before...

We were about fifty feet from *Heaven's Gate* when Rand abruptly cut the engine.

My pulse spiked. "Everything okay—"

"Sorry, guys. Give me a sec." Rand sent us an apologetic glance as he dug a hand into his pocket. "Got a phone call." He extracted his cell and frowned as he read the screen. "Hey, Eric, what's—*what?* Dude, slow down. Whoa. Are you serious?"

I shot a look at Jasper and saw his eyebrows raise from behind the rims of his ginormous shades. I could tell we were thinking the same thing. Eric?

As in Eric Brady?

"Dang. Of course, man. Anything you need," Rand continued his conversation, rubbing his temples furiously. "If you want, you're more than welcome to stay with us for a few days. Sage wouldn't mind." Sage Hattape was Rand's wife. They'd been together since high school.

He listened to the person on the other end of the line for a few seconds. "You think? Well, obviously. There's nothing to hide. Right?"

My ears perked up even more at the strained suspicion in Rand's voice.

"Look, I'm with clients. I'll swing by once my shift is over. Take care of yourself, bro." Rand punched the End Call button and stared at his phone momentarily before sliding it back into the pocket of his khakis.

"Everything all right?" Jasper cautiously asked.

Rand's frown grew. "No...not really." He sighed. "That was a buddy of mine. I guess a friend of ours passed away yesterday."

"Omigosh!" I did my best to appear taken aback. It wasn't too hard. I kinda was. How was Rand *just* learning about Kiefer's death now? Hadn't he seen it on the news? "I'm so sorry."

He shrugged. "Eh, it's okay. I didn't really know the dude that well. We only hung out a few times. He was a college friend of my buddy's." Rand started drumming his fingers on the boat's steering wheel, but he made no moves to restart the engine.

I elbowed Jasper, silently communicating to him that he needed to take the lead here. If I started asking questions, it might trigger Rand.

"You don't sound okay, man." Jasper summoned his best bro-y demeanor. "We're totally here to lend an ear if you need one."

Rand folded his arms, looking increasingly uncomfortable. "Maybe you can give me some advice since you've been involved with this kinda thing before."

The latter half of his statement was directed at me. "What do you mean?" I raised my chin defensively.

Rand reached for the back of his neck before answering. "A murder investigation."

"Murder?" Jasper and I both parroted. It would have been comical if I hadn't been so surprised by the turn in conversation.

"Wild, right? My buddy Eric thought his friend died from some medical condition, but the police have changed their tune. They're saying someone killed him while he was hanging out at the CSC grand opening yesterday." Rand swayed as the boat drifted up and down on the current. "I guess some detectives told Eric the news this morning. They just left his house."

"That would be Gavin McInnis and Adrian Riley, I bet," I offered cautiously. "I work with them through my consulting business. They did mention they were on a new case..." I trailed off, hoping my story was believable enough. "Did Eric say why the police think his friend was murdered?"

Rand shook his head. "Nah, he wasn't very forthcoming about what the heck is going on. He...he just told me that if the cops come asking around, I should say he and Kiefer were totally good."

"Who's Kiefer?" Jasper shaded his gaze against the sunlight radiating across the water.

"The guy that died." Rand didn't elaborate further.

I frowned. "Why would Eric tell you to say he and Kiefer were good?" I had a fairly keen idea, but I wanted Rand to connect the dots himself.

He began to fidget. "That's what I can't figure out. Unless the police think *Eric* had something to do with Kiefer's death."

"Yeesh." Jasper gave an elaborate shudder. "Why would they think that?"

I pressed my lips together, trying to keep a triumphant smile from spreading across my face. This conversation couldn't be going any better.

"Err..." Rand's expression contorted into a deep scowl.

I leaned forward, trying to appear sympathetic to his plight. "Were things not 'totally good' between Kiefer and Eric?"

Rand didn't answer right away. "I-it's not my place to say. Eric's my buddy."

"Dude," Jasper deadpanned. "A real friend wouldn't ask you to lie to the police. Who even is this guy?"

"Eric? He and I actually go way back. The guy grew up in Ocean Hollow. We played football together on the local travel team," Rand explained. "We lost touch after high school, but ended up crossing paths once he opened his sports memorabilia shop in the center." He ran a hand through his windblown hair. "We only just started hanging out again. Nice, laidback guy. Knows how to party."

Jasper pushed further. "I heard about someone dying at the CSC festival yesterday. I thought he was from out of town. How did Eric know him?"

"They played golf together in college. Also pledged the same fraternity. Took that whole 'brotherhood bond' seriously. They were tight." Rand drummed his fingers on the boat's console. "I guess Kiefer was dealing with some issues back home and needed a getaway. He'd been staying with Eric for weeks."

Issues in South Carolina? What did *that* mean? Had trouble followed Kiefer to Central Shores?

Chapter Fourteen

As I considered the possibility that Kiefer's killer may have trailed him from South Carolina, I opted to press Rand more about the extended visit with Eric. "Had Kiefer worn out his welcome or something?" Our source had been forthcoming with us so far and didn't seem to suspect our ulterior motive for being here.

"Or something." Rand gave a little *harumph.*

Jasper gestured to me. "Look, bro, we've both been in the hot seat with the cops before. It's not a pleasant experience. If you know something about why Kiefer's dead, maybe Coco and I can help you out." His last words inched upward in a tantalizing offer.

"Yeah, I'm aware." Rand's expression clouded, and for a moment, I worried he'd remembered our previous encounter a bit too vividly.

Jasper folded his arms. "Wouldn't want your clients thinking you were tangled up in this, either." He delivered the coup de grâce with refined poise.

Rand's skin lost some of its sun-worn color. "Jeez, I'm not tangled up in anything. I had no beef with Kiefer. I was smart enough to keep my woman away from that millennial Lothario."

I resisted the urge to cringe at his "my woman" comment as if Sage wasn't capable of making her own choices. "Millennial Lothario?" I thought back to the pictures we'd seen of a brunette wedged between Eric and Kiefer. "Did he hit on Eric's girlfriend or something?"

"Not girlfriend, per se." Rand gnawed on his lower lip before spilling the tea. "Eric's been simping for this girl, Janica Rice, ever since he moved back to Ocean Hollow. He was finally making progress out of the friend zone when Kiefer showed up. Janica became totally obsessed with him. Eric might as well have been invisible to her. And he wasn't happy about it, to say the least."

Jasper and I shared a look. "Who's Janica Rice?" My bestie won our invisible coin toss as to who should ask the million-dollar question.

"She owns Rice Design Co., a local interior design company." Rand pointed over his shoulder toward the mainland. "Her office is a few storefronts down from Eric's in the center." He sighed. "Honestly, I don't think Kiefer was all that serious about her. He still hit on girls whenever we partied without Janica. He seemed to have a thing for women with wedding rings on their fingers, if you get my drift."

Why am I not surprised? Charlotte's ex didn't seem like the type of guy who was great with commitment. "Do you know whether Eric confronted Kiefer about his feelings for Janica?" I asked.

Rand pushed his sunglasses up the bridge of his nose. "He was planning to, that much I know."

Jasper stroked his chin. "Hmm…so Eric and Kiefer clash over a girl, and now one of them is dead, and the other one is telling his friends to keep their mouths shut."

Rand flinched. "Sounds really bad when you put it like that. Eric's not a violent guy, though. He would never raise a hand to someone."

But Kiefer didn't die from a physical altercation. I debated sharing my thoughts aloud, but decided to keep the details of the crime to myself. I mentally replayed our conversation with Rand, and all he'd shared was that someone had killed Kiefer. He hadn't said how, so maybe he didn't yet know about the allergy poisoning. And I didn't want Rand to realize we knew more about Kiefer's death than we'd let on.

"Man, I should have gone with them yesterday." Rand stared up at the blue sky. "Help keep the peace and all."

"At the festival?" Jasper clarified.

Rand nodded. "I had the afternoon off, so Eric invited me to come along with him and Kiefer. But things had been so weird between them because of Janica, and I really didn't want to deal with their drama." His dejected gaze trailed along the floor of the boat. "Thought they could use the time to smooth things over. I ended up bailing and taking Sage on a cruise down the coast instead."

I stared out at the shimmering ocean as I considered his explanation. I supposed a trip out of town could explain why Rand hadn't heard the news about Kiefer's death until this morning. As I made note of the yacht broker's readily given alibi, I couldn't help but wonder why Rand was being so upfront with us. Was it the shock talking? Or something more calculated? Regardless, if he'd been out on the water with his wife, there was no way Rand could've poisoned Kiefer at the CSC festival. I just needed to figure out a way to confirm it.

"My advice?" I said, turning to hold the man's troubled gaze. "You should tell the police what you know. They'll uncover the truth sooner or later."

"Yeah." Jasper nodded his agreement. "And if they find out you lied or misled them, things could get bad for you real quick."

A low whistle sailed across Rand's lips. "You're right, you're right. I can't back Eric up the way he wants. Especially when I've already told Sage about their drama. If she found out I was keeping things from the police, I'd be in the doghouse. She always tells me, 'Lying wreaks havoc on our chakras.'"

I chuckled at his airy, whimsical impression of his wife. Sage owned a crystal shop in Central Shores and believed in the power of everything she sold, heart and soul.

Jasper maneuvered his way on shaky legs to the boat's helm to give Rand a pat on the back. "But don't put the cart before the horse. Who knows if the police will even reach out to you?"

I appreciated Jasper's careful reminder. The last thing we needed was for Rand to spread the word that Jasper and I had encouraged him to come forward and rat out his friend. That certainly wouldn't endear us to Eric Brady, with whom we undeniably needed to speak.

"Sorry for derailing our trip like that." Rand shot us both a grateful smile. "I appreciate the advice."

As he turned the engine back on, my shoulders sagged as tension eased out from me. Rand had presented us with the perfect opportunity to question him about Kiefer, and in return, we'd unearthed some sizzling intel. I was willing to bet that the beautiful brunette wedged under Kiefer's arm in Eric's Instagram photos was Janica Rice. It also wasn't a big leap to think that Kiefer and Eric's romantic rivalry could have imploded into a motive for murder. Clearly, Eric thought so if he was calling up his pals and asking them to lie to the police about the state of his friendship with Kiefer.

We sliced through the smooth crystalline waters toward *Heaven's Gate*, and soon, Rand pulled up alongside the grand yacht. I prepped myself to *ooh* and *ah* over the gorgeous vessel despite Jasper and I being there under false pretenses. Guilt roiled in my stomach as the speedboat gently buoyed against the current. Rand probably hoped he was about to hit a major payday.

But it wasn't hard for me to summon admiring words as Rand helped us aboard *Heaven's Gate*. It was stunning. While I'd never been on a yacht before, I'd watched enough reruns of *The O.C., Gossip Girl,* and *Revenge* to know that *Heaven's Gate* could float with the best of them. I didn't even want to imagine how much money one needed to buy and maintain a ship like this.

"You know, Rand," Jasper mused as he returned from examining the upper deck, "I'm not gonna lie. I kind of enjoyed our ride over here on Betty more than I expected."

Rand cocked an eyebrow. "Got a need for speed?"

I stifled back a giggle as Rand was totally serious about his question.

And surprisingly, it seemed like Jasper was, too. "Yeah." With a twisted grin, he turned to me. "What do you think, Cokes? Wouldn't it be fun to take the squad out on a speedboat?"

I eyed him up and down. "Would you be comfortable operating one?"

"I'm sure I could learn." His chest swelled with confidence. "Eli's mentioned a few times that he's had his boating license since he was, like, fifteen or something."

"Eli? Eli Holt?" A teasing grin spread across Rand's face. "You guys finally getting serious?"

Jasper's head whipped toward him. "What do you mean, *finally*?"

Rand threw a casual shrug. "Hey, you didn't hear it from me, but Eli's been yammering on about you for months. I think the dude's smitten."

"Really?" Jasper's cheeks blossomed pink.

Underneath my sunglasses, I felt my eyes double in size. In all the years I'd known my best friend, I didn't think that he'd ever sounded so...sweetly hopeful in his entire life. I pressed my lips together to avoid a traitorous smile. *Jasper has it baaad.* The words trilled around inside my head with a singsong voice.

Rand nodded and clapped the guardrail that ran around the yacht deck. "If you like speed over size, I've definitely got a few options for you," he said, changing the subject. "But I'm also going to a boat show next weekend where some new models are being unveiled."

Jasper reached for his wallet and pulled out a business card. "I'm sold. Something that can seat at least eight people."

Rand took the card before giving Jasper a fist bump. "It's a deal, man."

The ride back to Ocean Hollow Marine was more nautical in nature, with Rand showing Jasper all of Betty's bells and whistles while Jasper paid close attention. As for me, I was excited by the prospect of ocean adventures and water sports, as well as the fun development that Jasper and Eli were undoubtedly falling for each other. Add to that all the spicy drama we learned about Eric and Kiefer, and I'd consider the morning a success.

Chapter Fifteen

"I'll text you pics from the boat show." Rand waved the wish list Jasper had taken a few minutes to fill out upon our return to the dock. "And I'll let you know what meets these…standards." He chuckled as he held open the store's front door for us.

We bid the eager salesman goodbye, and as we strolled toward Jasper's car, I shook with bottled-up laughter. "I'm not sure asking for a wine fridge was a realistic expectation."

"Hey, if I'm going to drop a *boatload* of cash"—Jasper paused and waited until I acknowledged his pun—"I might as well see if Rand can procure the Taj Mahal of speedboats."

"You're really going to buy one?" I raised a skeptical eyebrow.

He admired his manicured fingernails. "I liked being out on the water today. And it would be fun, wouldn't it? Imagine, during our investigations, we could jet up and down the coast from suspect to suspect."

I rolled my eyes. "What makes you think there will be more cases for us to investigate? We're only stepping into this mess because Charlotte's involved."

He slid his shades down the bridge of his nose so I could see his icy blue stare. "Oh, come on, Cokes. You'd find a way to wiggle into anything Gavin and Adrian were dealing with. You can't help yourself."

I scowled at him but realized he was probably right. It felt weird to admit, but I really enjoyed teaming up with my friends to solve the crimes afflicting our hometown. There was something about it that filled me with purpose, pride, and accomplishment. I was making a difference in a way that felt real—much more than I ever did with *Trending Topic*. And as sad as it was that our local crime rate was inching upward, at least Central Shores could count on justice being served.

"So, what next?" Jasper asked once we'd buckled into his car.

I was already typing Janica Rice's name into my phone's browser. Her business popped up as the first result—great SEO configuration—and I clicked on her website. A professional headshot filled the screen, along with her logo for Rice Design Co.

"We've found our mystery Instagram lady." I leaned across the center console so Jasper could see.

He whistled appreciatively at her good looks. "Jeez, I'd be mad, too, if I was Eric. She's a total babe."

I giggled at his assessment as I navigated around Janica's website. A beige, sage, and robin's egg blue color scheme tied each page together in a serene, soothing manner, and her aesthetic mirrored the "tranquil approach" she claimed she took to her designs.

On her Contact page, I spotted the familiar row of social media icons situated at the bottom. I clicked the Instagram camera, and the app automatically loaded on my phone.

"What are you hoping to find on her Rice Designs profile?" Jasper frowned as a color-coded grid matching her website filled the screen.

"Her follower list." I tapped the modest number next to the Rice Designs profile photo. "I'd be willing to bet she follows her business profile with her personal account." I followed the official *Trending Topic* account from my Coco Cline profile to help keep tabs on everything. *Although*, both *will be relinquished to Rae Livingston if I accept the terms of her deal.*

I shook the nagging thought away and scanned the usernames following the interior design business, looking for any profile photo that remotely resembled Janica in any way.

"I know good bone structure when I see it." Jasper pointed to a pic of a glamorous, smiling woman beside the handle **@dolledupdarling**. "That's her."

I clicked the name, relieved to find the account was public. Once the user page loaded, the profile pic was a bit larger, and I could confirm that Jasper's deduction was spot on. "Good eye." But as my gaze moved down to the image grid of recent photos, my triumphant smile grew into an O. "Holy hashtags."

"Dang. Gurl had it bad." Jasper let loose a cringy shudder as we stared at row after row of photos of Janica's face smashed against Kiefer Marsh's cheek.

I scrolled down the page, doing mental math. "Good grief. She's got over two hundred photos of them together." Kiefer had only been in the area for three weeks or so. Miss Shutterbug had been pretty busy capturing memories.

Prior to Kiefer's arrival, Janica had posted photos of the ocean, pickleball courts, food, and garden flowers. The contrast in her content was quite stark.

Jasper tapped on one image to enlarge it. "Ugh, I hope a man never looks at me like that."

Indeed. The photo he'd selected had Kiefer staring at Janica's chest like she was a piece of meat, not a person. Her expression was all bright and bubbly, whereas his had an almost predatory look to it. It sent shivers down my spine.

"Okay, so clearly, Janica was into Kiefer." I navigated back to her profile grid. "But what isn't so clear is whether Kiefer was into her for anything other than carnal in nature."

"Rand didn't seem to think they were couple goals," Jasper mused. "And if Eric sensed his buddy was toying with the girl he's been pining after, that's a time bomb waiting to explode."

"Something bad must have happened between them if Eric's calling Rand to make sure he doesn't bring it up," I pointed out. "I wonder how serious their feud was."

Jasper raised an eyebrow. "What's your plan for finding out?"

Swiping away from Instagram, I tapped on the Google Maps app. "Why don't we swing by Ocean Hollow Center? See if we can chat with either Eric or Janica." I typed in the center's coordinates while Jasper put the car in gear and sped out of the marina's parking lot. "More so Eric. I'd like to see what he has to say about Kiefer's visit."

"He'll probably play it off as the best of times." Jasper shot me a sidelong look. "If he's calling his pals to make sure they all have their stories straight, I doubt he's going to tell *us* that he and Kiefer had beef."

He made a good point. "Right now, I'm more interested in whether Eric knows about Charlotte and Kiefer's history. If he learned they had bad blood, then it paves the way to proving that Kiefer's killer purposely framed Char for the peanut allergy debacle."

Jasper winced at the harsh reality we were facing. "Yeah, I guess we can't necessarily write off yet that whoever put those peanuts in Kiefer's cup just seized an opportunity, and poor Char is merely collateral damage."

I considered this whole nightmare to be a terrible coincidence. Stranger things had happened, I supposed.

Minutes later, the Google Maps Lady announced we had arrived at our intended destination. Jasper slid into an open spot on the street and parked.

"Wow," he murmured as we climbed out of the car. "I didn't realize downtown Ocean Hollow was so darn cute."

I grinned as I scanned the scene. We'd snagged a spot on the main road running through the center. Quaint, old-timey storefronts greeted us on either side of the street. Most were former residential homes converted into commercial spaces. Porches were peppered with geranium-covered gables and posts. Rainbow-colored flags celebrating Ocean Hollow's commitment to Pride Month fluttered from every business. Cheerful people milled about the cobblestone sidewalks. It made for a picturesque sight, even though the blue sky above us had clouded over.

Jasper puffed his chest out as he noted the Pride flags. "Oh, they are going to *love* me here."

I chuckled at his sassy delivery as we made our way down the street. Under Google Map Lady's guidance, we'd opted to park at the opposite end of the center from where Eric's and Janica's businesses were located in the hopes it looked like we were ordinary shoppers mulling over our options.

"Phew, where did this humidity come from?" Jasper tugged at his shirt, glancing nervously at the darkening sky. "Those look like storm clouds rolling in."

I noted the alarming change in weather. In decades past, we rarely had thunderstorms this early in the season. *Thanks, climate change.* "Let's hustle, then." I threaded my arm through his and hurried along the sidewalk.

Two blocks later, I spied a large green wooden sign blowing in the wind that reminded me of the colors on Janica's website. It dangled from a post in front of a tall, wrought-iron fence. As we neared, I could read the words "Rice Design Co." etched in bronze lettering. The font matched the logo on her website. "This must be Janica's place." And we'd found one of our persons of interest just in time. With the uptick in wind speed, I was struggling to keep my dress from blowing up. "Maybe we should chat with her first?" I eyed the stormy clouds barreling quickly across the sky.

"Good call." Jasper bobbed his head in agreement.

Behind the wrought-iron fence stood Janica's interior design studio. It was a beautiful Victorian home, although the front yard had been converted into a rather...*eclectic* garden. Tiny white pebbles formed curling walkways around massive topiary bushes.

"She must really like birds," Jasper muttered out of the side of his mouth as we approached the ornate gate to the boujee property.

I cackled at his dry observation. The topiary had been trimmed into oversized penguins and flamingos. An interesting aesthetic for coastal Delaware.

We entered through the gated archway. As we followed the pathway that looked like it led to the wraparound porch, a strange, garbled moaning reached my ears.

"Mrrr-oowwlp."

I placed a hand on Jasper's forearm in caution. "Do you hear that?"

"Hear—" Jasper stopped midsentence as a *crack* of thunder roared above us.

I jumped at the assault on my eardrums. I appreciated the majesty of Mother Nature, but I preferred to be safe indoors when she revealed her awesome power.

"Let's get inside before it starts pouring." Jasper tugged me toward the covered entrance.

The wind had picked up even more intensely, rustling the avian-shaped topiary all around us. Despite the leaves flapping, the strange *mrrr-oowwlp* sound cut through the air. "But don't you hear that?" I listened more closely, and I was sure of what I heard: someone calling for help.

Jasper realized I wasn't budging and relented to my request to listen.

"Mrr-oowwlp!"

"Hey, I hear it. What is that?" His hair whipped across his forehead, and Jasper's eyes widened as the moaning became even more high-pitched, accompanied by the sounds of vigorous splashing.

Struggling cries and splashing water? "Hashtags!" I grabbed his hand. "I think someone's *drowning!*"

Chapter Sixteen

My heart leaped into my throat as I swung my head around, trying to figure out where the moans were coming from. "Where *are* you?" I cried out helplessly to whoever was in need.

Crack. Another peal of thunder rang, followed by a streak of jagged lightning searing across the daunting sky.

"Mrr-oowwlp!"

"Around back!" Jasper dashed forward, bypassing the pathway to the porch steps. Instead, he took off around the side of the grand house.

I did my best to follow him as quickly as I could in my wedge heels. They made for fashionably fun walking shoes, but definitely weren't made for running.

I flinched as another *crack* of thunder ripped through the town. The storm was already upon us. We needed to get inside.

Just as I rounded the corner into the backyard, a shattering *splash* greeted me, and it took my brain a moment to process what I was seeing.

Janica—I'm assuming—had installed a huge koi pond in the studio's backyard, complete with lotus flowers, lily pads, and the bright orange-and-white fish. Add to that the six-foot-three figure of my bestie waist-deep, and you had quite the water installation.

I scanned the water's surface and saw nothing beyond floating bits of algae. Jasper, with his back to me, was totally alone in the pond, besides the fish. "What are you—"

He twirled around, the water sloshing in his wake. "Is she breathing?"

My jaw dropped as he held out a drenched little yowling creature who looked to be the size of a Birkin bag. "She's making noise, so yeah," I replied reassuringly. "Come on, get out of there!" I glanced nervously at the sky, searching for imminent signs of lightning.

Jasper trudged through the pond water, sending curious and confused koi scattering in all directions. "Help me out, will you?"

I grabbed his outstretched hand and tugged, giving it everything I had. He cradled the little critter gently in his other arm and, through gritted teeth, used his legs to propel his hulking form free of the pond's grip.

As he dripped water onto the mossy, manicured lawn, I took a step back to avoid pond scum ending up on me. "What happened?"

Jasper initially ignored my question. Instead, he stroked the soaked animal in his arms.

BOOM.

"Okay, we need to get clear of this lightning rod." I tugged Jasper away from the pond and toward the back patio, the only source of cover at our disposal. The second we stepped under the shelter of an overhang, the skies opened. Rain pummeled the ground. "Yikes. That was close."

Jasper scanned the decorated patio with a frown. "Do you have a blanket or something?" he asked me.

"A blanket?" I stared at him. "Where would I be keeping something like that?" I held up my clutch purse for emphasis.

He frowned. "I need to get her dried off." He hugged the critter closely. "Poor thing."

"Never thought I'd live to see the day." I shook my head at his uncharacteristic response. "Jasper Hastings, caring about something more than his own appearance." I studied the creature in his arms. From the looks of her, she had to be a long-haired cat.

Jasper scratched the matted, soaked kitty under her chin, and eventually, her yowls subsided into motorboat-level purrs. It was honestly impressive that we could hear her among the rain and high winds whipping through the yard.

"She doesn't look too traumatized." I scanned her sturdy body for any signs that she'd been harmed, but luckily found none.

My bestie shifted the cat to his other arm. "She was drowning, Cokes. She must have been looking at the fish and fell in."

I reached out a tentative hand to pet her, but the kitty swatted my hand away. My reflexes were quick enough to avoid her claws. "No collar." I noted her bare neck. "Maybe she's Janica's cat?"

"Let's get you inside." Jasper made a kissy face at the feline, and to my surprise, she tolerated him nuzzling her cute little nose.

I shot a wary look at the sky. The deluge of rain had already started to let up—at least, for now. "Let's get you both cleaned up." While I doubted Janica had any spare clothes for Jasper, hopefully, she had a towel we could use to wipe off all the pondweed and algae from his chinos.

Under the cover and safety of the wraparound deck, I led the way to the front of the house while Jasper muttered words of reassurance to the purring cat. Just as we approached the Victorian's front corner, the slamming of a door halted us in our tracks.

"Look, I'm sorry I'm not *sad* enough for you. I thought you—never mind." A male voice bellowed with evident frustration.

Footsteps thudded against the porch, and I slowly edged myself around the corner to see what was going on. Two very familiar figures faced off against each other. A petite, beautiful brunette woman folded her arms as she glared at the tall, gangly, brown-haired man. He then turned his back on her and stomped down the porch steps, his feet splashing in the puddles left by the rain.

"Come on, Eric. You can talk to me!" she called once he reached the entry gate. "Get back here. You'll get hit by lightning!"

He didn't listen, and he slammed the gate shut in response. A low rumble of thunder echoed in his wake.

Janica Rice stared out at her storm-disheveled front yard, her eyes leaking tears.

Over my shoulder, I shot Jasper a *stay here for a sec* look before I cleared my throat and stepped out from behind the building's shadows. "Um, excuse me?"

"Eek!" Janica yelped, her hand flying to her chest as she jumped back.

"Jeez! You scared the living daylights out of me."

I held my hands up to show her I wasn't a threat. "I'm so sorry."

She motioned to the ominous sky. "Taking shelter from the storm?" She did a quick double-take, and her jaw dropped open. "Omigosh. You're Coco Cline, aren't you? Oh, you totally are. I am such a fan!" Her squeals drowned out the remnants of the passing storm.

We're not in Central Shores anymore, I said to myself a la Judy Garland. While I knew there was a possibility that I'd be recognized for my online exploits, I hadn't been expecting this glowing reception. "I am. Hi, there."

Janica bounced up and down, the floorboards on the porch squeaking. "Wow. I can't believe I'm meeting you in person. This is so cool. What are you doing here?"

What *were* we doing here? What would be a believable excuse that I could placate her with? "You're Janica Rice, right?" I drew out the question, still scrambling for a reason.

As her brown eyes widened, I noticed how red and swollen they were. She'd obviously been crying. "Yep. That's me."

"Wonderful," I gushed. "I've heard fabulous things about your work. My friend and I were coming to speak with you about a possible renovation project." I then took a turn toward the truth. "But on our way to your front door, we thought we heard someone in distress. We wanted to help them, given the bad weather." I gestured toward the sky, hoping my excuse was believable. The storm seemed to be dissipating as rapidly as it had arrived. Already, sunlight poked holes through the dark clouds.

I then cleared my throat, a signal for Jasper to join me. Hearing me, he came around the corner, cradling the drenched fur baby. "We found a cat struggling in the koi pond around back," I added. "Is she yours?"

Janica's confusion morphed into immediate shock at seeing Jasper in her eyeline before ultimately settling into agitation. "Ugh, that pest has been assaulting my fish for weeks. I've tried calling animal control on the little beast, but she disappears whenever they come around."

Jasper clutched the poor kitty to his chest, his expression aghast at Janica's cruel words.

115

I guess we're not dealing with an animal lover. "You don't know who she belongs to?" I pressed sweetly, trying to soothe Janica's disgruntled nerves.

She tossed her expertly coifed tresses. "Nope. I don't care, either. Serves her right for terrorizing my koi." Janica snapped her fingers. "In fact, I ought to call animal control right now while you've got her captured."

"*That* won't be necessary." Jasper's nostrils flared with indignation. To me, he muttered, "The rain has already let up. I'll walk around to the other businesses and ask if anyone is missing a cat. *You* can deal with Ms. Bleeding Heart over there." His steely gaze flicked to Janica.

"What about..." I motioned to his messy appearance, wiping a few bits of pond scum off of his light-beige pants for emphasis. The Jasper I knew would *never* be seen in public looking like he'd just auditioned for the role of the Loch Ness Monster.

He shrugged. "Being outside will help me dry out. This stuff will begin to fall off when that happens. But I *could* use a towel for her." He held the cat out as water dripped from her grimy fur.

What has this cat done to my bestie? I blinked but then quickly composed myself and shot Janica a pleading stare. "You wouldn't happen to have a small towel we could use, do you? We'd really like to get her cleaned up."

"Oh, of course, Coco!" Her personality turned on a dime at my request. "Let me go find a towel for the precious thing."

"Precious?" Jasper mimicked Janica's chipper tone once she disappeared inside her studio. "What happened to *pest*?"

I tentatively reached out to scratch our new feline friend under the chin, and this time, to my relief, she let me touch her. "Just be glad she's cooperating."

"Looks like you've got yourself a fan," Jasper muttered as he nudged my arm. "Might be able to use that to your advantage."

"Are you really gonna leave me alone with her?" My tone was teasing, but I was a bit surprised he was opting to abandon me while questioning a possible suspect. The Sleuth Squad didn't often leave me to fend for myself—much to my chagrin.

His skin paled. "Shoot. I didn't think of that." He glanced nervously at the cat in his arms. Jasper was obviously concerned, both about the poor animal and leaving me.

"I'm not some helpless damsel." I patted his forearm in reassurance. "This pretty little maiden needs you more at the moment." I continued to rub my finger under the kitty's chin until her bright blue eyes narrowed in a way that said, *That's all*, with the cool precision of Meryl Streep as Miranda Priestly in *The Devil Wears Prada*.

I obediently whipped my finger back before I earned another swat.

Jasper shifted on his feet. "Well, okay. I'll be quick about it, though. And please don't tell Dad."

"What Hudson doesn't know can't hurt him." I held my hand up in promise.

Janica returned a few minutes later, waving a towel like she was the grand marshal of the upcoming Central Shores Pride Parade. "Here you go." She beamed as she handed it to Jasper. Although, the smile didn't quite reach her eyes as she shot a glare toward the cat.

"Janica," I hurriedly interjected, "as I mentioned earlier, I've been thinking about redoing the upstairs of my condo into a more…tranquil space," I fibbed, eager to get my mini-interrogation underway. Now that I knew she was a follower of my work, I had just the bait to entice her. "I was wondering if we could chat about a possible collaboration. One that we could chronicle on *Trending Topic?*"

The interior designer's eyes doubled in size with ambitious glee, but she played off the offer nonchalantly. "I'd certainly be open to something, should my calendar allow it."

I had to give her props for her *hard-to-get* attitude. "Great. Are you available to chat now?"

"Sure. I have some time before lunch." Janica beckoned me toward the doorway.

Jasper and I sent telepathic *good luck* looks as we went our separate ways. I felt a bit silly at the sudden lump in my throat as he took off toward the sidewalk. This wasn't the first time I'd been alone with a possible suspect, but I tried my hardest to have backup during my amateur investigations. It was the smart way to sleuth, after all. But I reassured myself that help was

117

just a phone call away, and given Janica's lithe, petite stature, I was pretty sure my size-eight, five-nine frame could handle her if need be.

Although the exterior of Rice Design Co. portrayed a stately Victorian, the inside had been totally gutted into a sleek, modern space. Sturdy metal beams ran across the ceiling to support the relatively open-floor concept. Pale green walls were covered with decals of flying bird silhouettes every few feet, and ornate potted plants were scattered across the grey laminate floor. I would have opted for less avian decorations, but overall, the vibe was serene and peaceful.

"Did you happen to bring any pictures of the space as it is now?" Janica motioned for me to take a seat on one of the low-back chairs facing a bay window.

I froze, trying to recall if I had any photos saved to my camera reel. "Um, unfortunately not. I'm in the *very* early stages of determining whether a remodel is feasible. And since I've heard such great things about your business, I thought, who better than you to guide me?"

Janica brightened at my compliment. "Well, I always tell my clients that I am their décor guru, a spirit guide to home renovation."

Since a remark about cultural appropriation probably wouldn't get me very far, I simply smiled in understanding. "Was that a client you were dealing with when we arrived?" I married coy and concern into my question in an attempt to get Janica talking about the heated scene I'd witnessed between her and Eric.

"Oh, goodness, no!" Her laughter had a frantic pulse to it. "I am *ever* the professional with my clients, even if we have disagreements about design. That was a friend of mine." She waved her latter comment away.

I plastered on a sympathetic expression. "I do hope everything is all right between you two. He seemed very...testy." I figured I'd get further with her if I painted Eric as the one in the wrong.

She rolled her eyes. "You know how men can be. Always denying themselves of having *feelings*."

I raised my brow in intrigue. "Oh, are you interested in him romantically, then?"

Again, manic laughter erupted from her. "Gosh, no. Eric is *just* a friend. Nice guy and all." Her expression clouded. "No, I was trying to get him to recognize his grief, but he wasn't having any of it."

"Grief?" I parroted.

Janica's hair swung back and forth over her slender shoulders as she bobbed her head. "A close friend of ours passed away yesterday, and Eric is carrying on like nothing happened."

Close friend, huh? Now we were getting somewhere.

"Oh no." My hand flew to my mouth to stifle a squeaky gasp. "I'm so sorry for your loss."

"Thanks." Her eyes glistened with unshed tears. "I'm still in shock over the whole thing. He was so young. So full of life. It hasn't quite sunk in that I'll never see him again."

If I hadn't already known whom she was talking about, I would've assumed Kiefer had been a fixture in Janica's life for years, not weeks. "I hope you're taking care of yourself, too."

"I'm trying to," she said, sounding sad. "I thought about taking the day off, but I needed the distraction."

I paused, tucking a strand of hair behind my ear to buy myself some time. "You said your friend was young. Do you want to talk about it? I know how cathartic it can be."

Janica's gaze dropped to her knees. "Well, uh, this may be hard for you to believe, but he was actually the guy that died at the festival in Central Shores yesterday." She twisted her fingers a few times. "I-I know that *you* were the one who found him. Gosh, that video circulating on X is just awful."

"What? Really?" I scrambled to cover my amateur faux pas. Of course, Janica, a millennial who clearly lived her life on social media, as evidenced by her Instagram profile, would have seen the posts about me being connected to Kiefer's case. "You knew Kiefer Marsh?" I opted to take a more familiar approach with her since I could no longer deny my involvement.

She nodded, her chin quivering. "I couldn't bring myself to read too much about how it all happened, but I appreciate that you tried to help him."

What social media posts has she been browsing? Relief fluttered through me that Janica wasn't of the opinion that I'd had a hand in Kiefer's untimely demise. *Take that, X.* "It was a tragic situation." This time, I didn't have to lie my way through a response. The haunted pain in my voice required no acting.

Janica shuddered. "I can't believe Kiefy is gone," she murmured, almost to herself.

Kiefy? I tried to keep the grimace off my face at the cutesy nickname. The Kiefer Marsh I knew of was anything but cute. "It sounds like you two were more than friends?" My voice inched upward, prodding her for more deets.

"Yeah. For sure." Janica wiped a lone tear from her cheek. "We'd grown, like, super tight. Gosh, he was the best. And so hot, too. We had such a special connection." She sighed. "Maybe that's why Eric thinks the police will want to speak with me."

I visibly perked up at the mention of the official investigation.

Janica noticed my reaction, too. "Are you helping them with their case? The police, I mean." Her question was curious rather than suspicious. Thankfully, she hadn't seen through my reasons for being here…yet.

"I don't think the police need my help." I felt my cheeks grow warm at her assumption. "I mean, his death was a terrible accident, wasn't it?" I asked, in the hopes she'd spill what she knew.

Janica folded her arms. "Accident? That's not what I heard." Her brow wrinkled.

"Really?" I leaned forward in my seat, playing the eager confidante. "Did Eric mention something while he was here?"

She wrung her hands. "Kinda. He was so weird about it. I mean, I knew from the report I read last night that the police are investigating the incident, but I thought it was just standard procedure since Kiefer was so young." Janica lowered her voice, even though we were alone. "Turns out, a pair of detectives came by Eric's house this morning, asking about Kiefer's visit. They wanted info on whether Eric knew anyone who might wish Kiefy harm."

I played the astonished listener. "Wish him harm? As in, *killed* him?"

"That's what it's looking like. How insane is that?" Janica's tone grew a bit more shrill. "I mean, he'd been here, like, three weeks. He was such a good guy—the best. How could anyone want to hurt him?"

The best, huh? I wondered if Kiefer's other cohorts would have described him as a "good guy." Based on what Rand had told us about Kiefer's wandering eye, I highly doubted it. "Did Eric have any ideas?"

"Not really. He was pretty freaked out about the whole thing." Janica sighed. "He seems to think that the police are going to look at him, given he's Kiefer's closest friend."

I gave an emphatic shudder. "Yeesh. I've been there before. I don't envy him at all."

She studied me for a moment, and I could practically see her cataloging the times I'd ended up on the news over the past year. "Maybe you can stop by his store and give him some advice about how to handle it all? Because him ignoring it and pretending like everything is all fine and dandy isn't going to make this go away."

Hmm. From the sounds of it, Eric hadn't directly asked Janica to lie about him and Kiefer being on good terms, which led me to believe she was most certainly the source of their beef. "Do you think Eric would listen to me?" Her suggestion gave me the perfect opening to chat with the guy, but it also seemed incredibly random.

"Of course! We both follow you on socials, and he's a *big* fan of your entertainment recommendations."

I tried to keep my expression neutral, as I couldn't help but wonder if Eric was truly a *Trending Topic* fan or if he used this shared "interest" to get closer to Janica. "Well, I'm always up for helping out my followers. Why don't you let him know he can DM me if he'd like to set up some time to talk?"

Janica whipped out her phone from her blazer pocket. "Omigosh, that's so nice of you to offer, Coco. You're like a crime consultant or something."

As she typed away enthusiastically on her phone, I prayed I hadn't done something I'd regret. My friends and I needed to chat with Eric about his ties to the victim and whether he knew Kiefer's turbulent history with Charlotte. Janica's suggestion seemed an innocent enough way to get in front of him. But I also saw the downside; Eric would now know I was in his orbit, and if he was our killer, that was never a good thing.

Chapter Seventeen

"I just texted Eric that you're open to helping him." Janica twiddled her phone in her hand before sliding it back into her pocket.

My smile felt strained. "Great." Me *helping* our number one suspect? Not exactly ideal. "In order to help Eric as best I can, will you fill me in on his situation a bit? Why is he so certain the police will be looking at him?"

Janica shrugged. "I told him he was being overly paranoid about the whole thing. Seriously, he's putting all his energy into it rather than processing the death of his friend." She rolled her eyes with a *tsk*. "He wasn't even at the festival when Kiefer collapsed, but he says he has no proof."

I stilled at this news. "Wait, he wasn't at the grand opening?"

"Well, he *was*," Janica clarified, "but I guess he took off. Told Kiefy he could find his own ride home."

This threw everything out of whack. "Why did Eric leave him at the festival?"

Janica's brow furrowed. "Eric said something came up, and he had to split. A client with a signed jersey to sell or whatnot."

"Wouldn't his client be able to alibi him?" I tilted my head, my skepticism growing.

"I said the exact same thing." Janica jabbed a finger in the air. "But Eric brushed it off, so I'm honestly not sure what the heck went down." The more she spoke, the more troubled Janica seemed to grow over the issue.

Something wasn't adding up with Eric's story. If he were with a client rather than at the festival when Kiefer was poisoned, the proof would be in his cell phone data. Also, depending on how new his vehicle was, his car would be able to give the police a readout of his movements, too. *Thank you, podcasts, for teaching me that fun fact.* But maybe Eric wasn't as obsessed with true crime as I was to know all the ways we could be tracked these days. Or maybe…the police wouldn't find proof of him leaving the festival because he actually hadn't.

"So, Kiefer was walking around the CSC by himself? Any idea why he stayed behind?" I mulled over the strange scenario. "Why didn't he just Uber back to Ocean Hollow once Eric bailed?"

Janica tucked a strand of hair behind her ear. "No idea." The corner of her lip twitched in the slightest manner, but just enough to catch my eye. Examining her closer, her nostrils also flared a bit. Was she angry? Over what, I wondered. Not being included in their little outing?

"Was there a reason you weren't with them?"

Janica's lip quivered again. "They didn't invite me. Even after I asked them if they were going." Her shoulders slouched in a pout.

Ah, the source of her souring mood. "That's rude of them."

"Right?" Janica shook her head. "I was so—ugh, I was so mad when I found out. Why didn't they invite me? I even closed my studio early and everything."

Her righteous anger made me pause. I could sympathize with being jilted, but her reaction seemed to take things to the extreme. I then thought back to the many photos she had posted with Kiefer. Was Janica the walking embodiment of a stage five clinger?

Her eyes suddenly filled with tears. "But then I remember I'll never see Kiefer again." This time, she lost her composure. "I-I just can't believe this is happening." She quickly swiped away the tears as they fell.

I glanced around her studio, looking for some tissues and for a graceful way to make my exit. I didn't think I could pry any more into her life without Janica growing suspicious of my true intentions for being here. She'd already been relatively forthcoming with me and had even paved the way for me to follow up with Eric. However, if both Janica and Eric weren't even at the CSC festival during the time Kiefer was poisoned, then where did that leave my pitiful investigation?

"You know, Janica, you really should give yourself more time to grieve," I cooed. "Take the advice you gave Eric." I finally spotted a tissue box and grabbed a swath. "Why don't I reach out to you in a few days to schedule an appointment to chat about the remodel?" I prayed to the karma gods that they'd forgive another white lie on my part. I sure was racking them up today.

Janica dabbed at her cheeks. "I'm sorry to be so messy. You're right. I need to listen to myself."

After ensuring she had a few more tissues within reach, I inched toward the front door, murmuring various sympathies. Only when I stepped off the outside porch did I speed up and dash toward the gate.

I took a deep breath once it clanged behind me, and I was safely on the sidewalk. My chat with Janica had gone reasonably well. Using my star power (if one could call it that) to weasel information out of her had worked in my favor. Folks in Central Shores often jumped right to suspicion when it came to me asking them questions. But if Janica and others viewed me more as a confidante or "crime consultant," as she had joked, who was I to dissuade them?

I was also incredibly lucky that Janica saw me as a Good Samaritan rather than Kiefer's killer after viewing that viral X video. If she'd sided with the vicious trolls calling me a murderer, then my presence in her studio would have undoubtedly raised her hackles.

I skimmed the center for signs of Jasper. In the thirty minutes since we'd parted ways, the storm clouds had all but dissolved, and sunny, blue skies stretched out overhead. Shading my eyes, I surveyed the various storefronts lining the street. Drew Wilson's bookstore was a block down the road on the opposite side, and I recalled my idea to stop in and chat with her about Eric and his houseguest.

While scanning the sidewalk, I reached for my phone to text Jasper. **Done with Janica. Where are you?**

His reply came immediately. **Pet shop. Finishing up. On your right, three buildings down.**

Obediently, I followed his directions, coming to a stop in front of The

Trusty Biscuit. It made sense that the pretty feline Jasper had jumped into a pond to rescue came from here.

I opened the door, a delicate bell announcing my arrival. Rows of toys, beds, cat condos, treats, and more greeted me with a warm color scheme. I didn't spy any cages or hear signs that there were animals for sale, but perhaps they were kept toward the back.

As I strolled down an aisle with every style of harness one could imagine, I heard Jasper's distinctive voice ask, "Do we really think purple is her color?"

"Well," came a matronly reply, "I may have something that might interest you. We just got it in yesterday. I'll be right back."

I rounded the end of the aisle to find Jasper lording over the check-out counter, studying a pile of pet necessities with a discerning eye. Perched beside the pile of goods was the most gorgeous, fluffy white cat I'd ever seen in my life. Her tail swished back and forth as she, too, assessed the scene.

"Hey. What's going on here?" I tapped Jasper on the shoulder to pull him from his reverie. "Who's this pretty lady?" I reached for the white beauty and gently scratched behind her ear. "Did you find the owner of the other cat?"

Jasper gave me a snarky side-eye. "Some detective skills you have."

Wondering what he meant, my focus returned to the glistening white kitty. It was then I noticed her strange, icy blue eyes, so much like Jasper's. "Wait, what? She's the same one?"

My bestie nodded with a smug smile. "She cleans up nicely, doesn't she?" He pointed to a sign hanging by the register. "They've got a pet grooming station here. I was able to bathe and blow-dry her."

"Omigosh." I whistled, impressed by the transformation. "She's stunning."

"A total Andi-goes-glam moment from *The Devil Wears Prada,* right?" Jasper chuckled.

I gave the cat one final chin scratch, thinking it was funny how she kept reminding us of our favorite movie in different ways. I then inspected the pet shop. "Did you find her owner?"

Jasper pointed a thumb at his chest. "You're looking at him."

"What?!" I whipped my head in his direction. "What the heck did I miss while I was talking with Janica?"

He scooped the cat into his arms, and she nestled against him with a contented expression. "Marla, the woman working here, told me this cat has been terrorizing the center for the last several weeks. Digging up flower beds, stealing food, wrecking outdoor displays... No one knows where she came from, and no one's reported her missing. I guess she's kinda worn out her welcome in Ocean Hollow because Marla said if I didn't take her, she'd have to call animal control to deal with her."

"Holy Hilary Duff." I glanced nervously at the purring feline. "Are you sure you want to take on a cat with such an...exciting reputation? I didn't even know you liked cats all that much."

He shrugged. "I like her. She might be a bit of a diva, but she's kinda a big ol' teddy bear, too."

Sounds like someone I know. I grinned as I took in the two of them together. "Well, what are you going to name her? Beyoncé?"

Jasper gave me a deadpan stare. "There can only be one Queen Bey." His gaze dropped to the cat snuggled up in his arms. "But this little lady does require an iconic moniker."

Just then, a short, stout woman emerged from behind a side door. "Here we go, young man. What do you think of this? Doesn't it match her eyes?" The elderly lady held up a small, teal diamond-studded collar.

Jasper gasped. "Is that Tiffany Blue?"

"Oh, no. *That* would be a copyright infringement." The saleswoman chuckled. "This is *Pawfany* Blue." She lowered her voice in a joking whisper, "The diamonds aren't real, either."

"No one will know the difference." Jasper waved away her comment. "I'll take it. She deserves a little luxury in her life."

I continued to observe the scene in amazement as the woman—whom Jasper introduced as Marla—rang up all the "essentials" a cat required. I could see food, a pet bed, and a litter box being needed, but I drew the line at a kitty spa massage pad. Yet, Jasper so willingly went along with anything and everything. I never thought he'd become a pet owner before I did. My chest thrummed with envy.

It took a few minutes for Jasper and Marla to coax his new companion into a blinged-out cat carrier, but once she was secure, I helped Jasper gather his many purchases. Marla also provided him with a few recommended vets in the area, and we were ready to depart.

"You sure you don't need anything else?" I teased as we struggled to squeeze through the doorway leading to the sidewalk.

Jasper lifted his nose. "That's all."

The lofty way he said it sparked an idea. Maybe there was a reason that references to *The Devil Wears Prada* kept coming to mind for us in the presence of this cat. "What do you think about the name Miranda *Purr-iestly?*"

He stopped in his tracks. "An ode to the Ice Queen herself?" He lifted the cat carrier so he could glance inside. "You know, Cokes. You may be onto something." Jasper's grin grew wide. "You've always been really good at building a brand."

A few minutes ago, I'd been concerned that Jasper didn't know what was in store for him as a pet owner. Now, I wondered if little Miranda was ready to be owned by Jasper Hastings.

Chapter Eighteen

By the time we had filled Jasper's trunk and packed his backseat with all of Miranda's things, I'd brought him up to speed on my chat with Janica.

"So, is Eric paranoid because he's watched too much *48 Hours Mystery* or because he has something to hide?" Jasper asked as he locked the car.

I handed him back Miranda's cat carrier, and her yowling mews immediately ceased. *A daddy's girl already, huh?* "Remains to be seen. He told Janica he wasn't at the festival when Kiefer went into anaphylactic shock, but who knows if that's actually the truth?"

"Shall we see if he's up for talking with you?" Jasper thumbed over his shoulder.

I pointed to Miranda. "Are you sure you don't want to head home and get her settled? I can Uber back."

"No can do." He shook his head. "If Char and Hudson found out I left you alone with our *biggest* suspect, then Miranda would end up an orphan again." He hoisted her carrier under his arm. "Come on, let's find his store."

I thought about the oddball picture we made. Jasper's clothes were still drying out from his dunk in the pond. Add to that a bedazzled cat carrier fit for the Queen of Sheba, and we sure drew some stares as we ambled through the Ocean Hollow shopping district.

While we walked, Jasper cooed over Miranda, and I focused on figuring out how we would approach Eric. Janica had already texted him that I'd offered to help him with his situation. I *could* say I wanted to drop by in person and make the introduction. But once we got past my reasons for being there, we'd enter scary territory. How was I supposed to question Eric about Kiefer without him getting wind of our suspicions?

I didn't have to stress over the situation for long. A hastily scrawled **Closed—Sorry for the Inconvenience** sign was taped to the front window of Gold Score.

Jasper squinted and peered through the glass. "I don't see him moving around inside."

My spirits momentarily deflated. Eric must've headed home for the day after talking with Janica. "I guess I'll have to wait for him to reach out to me. Or try again tomorrow." Even if I figured out where he lived, I couldn't very well show up at his house. At least, not yet. That would raise way too many red flags.

"Maybe he's been called to the CSC to chat more with Gavin and Adrian." Jasper nudged me back in the direction of his car, wordlessly telling me to throw in the towel for today.

I considered the possibility. I mean, I trusted Gavin and Adrian to do their jobs well. Really, I did. But there was an annoyingly silly part of my ego that wanted to be the one to crack this case open. Not only did I owe it to Charlotte, but I also seriously loved solving mysteries. And if Eric hadn't been at the festival when Kiefer was poisoned, where did that leave our investigation? Who else in the area could have had it out for Kiefer Marsh?

I decided to text Char and Deacon to see how their social media deep dive was going. By the time we were settled into Jasper's car, Charlotte responded.

Good news. We've covered a lot of ground. The woman we saw in Eric's photos is Janica Rice. She and Kiefer seemed to have gotten real close, real quick.

While reading her message, I realized we had much to debrief, as Jasper and I had already uncovered Janica's identity ourselves.

Neither Rand nor Sy have much about Kiefer on their socials. Sy posted an RIP tribute this morning, but it was pretty generic. Eric has been radio silent since yesterday.

I typed back, **Are you both at B2P? We're on our way back from OH.**

I can swing by once Jasper drops me off at home. I was careful not to mention Miranda. Jasper had sworn me to secrecy, as he wanted to do a big "baby reveal" to our friends, a la Cameron Tucker and Mitchell Pritchett in *Modern Family.*

We're here. See you soon!

It became clear within seconds of Jasper putting the Porsche into drive that Miranda was not a lover of car rides. She yowled the entire way back to our condo development. Jasper managed to find it endearing for the first few minutes, but by the time he pulled into his driveway, I could tell his rose-colored patience had reached the end of its thread.

"Well, you two have fun. Bye!" I burst out of the car, rubbing my ears as I booked it down the sidewalk toward my house. Behind me, I could make out Jasper fussing over Miranda. I felt somewhat bad for leaving him to deal with all his purchases alone, but then I reassured myself that he needed a solo pet-parent reality check. Besides, it was already past lunchtime. I desperately needed food, or I'd get hangry.

Inside my condo, I rummaged through the refrigerator, looking for anything that would be remotely satisfying. I wasn't a talented or frequent cook, and since Hudson wasn't here to grill the marbled steaks we had sitting on the bottom shelf, my options were limited to various forms of condiments and canned cocktails. Not exactly hunger-quelling stuff, so I decided to grab something to go before meeting my friends at the café.

After a quick check in the mirror, I hopped into my MINI Cooper—affectionately nicknamed Jolly—and drove to the strip. Even though it was past lunchtime, I had sugar on the brain, so I pulled into a spot behind Sweet Resolutions in the residential parking lot. One of Thomas's cocoa crème crullers had my name on it.

The rich scent of chocolate swept over me as I stepped across the threshold and into the bustling little shop. Tom was busy filling orders and grabbing treats from the shiny glass cases that made up the wraparound counter. Thomas appeared to be performing a demonstration as he spread melted chocolate over a big stone cutting board. I'm sure there was a fancy, chocolatier name for the slab, but what it was, I didn't know.

I searched for the end of the line and, amongst the sea of customers, spotted a familiar head of brown hair streaked with gray. "Hey, Dad."

My father, Simon Cline, turned his head at the sound of my voice. "Well, hello, Delia! Fancy meeting you here." He leaned in for a one-armed hug.

I couldn't help rolling my eyes at his greeting. My parents were the only two people on the planet who still called me Delia, as I'd rebranded from Cordelia to Coco during my high school days. "Whatcha getting?" I glanced at his empty hands. "Picking up some bourbon braised bonbons?"

He held a finger up to his lips. "Shh. Don't tell your mother."

"Your secret is safe with me," I reassured him. Mom currently had Dad on a diet because his cholesterol numbers had risen since his last doctor's visit. While he was still very much in the "safe zone" and fit for his age, Mom wasn't taking any chances with his health. Her militant measures had forced Dad to sneak treats behind her back.

He stepped aside and made room for me in line. "I'm actually going for one of those new espresso-dipped cookies. I think it will pair nicely with a slice of pizza."

"Mom's letting you have pizza, too?" I raised my brow as the line ambled forward.

His light blue eyes twinkled. "Your mother is on some spa trip this weekend with one of her girlfriends. The place you got her a gift card for. Reddy Serenity Spa, was it? And with Thea and Lucas off camping with the triplets, I've been the king of the castle for two days." He rocked back and forth on his heels, looking quite pleased by the situation.

I laughed. Oh, the simple joys in life.

"What's up with you, kiddo?" he asked as we took another step forward, getting closer to the counter.

"Jasper and I went boat shopping in Ocean Hollow this morning." I purposely omitted our snooping exploits. I didn't want to spoil my dad's special day by making him worry about me.

He smirked. "Boat shopping, huh?"

I gave him a sidelong look. "What's with that suspicious tone?"

"Oh, nothing." His elaborate shrug didn't put me at ease.

Two can play at that game, Daddy dearest. I lowered my voice. "Should we take a nice photo here and send it to Mom?"

"You wouldn't!" He held a hand to his chest in feigned horror. "Loyalties, daughter. Loyalties."

I nudged him. "I could say the same."

By now, we'd moved to the head of the line. Tom Kingsley beamed as we approached the counter. "Hello, Coco. Simon. Lovely to see you. What can I get you two?"

We placed our order, and I waved Dad's cash away as I held my phone out to tap the electronic payment reader.

Tom glanced at my arm and winced. "Yikes. That bruise still looks nasty, Coco."

I cursed myself for leaving the gold bracelet cuff I'd been wearing earlier at home, but it'd been rubbing against my skin uncomfortably.

Tom's concern drew my dad's attention to the marks on my wrist left by Kiefer. "How did that happen?" he asked, alarmed.

"It's fine. I'm fine. It's nothing, Dad." I answered each comment with a forced smile.

Tom leaned across the counter. "Your daughter is a hero, Simon. She tried to save the life of that poor man who died yesterday at the CSC festival."

My dad didn't look exactly shocked by this news. "That's my Delia."

Tom's head tilted, confusion spreading across his face at my dad's proud response.

"His pet name for me," I hurriedly clarified the use of my legal moniker. Hoping to change the subject, I added, "Business looks good."

"It's thanks to those Facebook campaigns you helped us with." Tom smiled as he reached for two espresso-dipped chocolate cookies. "It's been a madhouse. Kinda wish I hadn't given Rosie the day off." He wiped his arm across his forehead.

Thomas tossed a pair of latex gloves into a nearby bin as he sidled up to our conversation. "She deserved a break, Tom. You saw how tired she was this morning. We've been running her ragged." He clicked his tongue at his husband before turning to Dad and me. "Would either of you like to try a free sample?" He pulled on clean gloves and pointed to a display a few feet down the counter. Three trays of various goodies beckoned us to their side.

"Don't mind if I do." My dad plucked a cordial from the closest platter.

I took a chocolate-covered cherry and nearly fainted as the blissful sweetness spread across my tongue. "Holy Margot Robbie. This is incredible."

"Rosie made those." Tom's chest puffed with satisfaction. "Thomas is giving her lessons during down times. If she keeps producing this kind of delicious work, we'll have to give her a raise before some other place steals her away."

Thomas chuckled. "If the shop stays this busy, I doubt we'll have much downtime moving forward." He grabbed a few spare chocolate molds and headed back to his station.

Tom clicked his tongue after his husband before packing my cocoa crème cruller pastry. "I think all the foot traffic is due to yesterday's shocking events." He shot me a conspiratorial look.

My heart rate ticked up. "What do you mean?"

"Well..." Tom glanced around and pressed himself against the counter so he could lean closer to us. "Thomas takes yoga classes with two of the new CSC officers," he whispered. "This morning, he overheard them talking about how a latte might have killed that poor man. And we all know who was making lattes at the grand opening yesterday..." His voice trailed off, and he looked rather guilty.

My entire body felt like it had been dropped in an ice bath. "Tom, you aren't suggesting *Charlotte*, are you?" I hissed.

"Of course not!" He held his hands up in defense. "I'm just saying it's what Thomas overheard. And since you have a reputation for helping your friends out of sticky situations, I thought you outta know what's going around town."

While I appreciated his concern, protective anger still roared within me. "Has Thomas been telling everyone what he heard?"

"Of course not, Coco." Tom looked hurt by the question. "But he wasn't the only other person in this yoga class, mind you." His gaze traveled around the bustling store. "While I'd like to believe all this traffic is from your free-sample-with-every-purchase posts, we've taken a lot of caffeine-related orders, too."

Translation: locals were getting their coffee fix from Sweet Resolutions' mocha beverages rather than Charlotte's café drinks.

"How could anyone believe Charlotte had something to do with that man's death?" Dad huffed as he eyed a delectable-looking chocolate-glazed gingerbread loaf. "The woman is a saint."

I appreciated his support and smiled at him. "I'm sure the police will get to the bottom of this."

"The police?" Tom raised an eyebrow. "So, you're not helping them? Isn't that your MO?"

I swallowed the panic rising within me. The last thing I needed was for word to get out at the town's new gossip hotspot that I was officially looking into Kiefer's death. "I'm just their friendly neighborhood social media consultant." I plastered on my most chipper smile.

Tom's forehead furrowed. "Even though it looks like Charlotte's in their crosshairs?" He almost sounded disappointed in me.

My dad draped an arm over my shoulders. "I'm to blame for her sitting this one out, I'm afraid. Worrying about my daughter getting into trouble is the last thing my ol' ticker needs." With his other hand, he patted himself on the chest.

Tom grew immediately chastened. "Oh, goodness. I'm sorry to hear that, Simon. Of course, that's understandable." He gave me an apologetic smile and bagged our treats separately.

With Tom's attention diverted, I shot Dad an alarmed look. *What heart problems?*

He winked in reply, and I relaxed, pressing my lips together to avoid laughing. Dad had just pulled a fast one over the chocolatier to get him off my case.

Tom handed us our goodies before getting flagged down by another customer. Seizing the opportunity to escape without further questioning, Dad and I hurried outside.

"Okay, spill it, Pops." I knocked him softly in the arm once we were out on the sidewalk, heading toward Charlotte's. "What do you know?"

He chuckled. "I'm worried about your deductive reasoning skills, kiddo, if you can't figure it out yourself."

My cheeks warmed, annoyed by the teasing insult. "Why, you—" I cut myself off mid-thought. *Duh!* In his retirement, Dad volunteered a few days a week at the Central Shores Fire Department. A department that now happened to share the Community Safety Center facilities alongside the police and local EMTs.

"There it is." Dad snapped gleefully as he noticed the recognition dawning on my face. "Fire Chief Lowery called us in yesterday evening and debriefed the crew about the incident. Since McInnis and his team are leading the charge, I figured you wouldn't be able to keep away, either." His expression sobered as we neared Brewed to Perfection. "I had no idea, though, that the man collapsed in front of you or that Charlotte's involved."

"Charlotte's not *involved*, Dad." My snippy inner teenager shone through. "And like I said, I'm fine."

He put an arm around me. "Come on, hon. You can't lie to your ol' dad."

I paused and saw the genuine concern shimmering in his kind expression. "Well, I *am* fine. And Charlotte isn't a killer." I sighed. "But after hearing what Tom said, I'm worried about her. The test results on the supposed 'murder weapon' can't come soon enough."

Hashtags. How I'd come to regret those words.

Chapter Nineteen

"Why on earth would the police think Charlotte killed this guy?" Dad extracted one of the espresso cookies from his Sweet Resolutions bag and took a hearty bite. "The vic's name that Chief Lowery gave us didn't sound familiar."

"You're right. Kiefer wasn't from around here." I took a deep breath. "But he *was* an ex-boyfriend of Charlotte's from South Carolina."

Chocolatey crumbs tumbled from Dad's agape mouth. "Yikes, kiddo. That's not good."

"I'm aware. I'm on my way to check in on her." I threaded my arm through his and tugged him the remaining distance toward Brewed to Perfection's door.

A welcome bell jingled overhead as we stepped inside, and my stomach plummeted at the dismal sight. I'd never seen the café so deserted during this time of year—especially when everyone needed a caffeinated pick-me-up to make it through the rest of the afternoon.

"Welcome to—oh, hi Cokes. Hi, Simon." Charlotte glanced up from the pile of papers and electronics strewn across the countertop.

Beside her, Deacon waved to me in greeting. "Hi, Mr. Cline." He nodded respectfully at my father.

"It's Simon, young man. Mr. Cline makes me feel old." Dad chuckled as we joined them at the counter.

"What's all this?" I stared at their workspace, trying to make sense of the numerous scribbles and pictures spread out.

Charlotte grinned. "The intel we've gathered. We've spent all morning digging into the socials of our unsubs."

"Unsubs only works for suspects we *don't* know, sweetie." Deacon tapped the side of his temple with a teasing smile.

She shrugged. "Whatever. Saying all their names is too wordy, and it makes me feel like we're on *Criminal Minds* rather than experiencing this nightmare in real life."

My chest tightened with sympathy. I knew the feeling, but pretending we weren't in a world of trouble would do us no good.

"So, these are your suspects, huh?" Dad grabbed a picture that looked like an Instagram screenshot.

Charlotte sent me a panicked look.

"He knows." I reassured her that she hadn't blown my parental cover. "Fire Chief Lowery told his squad about Kiefer's death, so Dad already guessed I'd be looking into it." I didn't enjoy delivering the news that came next. "But Tom told us something unsettling while we were grabbing snacks at Sweet Resolutions." I quickly divulged what Thomas had overheard at his morning yoga class.

Deacon cursed under his breath. "Did Thomas mention which officers? That kinda sh—*stuff* can't be happening." He shot a spooked glance at my dad as if worried he'd be reprimanded for even contemplating the use of foul language. That's why I enjoyed using "hashtags" so much, even when I wasn't around my nieces and nephew. I didn't have to apologize for bad behavior.

Dad, though, could've cared less. "Yeah, McInnis needs to patch up those leaks fast. Now that the CSC is fully operational, there are a lot of eyes on how this first case is being handled. The county people are going to be especially critical."

I gnawed on my lower lip, thinking about Crime Lab Director Morrison and the honorable Detective Harriet Forrester, who'd assisted the Central Shores PD in previous investigations. Would they be called to assist if Gavin and Adrian didn't make meaningful progress?

"I'm going to give Gavin a ring." Deacon squeezed Charlotte's hand. "You wanna bring Coco up to speed on what we've found?" With that, he disappeared into Charlotte's office.

"Coffee?" she asked us, ever the warm hostess.

Dad and I accepted the offer, and while Charlotte brewed a fresh pot for us—or perhaps, her first pot given the ghostly state of the café—we traded information about what we'd learned during our separate missions.

"From what D and I can tell," Charlotte concluded, "it doesn't seem like Rand and Sy were all that close to Kiefer. There are only a few group shots of them together." She pointed out the relevant photos on the counter.

I studied one glam pic of the group on a boat as I began to nibble on my cocoa crème cruller, no longer able to tamp down my hunger. "Yeah, Jasper and I didn't get the sense that Rand was all that torn up about Kiefer's passing. He was mostly concerned about Eric asking him to lie about the state of their friendship."

"You wouldn't know Eric and Kiefer were going through a rough patch. At least, not according to their uploads." Charlotte placed our coffees on the counter, safely away from her paperwork.

My dad tapped on another printout. "This is Sid Ramone's kid, right?"

I studied the photo. "Yep. Sy. I think he was a grade ahead of Thea." My sister had just turned twenty-seven.

"Sy seems like he might be really tight with Eric." Charlotte collected her evidence and laid it out in front of us. "Between the group, they're the two who are pictured together the most. Usually at sporting events. Deacon was super jealous about the number of jerseys they each own. Guess I know what he's getting for his birthday." Charlotte tittered. "We also found a ton of comments between them on posts and such."

"Nice going." I grinned at Charlotte, impressed by all the ground she and Deacon had covered. "We know Sy was at The Beach Pit last night, and according to Noelle, he was super upset."

Dad took a thoughtful sip of his coffee. "About what?"

"TBD." I considered what we knew about this strange friend group. Kiefer and Eric were on the outs over Janica. But according to Rand's phone call with Eric, Eric had only learned this morning that Kiefer's death was due to foul play. "There's a chance Eric told Sy about Kiefer's sudden passing last night, and he was drinking away his sorrows."

"Or drinking away his guilt," Charlotte suggested. "Maybe he believed that removing Kiefer from the equation would help Eric out with Janica."

I shuddered. "Really puts a morbid spin on a ride-or-die friendship, doesn't it?" I studied a picture of Eric and Sy bro-ing out at a baseball game. The timestamp was two weeks ago. "Any pictures of Sy at the CSC festival?"

Charlotte shook her head, her amber ponytail swinging back and forth. "Nope. The only thing we got from Sy yesterday was an Instagram Story capturing the Orioles game against the Yankees on a flatscreen TV. The score was tied, three to three."

"Yeah, the Yanks tied it up in the ninth. The game went into extra innings," Dad interjected. "Didn't end until after eleven-thirty."

I frowned. So, the only social media record we had of Sy was after he'd been kicked out of The Beach Pit. "I guess he wasn't too sloshed to watch it."

"For friends who seem to live their lives online, it's pretty sus that yesterday was some sort of media blackout for them all." Charlotte shuffled through her printouts, her smooth, tanned skin furrowing slightly on her forehead. "Even Janica, who chronicles *everything* she does." She handed me a screenshot of Janica plucking her eyebrows.

My lip curled at Charlotte's slightly exasperated tone—she wasn't into social media as much as I was—and I examined the image from Janica's Instagram handle **@dolledupdarling**. She'd shared a GRWM—or a Get Ready With Me—post bright and early this morning. "She sure doesn't seem too grief-stricken to apply all that bronzer." I stared at the image, trying to reconcile the woman in front of the camera with the one who was supposedly devastated by Kiefer's passing. "But I guess we do all process grief differently." And who could forget that social media let us present our most polished selves, often hiding the reality unfolding behind the camera.

"So, these are your only suspects?" Dad asked before taking another gulp of coffee. "Who can you place at the CSC event?"

I sighed. "Right now, no one. Eric and Kiefer went together, but Eric told Janica he left Kiefer there. Janica wanted to go, but Eric and Kiefer went without her. Rand *was* invited by Eric but opted to take his wife on a sail down the coast, so he's in the clear. Sy is still an unknown." I drummed my fingers on the counter, the staccato rhythm the only noise in the quiet shop, other than Deacon's muted conversation coming from Charlotte's office. My assessment of our key players left me disheartened. We had nothing substantial to go on at this point.

"Well, kiddo, I mentioned I was getting pizza, right?" Dad nudged my arm, a playful grin curling on his face. "Why don't we see if Sy's working the counter at Saucy Sid's today?"

I brightened at the enthusiasm radiating from him. "You sure you can handle a covert mission like this? Subtlety isn't your strongest suit, Pops."

He chuckled. "I'll order the pizza. You do the talking. How about that?"

"You've got yourself a deal." I grinned.

"Thanks so much for helping us with this, Simon." Charlotte tugged awkwardly at her ponytail.

He reached across the counter and gave her a fatherly pat on the shoulder. "Of course, sweetie. Gotta do what I can to turn my favorite barista's frown upside down."

We giggled at his tender delivery, although I could tell Charlotte was touched by the sentiment.

From the back of the café, I heard a door open, and Deacon returned, his steps heavy.

"How'd it go?" Charlotte snuggled under his left arm.

He ran his right hand over his shaved head. "Eh, Gavin wasn't thrilled by the news, obviously."

"Is that all?" The poor guy looked like he had the weight of the world on his shoulders.

Deacon's gaze dropped to the floor momentarily before adding, "He slipped me some intel in return. The initial fingerprint analysis came back on the Brewed to Perfection cup."

His discouraged tone told me all I needed to know.

Charlotte gasped, and her eyes welled with frightened tears as she stepped back from Deacon's protective touch.

Dad, bless him, remained utterly clueless. "What'd they find?"

"Two sets of prints. The deceased's and…" Deacon's voice trailed off, his anxious gaze seeking out his girlfriend.

"Mine." Charlotte's whisper nearly broke my heart.

We now knew, without a doubt, that the B2P cup containing peanut bits had belonged to Kiefer. One of Charlotte's renowned yummy lattes had become a murder weapon.

"Are they coming to arrest me?" she squeaked.

Deacon pulled her close and stroked her hair. "No. No way. You made it very clear you made Kiefer a latte. Coco was there to verify that fact, so it makes total sense that your prints are on the cup. The police will need way more to issue a warrant since the only peanut-related item they can physically link to you is a tub of peanut butter. And we're all aware that Kiefer's cup was laced with peanut bits, not peanut butter."

"Can't they do peanut typing or something?" Dad scratched his head. "Find out what was crushed up and such? That might narrow down what vendor, if any, the peanuts came from. I'm sure I've seen that done on *CSI*."

I almost snorted at the silliness of "peanut typing," but then realized Dad's strange suggestion was probably within the realm of possibility. "You might be onto something. I saw plenty of booths selling peanuts that were roasted, candied, and everything in between. If they can find out what kind of peanut was used, Gavin and Adrian can trace vendor purchases at the festival." His theory also beckoned another annoying detail into my mind. "But if this was premeditated, there's a chance the killer *brought* the peanuts to the festival, thinking they'd lace whatever Kiefer ended up eating or drinking while he was there." According to Charlotte, peanuts or peanut dust would only need to contaminate whatever Kiefer ingested to trigger a reaction.

A small smile twitched on Deacon's lips. "The guys will run whatever tests they can, but tracking every transaction? That would completely over-extend the team. Lots of vendors were selling various styles of peanuts. Likely, Gav and Adrian will determine what type of peanut was dropped into Kiefer's cup and then look to see if any of their *suspects* made such a purchase."

My ears perked up. "Suspects, you say? So, Gavin and Adrian have eyes on people other than Charlotte?"

"Of course they do." He looked pained. "Gavin wouldn't tell me who, though. He's already broken a slew of rules by sharing the details he did with me. So, I suppose we can be grateful for that."

"Then why don't you look happier?" I retorted.

Deacon's expression grew pinched. "Part of the initial identification process is running a background check on their victim."

Beside him, Charlotte visibly stiffened, and her face drained of its color.

"And with that," he continued, pressing his lips together, "came Kiefer's criminal history."

Chapter Twenty

"Criminal history?" I repeated, stunned. "What for?" Was Kiefer involved in some shady dealings that got him killed?

Deacon glanced at Char, and after she gave a barely perceptible nod, he replied, "For domestic assault. He was arrested for attacking a young woman six years ago."

I felt like I'd been punched in the gut. Six years ago? Young woman? "What?" My head snapped toward Charlotte. I knew Kiefer had been violent toward her, but I never knew he'd actually been *arrested* for it. And so early into their courtship?

"I-I was stupid and dropped the charges." Tears ran down Charlotte's cheeks. "It should have been a sign to leave, but I-I thought it was just a one-time thing. He *promised* he'd n-never do it again."

"Oh, honey," my dad murmured his sympathies and patted her hand.

I unlatched the gate barring customers from behind the counter and came around to give Charlotte a bone-crushing hug. "You were not stupid. You were hopeful and full of compassion. *That's* the person you are."

She cried softly into my shoulder. "I'm sorry I never told you the full extent of what happened between us. I-I didn't want you thinking less of me."

I held her by the shoulders, demanding her attention. "There is *nothing* in the world you could do to make me think less of you. You are stuck with me as your biggest cheerleader for the rest of your life. Got that?"

A timid smile broke out through her tears, and she bobbed her head.

"How does Kiefer's criminal past affect the official investigation?" I asked

144

Deacon as I continued to hold my best girlie.

He folded his arms. "Fortunately for us, Charlotte was forthcoming with police about her connection to Kiefer, so it's not a terrible red flag. But it *is* legal confirmation that she had an unpleasant history with him, to say the least."

I scoffed. The *least,* indeed. My sense of justice, which I normally prided myself on, got more and more distorted as this case went on. Was I sad Kiefer Marsh was dead? If I was honest with myself, no, I wasn't. He'd hurt my friend in one of the worst ways possible. Did that make me a bad person? To some, probably. But I couldn't help these uncomfortable feelings. While I desperately desired to be a good human being, what I wanted more was justice for Charlotte, to ensure Kiefer and his violent legacy didn't ruin her life forever.

Deacon added, "Gavin says he and Adrian are briefing the DA tomorrow morning with what they have so far..."

"Which means, if *we* come up with something before then, Gavin wants us to clue them in?" I raised a searching eyebrow.

Deacon's nod was slight, but it was an affirmation, nonetheless.

"All right, then." I rubbed my hands together. "You guys continue your online deep dive. See if you can spot any of our suspects in pictures or videos under the #CelebratetheCSC hashtag. Dad and I will see what we can get from Sy about the whole Eric-Kiefer situation." The jury was still out on whether Eric was telling the truth about leaving Kiefer behind at the festival. Maybe we could get Sy to either confirm or deny this flimsy alibi.

"Sounds good." Charlotte's hands went to her hips as she surveyed her empty café. "I doubt we'll see much business for the rest of the day if word is spreading that one of my lattes killed Kiefer."

"Do you want to close?" Deacon asked.

She shook her head. "No. That will just cause more gossip." Charlotte held her chin high. "I've still got plenty of paper and ink in my office printer. We can continue our work from here."

I admired her strength and determination. A few cases ago, when I was in her shoes, I'd folded under the pressure of public scrutiny and hid myself away in my condo to avoid vicious whispers. Her inner warrior inspired me.

"Keep me posted!" I reminded the couple as Dad and I recycled our empty coffee cups and headed for the door.

Once we were alone outside on the sidewalk, Dad let loose a low whistle. "How anyone can have a negative thing to say about that young lady is beyond me. She is a credit to her generation."

"I couldn't agree more." I threaded my arm through his and strolled down the alleyway toward the residential parking lot. "Want to carpool to Sid's?"

He glanced at his watch. I did a double-take when I saw it on his wrist. It was the ancient *Lion King*-themed Casio I'd given him for his birthday when I was four. *Aww.*

"I've got to be at Omar's place in an hour, so I'll drive myself."

"Omar Jackson?"

He nodded. "I'm helping him install a new stereo in his game room."

I smiled sadly at the underlying subtext. While gym entrepreneur Omar Jackson was wealthy enough to pay for the professional installation of just about anything, I imagined this was Dad's way of checking in on his friend, who was still recovering from the devastating loss of his only daughter last year.

We arrived at Dad's road-worn sedan first ("if it ain't broke, don't upgrade it" being one of his favorite slogans in the tech-driven millennium), and I assured him we'd reconnect at Saucy Sid's. I then made my way toward Jolly, checking the notifications that had come in.

Ignoring all the social media alerts for now, my heart jumped into my throat at the red badge next to the iMessage app. Seventy-eight texts?! What the hashtag?

As panic jolted through me, it was quelled just as quickly when I realized the culprit. Jasper. More specifically, Jasper and Little Miss Miranda Purriestly.

He'd sent me a seemingly endless picture stream featuring the refined feline perched on various pieces of furniture around his condo. My thumb got sore scrolling through them all. While Miranda was stunningly beautiful—she needed her own Insta account, stat—I searched for any actual words Jasper had sent, assuming he'd want to know about my chat with Charlotte and Deacon. But nope. My bestie was currently in cat-dad heaven without a care in the world.

I hearted some of my favorite photos, but I didn't send a text response. I'd fill him in later after swinging by Saucy Sid's.

Hudson, on the other hand, had sent a few messages inquiring about the case and how Charlotte was doing. Ever the thoughtful fiancé.

Just leaving B2P now, I tapped on my keyboard. **Things aren't going too great. Word is out that Char's latte supposedly killed Kiefer, so it was a ghost town at the café.**

Hudson responded by the time I was buckled in Jolly. **Yikes! How did that get out so soon?**

Instead of texting a long-winded response, I called him via Jolly's Bluetooth.

"Everything okay?" His greeting was hesitant, as Hudson knew more than anyone how much anxiety I got while talking on the phone.

His wary tone coaxed a chuckle from me, allowing me to relax as I drove inland toward the strip mall where Saucy Sid's was located. "As fine as it can be. I thought I'd give you a quick rundown of the day so far." I didn't have much time because the drive to the pizza parlor was only ten minutes, so I touched on the major case points, leaving Miranda's harrowing rescue and subsequent adoption for later.

"It's not much," I concluded with our mission to chat with Sy, "but it's all we've got."

"I'd say you've covered a lot of ground, babes." Hudson's pride was evident, and it warmed my soul. "This Eric dude sounds like he's got a reason to be nervous about cops poking around."

"But if he wasn't even at the festival when Kiefer was poisoned..."

Hudson jumped in, "All you have is his word—through Janica, mind you—about that."

"You're right." I clenched my fingers against the steering wheel. "I need receipts." But how would I get them?

"Speaking of receipts." I heard shuffling on Hudson's end, and when he spoke again, his voice was lowered. "Sorry, I'm at the studio going through the footage we got with Ivy."

I wanted to ask him how his interview went, but it sounded like Hudson had something important to share.

"Cokes," he began, his voice compassionate and soft, "I asked Diamond to run a background check on Kiefer Marsh, and some...unsettling information came to light."

I flinched. "I think I know where this is going." When I'd recapped everything for Hudson, I hadn't mentioned the news about Kiefer being arrested for domestic violence against Charlotte. "Kiefer's criminal record, right?"

Hudson's sigh carried through the phone line. "Poor Charlotte. I had no clue things had escalated that badly for her. What a terrible situation."

"I never realized the full extent either." Tears welled in my eyes. "I knew things were awful, but I had no idea she'd endured so much for so long." I wiped my cheeks, wondering how Charlotte managed to be such a bright ray of sunshine despite what she'd survived. Her strength was humbling, to say the least. "Deacon says that it's a good thing Char didn't hide her history with Kiefer from the police. Otherwise, she'd probably be in more hot water than she currently is."

"Well, he says that now," Hudson challenged, "but once Gavin and Adrian talk with the DA, it might be another story." His tone grew grave.

My heart skipped. "What do you mean?"

"Gavin and Adrian are confident that there's more to the story because they *know* Charlotte," Hudson reminded me. "The DA doesn't. She'll listen to the evidence so far and probably wonder why Charlotte isn't being looked at more closely. So, I would prepare for things to get a little dicey after their meeting tomorrow."

I turned into the strip mall parking lot, snagging a spot in front of Saucy Sid's. "Unless I can uncover something this afternoon that totally changes the playing field."

"That's a lot of pressure to put on yourself." Hudson's remark was gentle.

"It's barely been twenty-four hours since Kiefer was killed—"

"That's twenty-four hours too long for Charlotte's name to be dragged through the mud," I interrupted, my nostrils flaring. "You should've seen the café, babe. I think my dad and I were the first people there all day."

"I know you're worried about her, but I'm worried about *you*," Hudson replied with the patience of a saint. "If you go a hundred miles an hour trying to solve this thing, you're bound to make a mistake or put yourself at risk."

My cheeks heated with shame. Hudson didn't know it, but I'd already put myself at risk. I hadn't told him about Jasper leaving me to question Janica solo, nor had I revealed we'd questioned Rand, a potential suspect at the time, in the middle of the ocean (okay, maybe not the middle, but you get my drift). As much as I hated the idea of Charlotte being sullied by this investigation, I had to be smart about how I continued to work the case. I was no use to my bestie if I got myself thrown in jail for obstructing justice...or worse.

Chapter Twenty-One

"All I'm saying is, please be careful."

A small smile spread across my face at Hudson's concern. I knew he was only trying to look out for me. "I will."

"I'll be waiting to hear how your dad's detective skills rate, too." My fiancé chuckled before we said our goodbyes.

I climbed out of Jolly and checked the parking lot, spotting Dad a few rows down. He was chatting on the phone and hung up just as we met in front of Saucy Sid's.

"Your mother." His eye roll rivaled my most sassy attempts. "She wanted to make sure I was eating enough vegetables. Tomato sauce counts as a veggie, right?"

I giggled. "I think tomatoes are a fruit."

"Same difference." He shrugged before assessing the entrance of the pizza parlor. "What's the plan?"

Before I could make a suggestion, a loud *clang* blasted through the air. Dad and I whipped our heads in the direction the sharp noise had come from.

"Sounds like it might be around back?" Dad pointed to the slim alleyway between Saucy Sid's and Trove, the local consignment shop.

I thought about finding Miranda in Janica's koi pool earlier today. "Maybe it's just a stray cat. Or raccoon, even."

Dad looked like he was about to agree when another *clang* echoed, followed by a pained grunt. A very *human* grunt.

"Someone's hurt." In a flash, Simon Cline morphed into heroic volunteer firefighter mode. He straightened his shoulders and balled his fists as he hurried toward the alley.

"Hey, Dad, wait!" I hissed after him, a bit more wary about what—or who—we might be running into.

However, he paid me no heed. *Must run in the family*, I grumbled to myself as I pursued Dad down the shadowy, tight passage.

Another *clang* followed by a deep voice bellowing, "This is what you get, punk," reached us, getting clearer with every step.

"Please," a nasally reply whimpered. "I-It's not my fault."

"Then you tell your guy that he better get his act together and deliver the real thing." A third person punctuated his words with a juicy spit.

At the end of the alley, Dad and I stuck our heads out just enough to see around the corner. Two lanky white guys who were tall enough to be threatening loomed over the cowering figure of Sy Ramone. Sy lay curled in a ball next to a dumpster, sniffling.

My hand flew to cover my mouth, although I was too scared to summon even a small shriek. *Hashtags, what have we walked into?*

As one of the men raised a metal trashcan lid to deliver a blow to Sy, Dad reached for a discarded rusty pipe propped up against the side of the building. "Hey, you jerks. Pick on somebody your own size." He stepped out into the back alley, swinging the pipe like he was some seasoned mobster.

"Dad!" The exclamation got stuck in my throat. What in the name of Marlon Brando did he think he was doing?

The two thugs whirled around, clearly startled by the interruption. But when they saw Dad was alone, their jeering grins returned. Even though he had a good thirty pounds of muscle on each of them, it was still two against one.

"Come to play, old man?" The spitter beckoned Dad forward with a smug flick of his wrist.

Jumping out from the shadows to assist my father, I whipped out my phone and had my camera app open a second later. "You bet we have." While I tried to sound like I meant business, my words came out more high-pitched and strangled than I would've liked. There was a reason Hollywood hadn't come calling after my acting talents. "We've already called the police, and

I'm streaming this on Instagram right now." I'd done neither of those things, but these buffoons didn't have to know that.

The other guy grabbed the spitter by the arm. "Dude, that's the influencer girl my sister always watches. We can't have our faces caught." He continued to pull his buddy back, shielding himself with his other hand. "She's with the cops."

The spitter yanked his arm out of his pal's grip. "If you don't deliver, we'll be back." He spat once more on Sy's shivering figure before he and his cohort hightailed it into the thick woods behind the strip mall.

"Omigosh, Sy, are you okay?" I dashed forward to check on the poor guy.

Dad knelt beside me. "What'd they do to you, son?"

Sy moaned as he pushed himself into a sitting position on the asphalt. "I-I'm fine." He winced as he shifted on his bum. "They just knocked me around a bit with those lids." He motioned to the discarded metal trashcan tops.

Relieved he didn't seem too hurt, I held up my phone. "I'll call the police—"

"No!" Sy grabbed my right wrist, the action causing us both to hiss in pain. "Oops. Sorry, Coco," he murmured shamefully, releasing his grip once he saw the bruises on my skin.

I smiled reassuringly through gritted teeth. "It's okay." As I massaged my arm, I added, "Those men assaulted you, Sy. You should file a report."

He shook his head as he began to pull himself off the ground. "That will only cause us more trouble," he muttered.

"Us?" Dad hoisted him upright, his glare stern. "What kind of trouble are you in? With whom?"

Sy dusted off his Saucy Sid's uniform and apron, clearly uncomfortable with our attention. If I hadn't known he worked at a pizza joint, I would've wondered if those tomato sauce smears were blood stains. "Er, I just owe those guys some…money. You know how it is."

Dad and I shared a telepathic glance. *No, we did not know how it is.* And I very much doubted Sy owed "money," based on how unconvincingly he'd uttered the explanation.

"Thanks for the help, though. You guys saved my butt." Sy smoothed down his out-of-control black hair. "When you came barreling in with that pipe, Mr. Cline, I thought I'd lost it."

Dad placed the pipe back in the spot he'd grabbed it from. "Probably wasn't the smartest move on my part," he murmured so that only I could hear. "Let's not mention this to your mother, okay, Delia?"

I snorted. "Sure, Pops." He couldn't keep a non-food-related secret from Mom if his life depended on it, so I doubted our pact would last long.

"Can I offer you guys some pizza on the house?" Sy asked.

I sensed we were being bribed, but if Sy didn't want to involve the police, that was his decision. His wishes, though, wouldn't stop me from informing my detective pals about what I'd witnessed.

"That's what we're here for, so who am I to say no?" Dad patted his stomach and smacked his lips.

Sy ushered us through the back door of the pizza parlor, and before long, we'd taken our place on the customer side of the 1960s-style counter. "You're the only one working today?" I asked, although the answer was evident.

Sy nodded as Dad pointed out the slices he wanted boxed up. "Yeah, at the moment. Pa had a church event this afternoon, so I'm covering for him until four." He tossed a glance at the clock as if pleadingly counting down the minutes.

"So...you're really not gonna tell us who those guys were?" I raised an eyebrow.

His cheeks colored. "Like I said, just some Ocean Hollow dudes I owe money to."

"Ocean Hollow, huh?" I paused, considering how to best approach things. As much as I was curious about what trouble Sy was in, his mention of the neighboring town opened the door to chat about Kiefer. Perhaps I could accomplish both. What's to say they weren't somehow related? "Wasn't the guy who died at yesterday's CSC festival from there?"

The embarrassed color in Sy's cheeks drained to white.

Even my dad picked up on Sy's nonverbal response. "I take it you knew him, son?"

The serving spatula in Sy's hand scraped loudly against the pizza pan

153

holding Dad's sausage and cheese. "Kinda. He was an old buddy of my pal, Eric."

"I'm sorry for your loss," I offered gently.

Sy shrugged. "I'm sorry what *you* had to go through, Coco. My dad was there when it went down. He said you tried to help the dude."

Again with the helping narrative. It was very different from the one trending online. "Thanks. It was pretty awful." I shuddered involuntarily as the memory rammed through me. "How's your friend Eric handling things?"

"I think he's still in shock. He feels guilty, of course."

The hair on the back of my neck stood at attention.

Sy continued, "He's blaming himself because he left Kief alone at the festival. Eric thinks whoever Kief pissed off wouldn't have made a move on him if he'd been with a buddy."

"Made a move?" Dad's brow furrowed. "I thought the poor guy died from some medical incident."

I pressed my lips together to conceal a smile. Dad was pretty good at this amateur detective thing. Must be thanks to all those *PBS Masterpiece* shows he and Mom watched.

Sy's eyes widened. "You haven't heard?" He turned to me. "I would have thought *you'd* be in the know, Coco. Since you work with the police and all."

I cringed. I guessed after being tied to three well-publicized cases, it was a bit naive of me to think I could completely fool the people of Central Shores. "I'm trying not to interfere this time around." I smiled sweetly through the lie.

"Eric called me this morning and told me the news. The police came and questioned him. Something about his friend's allergy being *purposely* triggered." Sy shuddered. "Coldhearted stuff, if you ask me."

Hmm. Interesting. It sounded like Eric had confided in Sy about Kiefer's cause of death. Why hadn't he shared it with Rand or Janica? Did Eric trust Sy more? Or had Sy persuaded him to keep the details from their other friends?

"Triggered?" Dad crossed his arms. "Now, who would do that? I thought the kid wasn't from around here."

I resisted a scoff at his somewhat patronizing phrasing. In his early thirties, Kiefer was hardly a kid.

But Dad's "boys will be boys" approach worked with Sy. "I've been wracking my brain with the very same question. Although, the guy was kinda a tool, so I suppose he could've made a few enemies fairly quickly." His expression grew pained. "Sorry. Shouldn't say that about the dead. Pa would wallop me."

"Was Kiefer in trouble with anyone?" I gnawed my lower lip.

Sy snorted. "Probably any guy with a wife or girlfriend under the age of thirty-five." He lowered his voice, even though it was just us in the pizza parlor. "Kief had a nasty habit of wanting what wasn't his, if you get what I mean."

I certainly did. But tracking down all the scorned male partners he could've offended during his stay in the area seemed like an impossible task. So, I chose to narrow my focus closer to home. "What about those guys who were here? Did Kief owe them money, too?"

"What? N-No. No way." Sy's reply was adamant, but there was an underlying current of panic in his response. "That was just a…poker game dispute. A pal and I haven't paid in full. Nothing to do with Kief." He finished boxing my dad's selection of pizza slices and slid the container across the counter. "Thanks again for bailing me out."

His tone had a clipped note of finality to it. He gave Dad a friendly salute, but I could tell Sy wanted this conversation to be done without being rude in front of one of his father's friends.

"Of course. But get it handled." Dad's glare became stern. "I spoke with Sid yesterday at the festival. He's proud of your progress, Sy. So, my advice? Get yourself back on the straight and narrow."

Sy looked like a six-year-old being chastened. "Yes, sir."

I seized the small opening Dad had given me. "Did you get to enjoy the festival at all yesterday, or were you there helping your dad out?"

Sy shook his head. "Nah. I couldn't make it. I had some business to take care of." His gaze trailed off to the side. "That's why I'm stuck here today while the rest of the crew has the day off."

Business, huh? *I wonder what that could be?* As far as I knew, Sy only worked for his dad.

His answer also added another kink in our investigative chain. Unless we could prove otherwise, Sy hadn't been anywhere near Kiefer when the peanuts had been dropped into his latte. That meant he couldn't be our killer.

Chapter Twenty-Two

"**D**o you often leave a suspect interrogation with more questions than you had going in?" Dad asked with a light chuckle as we walked to our cars.

I blew a defeated burst of air across my lips. "Honestly, it's par for the course."

He popped open the top of the pizza box to offer me a slice, and I gladly accepted a gooey piece of pepperoni. "It didn't sound like this Eric guy was paranoid about being on the hook for Kiefer's murder when he told Sy about it."

I mulled over our conversation as I chewed. "Or Sy was more comfortable covering for his friend than Rand Windham was."

"Yeah…it seems like Sy is no stranger to shady dealings," Dad admitted.

I swallowed a delicious bite. "Did you really chat with Sid Sr. yesterday about him?"

Dad's expression became meek. "Nope. I didn't even go to the festival. But since Sy told us Sid saw you helping out the vic, I figured it was a safe enough bet."

I grinned. "Good instincts, Pops."

He puffed out his chest. "High praise from our resident crime influencer."

"Now, where did you ever hear *that* term?" I did a double-take.

"Thea. She prattles on about your online stuff all the time." Dad held my gaze. "She's quite proud to be your little sister, you know."

"Aww, that's sweet." Because of our very different lifestyles, Thea and I didn't always see eye-to-eye, but we'd been making an effort in recent months to nurture our sisterly bond.

Dad gave me a one-arm hug, careful to avoid getting pizza sauce on me. "Your mother and I are proud of everything you do, too. Especially how you've helped the community."

"Thanks, Dad." I kissed him on the cheek. I knew I walked a very different path than my parents had expected of their eldest daughter, but it was good to know they supported my decision to live life on my own terms.

"So, what's next?" he asked once our tender moment passed.

His question brought forth a frown. "All roads lead to Eric Brady. I've got to find a way to chat with him." Had he responded to Janica about my offer to help? I hadn't seen any DMs come through from either of them. If Eric wasn't willing to engage with me voluntarily, what was the best way to approach the situation?

"Why don't you take the night to think about it, kiddo?" Dad patted my back. "Maybe a relaxing evening at home will spark an idea."

I checked my watch, noting it was nearly three thirty. The day had flown by, and all I'd eaten was a chocolate cruller and a piece of greasy pizza. A salad was warranted to help balance everything out. "I think that's a good plan of action. Are you still heading to Omar's?"

He nodded. "Wish me luck."

"Enjoy the rest of your weekend." I eyed his pizza box. "Make sure to hide all evidence from Mom."

He laughed, and we parted ways.

As I strolled toward my car, a fluttering Pride flag caught my eye, drawing my attention to Bright Auras, the local crystal shop owned by Sage Hattape, Rand's wife.

"Maybe I should swing by and see if she can alibi her husband," I mused aloud to myself. Rand had mentioned he'd filled Sage in on the Eric-Kiefer drama. Perhaps she'd have something insightful to add to the mix.

I was a few yards from the entrance when a familiar figure stepped out, her expression much more downcast than I was used to seeing.

"Heya, Rosie!" I beamed as I hurried toward her. "Fancy meeting you here."

She removed her sunglasses and appeared to brighten slightly. "Oh, hi, Coco. I didn't realize you were into crystals."

Only when they can help me with a case. Unable to say that out loud, I searched for an answer that wouldn't be a lie but also wouldn't offend someone who was truly into crystals. "I'm always up for exploring new things. Doing some shopping on your unexpected day off?"

Rosie tilted her head in confusion. "How did you know it was unexpected?"

"I went by Sweet Resolutions earlier, and Tom mentioned it," I explained. "He and Thomas are worried about you. They think they're working you too hard."

Rosie tugged at a lock of her brown hair. "Well, I hope they don't cut back on my hours too much. I need all the time I can get." A cloud of apprehension descended on her pretty face. "I was actually asking Sage if she had any part-time work available."

That's when I realized she wasn't wearing her trademark UNC Tar Heels cap. Without it, the lighter roots of her dyed tresses were on full display. As I studied her reddening cheeks, I also doubted the holes in her tank top and shorts were there for fashion reasons. "Oh, cool. Did she?" I didn't want to pry into her financial situation, but the girl looked stressed.

Rosie shook her head. "Nothing that works with my current schedule, anyway. She recommended asking the local supermarket if they needed anyone to stock shelves overnight."

Overnight? That sounded like a lot of hard work. "You know, I actually might have something if you're interested?" The offer was out of my mouth before the idea had even fully formed.

"Really?" Her watery-red eyes widened with hope. "You mean for *Trending Topic* or CoA?" She quickly tamped down her excitement. "Because you know I'm not the best person when it comes to social media. I tend to avoid it like the plague."

I recalled a conversation I'd had with her while working on the Sweet Resolutions website. She'd deleted all her accounts because she was fed up with reading disinformation and political rants on people's timelines. "Actually..." I searched my brain for an offering she might feel more comfortable with.

"You and Hudson must be so busy these days—what if I took care of some housework for you?" Rosie shyly swayed on her feet, not quite meeting my gaze. "You know, like laundry, meal prep, and stuff like that."

I stared at her, wondering if she was a gift from the karma gods. "You'd be up for that?"

She bobbed her head furiously. "Of course. I could come by after my shifts at the shop and do whatever housework you need."

Hudson had wanted to hire someone to clean our condo since we'd moved in together, but I'd always opted to do it myself. The idea of having a housekeeper made me feel uneasy as if I was getting too big for my britches. My whole online persona revolved around being the down-to-earth girl next door, and I worried that paying someone to take care of my house would spoil me. But Hudson and I had so little time together these days that I didn't really want us to spend that time cleaning. And it sounded like Rosie was in need of some extra cash flow.

"You've got yourself a deal." I held out my hand. "How does one twenty-five an hour sound?"

"What?" Her eyes doubled in size. "T-that's way too much."

"Hey, you haven't seen my laundry mountain yet." I grinned, refusing to budge on my offer. "I'm no easy customer."

Rosie giggled. "I highly doubt that, Coco. But I appreciate it, and I will accept." We shook on it. "When would you like me to come over? Today?"

"Gosh, no. You rest up. You do look a little under the weather." I examined her freckled face. Between her watery eyes and pasty skin, she looked like she'd spent some time crying. I hoped this new gig would help alleviate the financial stress she was under.

Rosie put her shades back on. "I'm feeling better already. But I suppose you're right. Maybe I'll treat myself to the salon. I'm way overdue." She motioned to the roots of her hair.

"I love a good spa day." I smiled sympathetically, knowing all too well the hoops we had to jump through to maintain the color of dyed hair. My strawberry-champagne hue had masked my natural mousey brown for years.

"If you're free Tuesday evening, why don't you come over then?" I was already mentally searching my and Hudson's schedules. "Hudson has a game night with the boys, and I can hole myself up in my office, so I'm not in your way."

"Tuesday works great for me! Thanks so much, Coco." Rosie reached for my left arm and squeezed, her gaze moving to the bruises on my right wrist. "Gosh, that looks terrible. You sure you're okay?"

"It's all good. You should see the other guy." I regretted the awful joke the moment it crossed my lips. "I-I mean…hashtags, that was rotten of me to say."

Rosie had paled slightly, but she didn't look at me like I was a heartless monster. In fact, her expression was one of compassionate understanding. "It's okay. I won't tell on you." She mimed zipping her lips with a sad smile.

"Thanks." I grimaced, ashamed of my actions. I may not have been upset that Kiefer was dead, but his death was no joking matter, even among friends.

With a plan in place to have Rosie clean the condo on Tuesday, we bid each other goodbye. Seeing her walk toward her rusty car with her head held high allowed the warm fuzzies to return. I was happy I could help out a friend going through hard times. "Go Tar Heels!" I called after her.

Rosie whirled around with a puzzled expression. "Huh?"

I pointed to my forehead, where a baseball cap would typically rest. The action seemed to clarify my words as realization spread across Rosie's face. "Ha ha, you bet!"

Feeling slightly foolish at my failed attempt to be a UNC sports fan, I turned to face Bright Auras' storefront, reminding myself of my current mission: get Rand's alibi and see if Sage had any dirt to share on her husband's Ocean Hollow friend group. Although, I had to be smart about getting her to spill the tea. No doubt, Sage viewed gossiping as toxic to one's chakra.

I stifled a giggle as I reached for the door handle, briefly recalling the last time I'd been inside the crystal store. My sister Thea had accompanied me, and Sage's earthy stones weren't the only thing we'd found "au naturel."

I opened the door, and it took a moment for my eyes to adjust to the dark light. New age music hummed lightly through the store's speaker system, and the smell of intense incense hit me like a brick. As I tried to stifle a cough, I heard murmuring from the back of the narrow shop.

Sage Hattape's lilting, deep voice reached my ears. "Yes, it's about the man on the news. The one who died."

Who was she talking to? I sidestepped to check down an aisle, spotting the customer service desk. Sage stood behind it, a landline phone pressed to her ear. She appeared engrossed in her conversation and didn't acknowledge me.

I moved closer, hundreds of colorful rocks shimmering in the dim overhead light on either side of me.

"Yes, hello, officer. I'm calling about the man from the CSC festival. Kiefer Marsh?" Sage's voice quivered as she spoke. "I know who killed him."

Chapter Twenty-Three

My jaw dropped open, and I nearly stumbled into a display of pink quartz. Hashtags, what was going on here?

Sage took a deep breath. "You see, I did a reading, and the cards told me—what? Yes, a reading. With my cards. No! Sir, you don't realize—sir? Officer?" She pulled the phone away from her ear, her expression miffed. "What kind of tipline is that?"

I swallowed the awkward laughter gurgling within me. Sage had called the CSC tipline to share a tarot reading she'd done on Kiefer? A bold move, for sure.

Yet, despite her somewhat unorthodox method, I didn't like that whoever answered her call had simply hung up on her. Weren't the police supposed to record every tip that came in, even the kooky ones? I made a note to relay the oversight to Gavin or Chief McInnis. The CSC couldn't afford to make amateur mistakes like this.

I cleared my throat to announce my presence. "Hey, Sage. Long time, no see."

She glanced away from the phone, slamming it on its cradle as she did so. "Coco! Sorry, I didn't hear you come in."

"No worries." I ambled toward her. "That sounded like an important call."

"It *should've* been." She folded her dark tan arms with a huff, and with her sleeveless floral dress, I spotted the intricate design of a turtle tattooed on her shoulder. A symbol of her tribe, the Lenape.

"New ink?" I pointed at her arm, attempting to ease my way into the conversation I'd just overheard. I didn't want her clamming up on me if she thought I was fishing for information.

Sage proudly glanced at her tattoo. "I got it a few months ago. It matches the one on Rand's forearm."

"Looks great." I leaned casually on the countertop and nodded toward the landline. "Someone not taking your reading seriously?"

Her frown returned. "No. You'd think the police would at least *listen* to what I have to say, given that they're asking for the public's help with the matter." For emphasis, she held up a copy of the *Central Shores Gazette*, the town's local newspaper. "I was reading about it just now. What a dreadful situation." Sage then pointed to the big, bold words, "Tragedy Strikes Safety Center."

I winced at the unflattering Sunday morning headline. It also sounded like Rand hadn't yet told his wife about Kiefer's passing. "Did you know the victim?"

Sage's brow furrowed. "Not really. But Rand did somewhat. They shared a mutual friend, I guess. I wonder if he's heard about this." She glanced once more at the headline, a black-and-white photo of the CSC parking lot covered with crime scene tape right below the text.

I stopped myself from suggesting that she text him and check in because I knew from previous encounters that Sage didn't own a cell phone—bad for those chakra channels and all. "So, what information did you want to share with the police? Perhaps I can help get it in front of them." I smiled sweetly.

Sage shuffled further down the counter. "Well...I think I know who killed this Marsh fellow."

"Who?" I followed her, mindful to stay on the customer's side. "How did you find out?"

She pointed to items lying on the glass countertop in front of her. "The cards told me."

I prided myself in being open-minded about other people's belief systems, but this tested my inner willpower. "I see." I stared at the beautiful artwork adorning her tarot collection. I didn't know what any of the symbols meant, but I doubted they revealed our murderer.

"It was quite enlightening." Sage gestured to three cards laid out equidistant from each other. "The Fool, The Empress, and The Tower." She paused to make sure I was paying attention. Which I was. Kinda.

"Note their positioning," Sage continued. "A Reversed Fool means recklessness or being taken advantage of. The upright Empress signals motherhood and fertility, whereas the upright Tower reveals upheaval or broken pride."

Her explanations swirled in my mind. "What does that mean? That Kiefer was killed by an angry mother?"

Sage tapped her chin. "I was going to suggest the police look into anyone Kiefer might've been dating. Perhaps someone with an unplanned pregnancy."

I opened my mouth to scoff when Rand's and Sy's comments about Kiefer pursuing women—regardless of their relationship status—pushed to the forefront of my mind. "Or it *could* mean that Kiefer was reckless with a married mother, and her husband violently retaliated over his wounded pride." I couldn't believe I was considering that Sage's tarot card reading illuminated the truth, but here we were.

Sage stared at me, impressed. "Wow, Coco. You may have an affinity for this."

I wasn't sure that was the compliment she thought it was. "Do you mind if I take a picture of this? I can show the guys at the PD and float the theory by them. You know, since I have to go in and help out with their social media," I quickly added to cover for myself.

"Of course."

I noted that she took a few steps back once I had my phone out. Not wanting her to worry about her chakras getting fried, I snapped a quick pic and slid my phone back into my clutch. "All set."

Sage clasped her hands in front of her, her expression expectant.

I realized I had to come up with an innocent reason for being here. "I looked for your stall yesterday at the CSC event but didn't find you," I fibbed. "I was hoping to get some stones for my nieces and nephew."

"Oh, I didn't have a booth at the festival." Sage batted the notion away. "By the time I found out about it, it was too late to sign up for one."

Probably because Bernie and I did most of our vendor marketing on social media.
My cheeks heated at the oversight, realizing we'd probably missed out on a
few other local businesses this way. Not everyone was as firmly planted in
the twenty-first century as I often assumed.

"But no matter. I decided to close the shop due to the meager foot traffic
over this way." A dreamy smile stretched across her pretty face. "Rand and I
ended up taking one of his company boats for a sail. It was a beautiful day
out on the water. We made it all the way down to Fenwick."

I did some mental math. Fenwick was at least thirty miles from Central
Shores. I wasn't a nautical expert by any means, but I wagered it would take
at least a few hours by sailboat. Meaning Rand's alibi checked out.

"Sounds like a perfect day date," I gushed appreciatively.

Sage motioned to her glittering inventory. "So, what were you thinking
for your nieces and nephew?"

Ten minutes and waaaay too much money later, I escaped Bright Auras
with shiny presents for the triplets and a hodge-podge of case intel to sort
through. I hurried toward my car, eager to get home and eat something
more substantial than pastries and pizza.

As I buckled myself into Jolly's front seat, my phone buzzed with a text
from Hudson.

Wrapping up at the studio. Be home in 30!

I smiled at the prospect of seeing him. **Drive safe. I'm getting stuff for
dinner.**

I made a quick detour at the local supermarket to grab red leaf lettuce,
tomatoes, carrots, prosciutto, parmesan cheese, and corn. I may not have
been the world's greatest cook, but I could throw together a nice salad.

While I waited in the checkout line, I texted Gavin and Adrian the picture
of Sage's reading. **She tried calling in a tip about this, but whoever
answered hung up on her,** I added, once I'd explained the meaning Sage
had seen in the cards.

Great, came Adrian's reply. **Just what we need. Our people turning
away tips.** The message was accompanied by several angry-face emojis.

We'll make sure to speak to the team about this, Coco, Gavin chimed in. **We can't be making mistakes like this. Thanks for bringing it to our attention.**

Ofc, I responded. **Have you guys come across any jilted husbands that might fit the bill?**

Both detectives left me on read. Oh well, at least I had shared Sage's tip with them.

As I helped bag my groceries, I wondered how we could trace other women Kiefer might have been involved with during his visit. At this juncture, the only one we knew about for certain was Janica.

The question made my head spin, and I remembered Dad's suggestion to take the night off. So, once I arrived home, I put the case details to the side and focused on dinner prep. I whipped up a homemade dressing using herbs de province-flavored olive oil and blood-orange-infused balsamic vinegar. By the time Hudson stumbled through the front doorway, looking worn out from a long day, I had our deck set up for dinner outside.

Over a nice meal, we traded stories about our adventures. Rather than focusing too much on Kiefer's case, I shared the good news that Rosie would be taking care of our housework for the foreseeable future. Hudson was thrilled, both that we were helping a friend and that we'd no longer have to argue over who loaded the dishwasher correctly. I saved the pièce de resistance for last by delivering an animated play-by-play of Jasper rescuing Miranda and his journey to becoming a cat dad.

"I'm technically not supposed to tell you about her because Jasper is doing a reveal party tomorrow night." I shook my head at my bestie's silliness.

"Yeah, I got the e-vite just as I pulled into the garage." Hudson laughed. "I'll do my best to feign surprise."

"How are things going with *Crime Sweet Home*?" I asked as I speared a tomato and popped it into my mouth.

Hudson shared how Ivy Chu remained tight-lipped on numerous topics concerning her former boyfriend's disappearance. "Millie and I both know she's hiding something." His brow pinched with frustration.

"Because she's involved?"

He sighed. "I'm more inclined to think she's afraid."

I gave his hand a sympathetic squeeze.

"What about you?" Hudson turned the spotlight over to me. "How did your chat with Sy go?"

"Eventful, to say the least." It was time to come clean about the scary scene Dad and I had encountered in the alley behind Saucy Sid's. As expected, my fiancé wasn't exactly pleased with the fact that we'd put ourselves in unnecessary danger.

Hudson rubbed his temples as if my antics gave him a headache—which, to be fair, they probably did. "Jeez, Cokes," he groaned. "Well, at least Simon can't give me a hard time anymore for not reining in your escapades."

I knew it took a lot for Hudson to find humor in the situation, even after the fact. "I promise, I would *not* have engaged if my dad hadn't been the one to run in swinging a rusty pipe." I shuddered at the wild memory.

Hudson propped his elbow on our outdoor table. "So, what were those guys really after, you think? Something to do with Kiefer?"

I flopped back in my lounger. "I have no clue, to be honest. I feel it in my gut that Sy was lying about defaulting on a poker game, but he didn't seem all that concerned, quite frankly, about Kiefer."

Hudson stroked the stubble on his bronze skin. "And if he wasn't even at the CSC event to begin with…"

"All known roads currently lead to Eric." I dug my phone out of my dress pocket and did a quick search. "But getting to him is the big issue." I slid the device toward Hudson so he could see the store hours I'd Googled. "Gold Score isn't scheduled to open until Wednesday, but I'd like to talk to Eric sooner rather than later. I can't exactly show up at his house, though. I have no idea where he lives."

Hudson raised an eyebrow. "Well, that's easy enough to uncover." He reached for the discarded messenger bag he'd dropped by his lounge chair and pulled out his laptop.

I scooted closer to watch him work. He opened a browser window, typed **Ocean Hollow Zip Code**, and within seconds, a long list of websites appeared.

"What do you need the zip code for?" I asked.

He smiled. "Just watch." He then typed in ListedPeoplePages.com. Once the site loaded, my gaze darted to two text boxes in the middle of the page. Hudson typed **Eric Brady** in the name box, then the Ocean Hollow zip code in the other. My jaw dropped when Eric Brady's personal information loaded. Some things, like his email address and mobile number, were blurred out, but not his current address. The website even provided a map with a pin marker.

"Are you a subscriber to this site or something?" A super creepy, tingling sensation ran up my arms as I continued to take in all the info available on Eric. His parents' and siblings' names were even listed.

Hudson shook his head. "Nope. This is all free to access. Scary as you-know-what, huh?"

I prided myself on being savvy when it came to protecting myself on the Internet, especially given my level of notoriety. But to know this kind of information was just floating around for anyone to find was deeply, *deeply* disturbing. "Is our stuff listed here?" I was almost afraid of the answer.

Hudson reached for my hand and kissed it. "Diamond helped me remove our records the first time she showed me this site."

My relief was fleeting as I studied Eric's profile. "Okay, so we know where to find the guy. Now, I just gotta figure out how to show up at his front door without raising all kinds of alarm bells."

"You mean how *we* show up." Hudson held my gaze. "Why not say that Janica was concerned about him and gave you his info?" he suggested as he closed his laptop.

I tapped my chin as I considered the underhanded approach. "Eric might soften to us if he thinks Janica is fretting over him." A grin spread across my face. "It's worth a shot."

"Why don't we scope it out tomorrow after you're done with your client work? I've got some research to compile in the morning, but I should be good to go by two or so."

I'd actually forgotten tomorrow was Monday. Oops. As much as I wanted to continue full steam ahead with the case, I had client projects to finish and meetings to attend. "It's a date."

Chapter Twenty-Four

Hudson and I enjoyed a rare night together at home, the only interruption being more Miranda photos from Jasper. When we woke up to Hudson's seven AM alarm the next morning, I had a fresh batch of cat pics waiting for me.

As I brushed my teeth, I hearted a slew of them. It wasn't until Hudson kissed me goodbye and my morning coffee percolated from the Keurig that I received an actual text message.

You have NOTHING to say other than swiping hearts??!?!?!?!

Oh, dear. I'd offended the proud parent.

Her beauty leaves me speechless. I chuckled at my own remark as I collected my coffee and curled up on the sectional.

Fine...I'll allow it. Everyone is coming over at seven for the big reveal. You didn't tell anyone, did you? Not even Dad?

I rolled my eyes at his dramatics. **Are you sure you don't want to loop Charlotte in earlier?** I skillfully ignored his question about telling Hudson. **She might appreciate some pretty kitty pics.**

I was hoping you'd have the case solved already so Miranda can be the sole focus of the evening.

I wasn't a hundred percent sure Jasper was joking. **Maybe I will. Hudson and I are going to OH today to chat with Eric.**

Ooh? When? Do you need backup?

I appreciate the gesture, I typed, **but we'll be fine.**

Okay, phew. I can't leave my baby alone just yet. She gets anxious when I'm away.

Miranda and Jasper seemed like a match made in diva heaven. **Have you told Eli that he has new competition for your affection?**

He'll find out tonight. Along with everyone else, RIGHT?

I'd walked right into that one. Lucky for me, I noticed the shadow of a familiar, willowy figure walking up the driveway.

Can't wait to see that play out. Gotta go! Amanda is here.

I tossed my phone on the countertop and hurried to the frosted-glass front entrance. "Hey, girl." I plastered on a cheerful grin as I threw back the door to greet my coworker.

Amanda Highgrove summoned a warm smile, although it didn't quite reach her eyes. "Hi, Cokes. Happy Monday."

I gave her a quick hug as I welcomed Amanda inside. "Can I get you anything?" I cursed inwardly as I'd forgotten to grab chocolate chip espresso muffins from Charlotte's yesterday. Whenever we met at Amanda's house in the swanky part of town known as Mill Row, I was provided with a lavish continental breakfast spread. So, in an effort to return the hospitality, I tried to serve yummy goodies when Amanda came over to my place to work. But given my preoccupation with Kiefer's death, all I had on hand were four-day-old bagels and K-cup coffee.

Perhaps Amanda saw my inner panic written across my face because she waved away my offer. "I'm fine. Arthur made me breakfast in bed."

"That's sweet of him," I gushed as we made our way out onto the back deck. With summer upon us, we worked outside whenever the weather allowed for it.

She tucked a strand of her buttery blonde hair behind her right ear. "Yeah. He's been taking good care of me ever since…" She didn't need to voice their tragedy out loud to convey her raw pain.

I reached for her hand and squeezed. I had no idea how to comfort someone in her position. I felt incredibly helpless, which, in turn, made me feel guilty. It was a strange cycle, but one I would continue to endure if it supported Amanda in any way.

She sank into a lounger and dug out her laptop, her expression all business. "I have a webpage layout I'd like your feedback on. Drew is launching a book club for The Twisted Candle, and she called yesterday about having us whip something up to showcase it online."

While I loved the idea of creating a book club to draw more people into her store, I wasn't thrilled that Drew had reached out to Amanda on a Sunday. "You know you don't have to address client requests on the weekend, right?"

"Oh, I don't mind." She shrugged off my remark.

A flash of exasperation welled within me. "Well, I do. Weekends are our time to rest and recharge. If we begin setting expectations with clients that we're at their beck and call whenever is convenient for them, our work-life balance gets thrown out the window." I already had limited time to spend with Hudson as it was. I didn't want our days off sabotaged by client needs.

Amanda's stunned gaze landed on me, and I realized I'd spoken to her more authoritatively than I had since...

"I mean—"

She broke into a relieved smile. "Relax, Cokes. You're totally right. I'm setting us up for failure by coddling people like this." She reclined in her chair, a musical chuckle floating across her glossed lips. "You know, that's the first time you've spoken to me like an adult since I lost the baby."

Anxiety welled. "I-I'm sorry. I didn't mean to—"

She placed a calming hand atop mine. "I'm saying that's a *good* thing. It makes me feel somewhat normal." She sighed. "Everyone's been treating me like I might shatter into a million pieces at any moment. Even poor Arthur. Don't get me wrong, I appreciated the space the first month or so. Really, I did. But I also need to learn to move forward." Her expression grew resolute. "I'm capable of moving forward. And that will never happen if we keep doing this weird tippy-toe dance." Inner strength radiated from her.

I swallowed my own emotions and nodded. "Just tell me what you need from me. I'm here for you, Amanda. I've got your back."

"I know you do. And I love you for it." She straightened in her chair and opened her laptop. "What I need from you now is your opinion on this book club landing page."

For the next thirty minutes, we reviewed the page she'd designed on Drew's Squarespace platform, tweaking the text copy and organizing stock images that promoted the idea of a fun, engaging book club.

"Gosh, this looks so much better." Amanda clapped her hands once she saved our final changes. "I love how you incorporated the bookstore's logo behind the club header."

I closed out of BrushUp, my go-to user-friendly graphic design application, on my laptop. My work as an influencer had forced me to become a semi-professional digital designer since I often needed visual content to support my posts. Finding an easy-to-use program like BrushUp had been game-changing for my graphic needs. "I can't wait to see what Drew thinks."

In fact, speaking of Drew, I wondered if *I* should go through the website update with her in person. That way, I could pepper her with questions about Eric and whether she knew anything about his relationship with Kiefer.

"What's with that curious look on your face?" Amanda tilted her head.

I thought about shrugging off the morbid topic, but then I realized I'd be doing exactly what she had asked me *not* to do. I shouldn't be hiding from her that I was involved in another murder investigation. "Did you hear about the man who died at the CSC grand opening festival on Saturday?"

Her fingers paused, hovering over her keyboard. "Of course. Something about a medical emergency due to the heat, right?"

I considered her response a win. Amanda was tapped into the gossip circulating around Central Shores, so to hear this version of events from her made me hopeful that Charlotte's reputation was still somewhat intact. At least among Central Shores's wealthier crowd. "Not exactly..."

Since we'd chatted about our current client tasks while designing Drew's book club page, I figured I could hijack the remainder of our CoA meeting to bring Amanda up to speed on our amateur investigation. The perks of being your own boss.

"Oh my gosh! Poor Charlotte." Amanda's brow pinched with sympathy once I'd divulged everything we'd been dealing with since Saturday after-noon. "She's the last person to deserve something like this."

I nodded in agreement. Amanda didn't know how right she was. While I'd let her know Kiefer had been Charlotte's ex, I hadn't revealed the intimate details of their horrific relationship. It wasn't that I didn't trust Amanda to keep sensitive info to herself; it just wasn't my place to share.

"Of course, Gavin and Adrian don't believe for a second that she was behind the crushed peanuts in Kiefer's cup," I added, "but Hudson's got me worried the DA will see things differently."

"So, you guys are going to track down this Eric guy and see what he has to say?" Amanda chewed on her lower lip. "Isn't that a bit dangerous? Even if Hudson's with you?"

"Janica already reached out to Eric about me being willing to offer him advice, so I'm approaching the sitch as if I'm merely there to lend my aid," I reassured her. "We're going to do some fact-finding to get the real scoop about him and Kiefer. It rubs me the wrong way that Eric's asking his friends to lie about how good things were between them. Why lie if he has nothing to hide?"

"But didn't he say he wasn't even at the festival when Kiefer collapsed?" Amanda countered. "How could he have put peanuts in Kiefer's drink if he wasn't there?"

I drummed my fingers on the tabletop. "He might be lying about that, too. As far as I know, Gavin and Adrian haven't been able to prove or disprove his whereabouts."

The corner of her lip curled into a smile. "I'm glad those two are in Charlotte's corner." She folded her hands. "Now, what can I do to help?"

I debated her offer, somewhat concerned that I would be dragging her into a murder investigation while she was processing personal trauma of her own. But then I recalled her earlier plea and asked, "Got any intel about Eric, Janica, or that friend group?"

Her pert nose crinkled in thought. "Eric runs Gold Score, right? Both Daddy and Arthur have snagged a few autographed pieces from his collection. Daddy's signed Cal Ripken Jr. glove is his pride and joy." Her smirk twisted into a frown. "Arthur, not so much. Just yesterday, he noticed the signature on his Ray Lewis jersey starting to smudge. He's been trying to get in touch with Eric for assistance, but the store's number keeps going to voicemail. Guess we know the reason why."

The names Cal Ripken Jr. and Ray Lewis were familiar to even a sports noob like me, so they must've been big deals to fans. "Yeah, Gold Score was closed yesterday when Jasper and I swung by."

Amanda whipped out her phone. "I'll let Arthur know so he can stop wearing down our carpet with his incessant pacing. I told him just to Google a solution, but he wants to ask a pro. So, beyond Gold Score, I don't know much about Eric. Janica, on the other hand," she paused as a grin spread across her lips, "is on the board of Beds by the Bay with me."

I steepled my fingers, waiting for more deets. Beds by the Bay was a local non-profit that provided clean, safe housing for people experiencing homelessness in the area.

"We chatted before our last meeting. About a week ago." Amanda twirled a strand of hair. "She was telling me all about the 'dreamboat' guy she was seeing and how she thought he might be *the* one."

My jaw dropped. "Do you think she was talking about Kiefer?"

"She didn't mention the guy's name." Amanda held up a finger when she saw me slouch with disappointment. "However, she *did* say he was new to the area. He'd come to help a friend with a remodeling project and was thinking about remaining indefinitely."

Indefinitely? While helping a friend with a remodel certainly described Kiefer's situation, when Charlotte and I spoke with him at the B2P booth on Saturday, he hadn't mentioned anything about staying in the area permanently.

"Interesting. So, Janica thought things were serious between them." Her Instagram feed kinda gave off that impression, what with her countless photos of the two together. And Rand *had* mentioned that Janica was "obsessed" with Kiefer. Yet, thinking back to my conversations with him and Sy, it didn't seem like our victim was all that dedicated to Janica, given his playboy tendencies.

Amanda bobbed her head. "She couldn't stop gushing about him. But then again, she has a history of falling fast and hard. It's caused her a lot of heartache in the past."

"Heartache, huh?" I tapped my chin as I considered Amanda's insider information. Had Janica and Kiefer been more committed to each other than his acquaintances led me to believe? Playboys had to grow up at some point, right? But if they were in a serious relationship, why did Keifer go to the CSC festival with Eric and not Janica? Going together seemed like something Janica really wanted when we'd chatted about it. "She got all riled up that Eric and Kiefer went to the festival without her. It was a bit weird how upset she was."

"Maybe it was her grief over his death talking?" Amanda suggested. "It causes all types of emotions to engulf you. Believe me, I know."

I replayed my chat with Janica, and as I did, I typed away on my laptop, navigating to her Instagram account **@dolledupdarling.** One of Janica's first remarks tickled my mind as I stared at her profile.

I appreciate that you tried to help him.

Sy mentioned that his dad had said the same thing because Sid Sr. had been there at the festival to witness my efforts. How exactly did Janica know I'd tried to help Kiefer? She told me she hadn't read too much about the situation, but even then, my name wasn't in the official police reports. She'd also seen that viral X video, but that made me out to be a harbinger of death, not the good Samaritan she perceived me to be.

To illustrate my inner thoughts, I opened another tab and loaded X. Sure enough, my mentions were still blowing up with rude and unhelpful comments regarding that awful video. How could these people seriously think Kiefer had died because I'd touched him?

The original tweet containing the video upload wasn't hard to find. It was the top result under the #DeathByCocoCline hashtag.

"What's got you so glum?" Amanda came around to my side and stared at my screen. "Oh, jeez. Why are you looking at this trash? Trolls will try and tear you down over anything."

I was about to take her advice and close the tab when a thought crossed my mind. Yes, the trolls had been vicious, but what if Janica wasn't getting her information from second-hand accounts?

"How could I be so foolish?" I snapped my fingers as my mental gymnastics vaulted over the final hurdle. "I've been assuming that because Janica said

Eric and Kiefer went without her, she didn't go to the CSC festival at all. But what if she was actually *there*, and I've been overlooking it this whole time?"

Amanda's eyes widened. "You think she saw them palling around without her and went nuclear?"

"Maybe. If she felt she'd been rejected by Kiefer," I added, "she could have been feeling vengeful, especially if she thought he was 'the one.'"

Amanda's smooth skin went ashen. "But would she really kill him over that?"

"People have done so for less." I mulled over the puzzling situation a bit more, and an unsettling realization hit me. "But there's also the possibility she didn't *mean* to kill him. Only trigger a reaction."

Amanda frowned. "But what about the discarded EpiPen?"

If Janica had poisoned Kiefer's drink, there was the very real possibility that she sabotaged any hope of recovery by tossing his medication in the nearest garbage can. But that wasn't the only unfortunate scenario at play here. "We've been operating under the assumption that the person who added the peanuts to Kiefer's drink and threw out his EpiPen are one and the same." A pit grew in my stomach. "But what if Kiefer's meds simply fell out of his pocket, and someone innocently discarded the tube, thinking it was just a piece of trash?"

Amanda shivered despite the warm sunlight bathing the deck. "If that's the case, Kiefer's luck certainly picked the wrong day to run out."

Chapter Twenty-Five

To test this new theory, I typed **EpiPen** into my laptop's browser and scrolled through the image results. My initial reaction was that the yellow tube with an orange cap kinda resembled a glue stick.

Amanda leaned closer to check out my screen. "Wow, that's not what I pictured them looking like. If I saw that on the ground and didn't examine the label closely, I might think it was litter." She then glanced my way, impressed. "You may be onto something with this Janica angle."

I snapped my laptop shut as my stomach suddenly churned. "The idea that Kiefer's death was unintentional makes me feel even worse about the whole situation. Is that weird?"

Amanda raised an expertly groomed eyebrow. "You'd rather a cold-blooded killer be on the loose?"

"When you say it like that, perhaps not." I ran a hand through my hair, detangling it as I went.

The chirping tone of my RingCam doorbell interrupted our conversation.

I hurried through the condo and opened the front door, surprised to find Deacon standing there with his arms folded. "Hey, neighbor. What's up?"

His dark eyes were steely. "Got a minute?"

"Sure. Come on in." I gestured toward the deck. "Amanda and I were just chatting about the case."

Deacon suddenly grew wary. "Does she know about Charlotte being dragged into it?"

I nodded and noticed how worn out he looked. "Did something happen?"

"I'll fill you both in." With hurried steps, he headed toward our outdoor workspace, greeting Amanda warmly as he claimed a lounge chair opposite us.

My heart dropped as I sank into my seat. "You look like the Grim Reaper."

Deacon massaged his temples. "Gavin and Adrian came by the house asking Charlotte to accompany them to the CSC for questioning."

Amanda gasped.

"*What*? When?" Anxiety jolted through me.

"Just a few minutes ago," Deacon muttered defeatedly. "I came here as soon as I called a lawyer I know through the system. Gloria's defended a lot of clients I've been called to testify against. She's ruthless in the courtroom. She's meeting Charlotte at the station."

"Char knows not to say anything, right?" Amanda wrung her hands.

Deacon nodded. "Adrian specifically told her not to. They weren't happy with the situation, either. The DA sent them for her."

Hearing that neither Adrian nor Gavin was happy about the circumstances made me feel a little better. But only a little. Hudson's bleak premonition about the DA being all over Charlotte had come to fruition.

"The guys did have some good news to share." Deacon still looked tense despite his words. "The initial fingerprinting results came back on the EpiPen. There was a partial print located alongside Kiefer's."

I sucked in a breath. "You said this was good news, right?"

Deacon nodded. "They compared it to Charlotte's, and it *wasn't* a match. So, Charlotte can't be tied to that piece of evidence. At least, not yet." He steepled his fingers together. "It will be some time before touch DNA results come back, so we're not completely out of the woods."

"Do you know whose fingerprint they *did* find?" Amanda pressed.

"Unknown at this point. It could be someone from the pharmacy who handled the 'script. But since it's a partial, it will take longer to run through our databases." Deacon ran a hand over his shaved head. "But another foreign print is darn good news for Charlotte's defense."

"It most certainly is." I felt a little bubble of relief burst within me. "And it aligns with what Amanda and I were discussing." We shared with him our thoughts about the EpiPen accidentally being discarded in the trash, as well as our growing suspicions regarding Janica.

Deacon pulled out his phone. "Char and I were up late last night combing through the CSC event hashtag, and we pulled together some videos that might be helpful. Charlotte's pretty confident they all capture Kiefer while he's walking around the festival."

"Can you send me the links?" That way, I could pull them up on my laptop so we could all see the media clearly.

Deacon tapped rapidly on his phone, and a moment later, a text message from him popped up on my end. "Sent."

I accessed iMessage on my Mac laptop and clicked the first URL Deacon provided. A browser window opened, revealing an Instagram Reel upload. The account was @littlesplashofsun, and the video was a sweeping cinematic of the crowd milling around the festival.

It didn't take me long to spot Kiefer's hulking frame near the foreground of the shot. But what surprised me was the lanky figure standing beside him, drinking from a red Solo cup. "That's Eric, right?" I'd only seen the guy in expertly curated social media pics, but this scruffy-faced dude in sunglasses looked the part.

"Yep. Check the next clip," Deacon encouraged.

I clicked on the second URL, and another Reel loaded. This time, the video showcased a vendor booth filled with whirling blenders. I took note of the familiar business handle. "This was posted by Squeezed." Lacie Burbank must've shared videos of her working the makeshift juice and smoothie bar.

The Reel showcased a group of kids looking eagerly at the strawberry and banana smoothies being made, but it also caught people enjoying the festival in the background. Kiefer's towering figure was one of them.

"He doesn't look happy in this one." Amanda gestured to the scowl etched into Kiefer's face.

I nodded in agreement. "It also looks like he's alone." I didn't see Eric anywhere. "Too bad there isn't a concrete timestamp available on Reel clips." I checked the video's comments section to get a sense of when it had been posted. At least I could see the timestamps on the clip's comments.

Unfortunately, the oldest ones only said "2d" to indicate that two days had passed since their reply. Not exactly helpful for narrowing down a specific timeframe.

Feeling somewhat discouraged, I clicked on the final link Deacon had sent. The main focus of this Reel video was a cluster of kids blowing giant bubbles with some wand-like contraption, but in the background, Kiefer stood with his arms folded. He looked like he was searching for someone. "These are the only posts capturing Kiefer?" I felt bad, but I couldn't keep my disappointment from showing.

"Unfortunately, yes." Deacon gave me a pitying grimace. "Folks mostly used your customized hashtag to post selfies, so there wasn't a lot of background footage to review."

It was my turn to wince. "That tracks, I suppose. On social media, people generally want to advertise *themselves* being at an event, not the event itself." I felt a little foolish assuming the greater public would chronicle the festival goings-on in detail. "But maybe all hope isn't lost." I opened a new tab and navigated to the search bar on Instagram. Instead of typing in the #CelebratetheCSC hashtag, I put **CSC festival** in the hopes attendees had at least included the event name in their captions.

"Dang." Deacon whistled as a full page of results loaded. "Char and I definitely did not come across this digital treasure trove."

Amanda had her laptop open and copied my steps so that our screens were identical. "Should we get started?"

I glanced at my smartwatch. Neither of us had a client meeting until eleven, so we could make a dent in the video footage before us. "If you're up for it." I welcomed her offer to help.

Deacon rose from his chair. "I'm gonna head down to the CSC and wait for Char. I'll keep you guys posted about how it all turns out."

"Thanks for stopping by." Amanda and I wished him luck and asked him to pass on our well wishes to Charlotte.

For the next two hours, we scoured any Insta Reels that mentioned the Central Shores festival in their caption. In addition to the three videos Deacon had already provided, Amanda found Kiefer appearing solo in five uploads, whereas I came across three.

"Hold up, check this out, Cokes." Amanda slid her laptop over my way. "Watch the back-left corner closely."

I did as instructed and was surprised to see Eric Brady instead of Kiefer. The clip captured him waving his hands around before he shook his head and stomped off-camera.

"He's totally arguing with someone, right?" Amanda nudged me as soon as the clip began to loop back.

I squinted at the screen, focusing on Eric's sharp body language. "He does look annoyed." But the video cut off who he was speaking to, so we could only guess who.

I rewatched the Reel several times, noting the layout of the festival and its immediate surroundings. "When Eric stomps out of frame, he's heading in the direction of the parking lot." I tapped my finger on the laptop's bezel. "This could be when he decided to leave."

"Any guesses as to the time?" Amanda's brow furrowed.

I studied the clip's surroundings. "Well, the CSC faces east, and the sun is clearly sinking behind the building by this point, so it's gotta be at least after noontime."

"And how do you know the CSC faces east?"

I laughed at her dubious question. "Maude Langford is always talking about the nice ocean view she has from the reception desk." It was the one thing the seventy-something receptionist appreciated about the new, high-tech CSC. "Hence, the entrance of the building faces east."

"Good detective skills." Amanda smiled before turning her attention back to the video. "So, if he really did bounce, where does that leave Eric as a suspect?" Her blue-eyed gaze tinged with worry.

"I don't know," I admitted with a sigh. We'd seen plenty of footage of Kiefer wandering the festival on his own, but that was partly due to his recognizable stature. Eric, on the other hand, we hadn't come across solo in any clips beyond this one.

I clicked the arrow to proceed to the next result, this one highlighting three guys double-fisting corn dogs. I looked past the activity in the foreground and scanned the crowd behind the proud eaters. Kiefer's swept-back blond hair caught my attention, but when I realized who stood in front of him, my jaw dropped. "Holy, Anne Hathaway! Is that who I think it is?"

Amanda waited for the Reel to replay before a gasp whispered through her fingers. "Omigosh. That's totally Janica."

I grabbed a screenshot of the two of them together. "So, this proves without a doubt she was at the festival." *Hashtags.* I still couldn't believe I'd made such an amateur assumption when I'd spoken with her.

"I don't see Eric anywhere in this frame." Amanda motioned with her finger. "Think Janica waited until Eric left to pounce on Kiefer?"

I tugged at my hair. "If only this clip were longer." The video hadn't captured much interaction between the couple; the person behind the camera had zoomed in on the unofficial corn dog eating contest. "But wait a sec." My internal dialogue had given me an idea. I checked the Reel's caption, and my heart skipped a beat as I read it.

My man going all out for the win. Love u bae <3 Sorry, boys.

The caption was followed by three tagged accounts, which I assumed belonged to the college-age guys in the video. Hoping that perhaps other friends or partners had captured the eating contest, I clicked on the last username tagged. Their profile grid loaded, and I skimmed the uploads for the telltale Reels icon. Seeing the Play arrow, I selected the video, waiting to see if my hunch panned out.

The screen filled with the same three young men waiting while someone counted down off-screen, "Three, two, one, EAT!" The caption? **I was robbed.**

As the lads began stuffing their faces, my gaze darted to the crowd behind them. Sure enough, Kiefer was speaking to a grim-faced Janica. He motioned behind her several times, and at each instance, she batted his arm away. She was clearly not interested in taking direction from him.

Finally, the video caught up to the first clip that Amanda and I had seen, and luckily, it continued from the cut-off point. As the guys drew closer to their corn dog finish line, Kiefer and Janica grew increasingly testier with each other. As the middle guy swallowed his last bite and began doing a victory dance, the camera angle changed slightly. All I could see was Kiefer shoving himself deeper into the crowd while Janica swiped at her eyes.

"*That* doesn't look like a friendly chat to me." Amanda's gaze twinkled with intrigue.

I nodded as I rewatched the strange scene. "He storms off, and she's left in tears." I pressed my lips together as I grabbed a screenshot of Janica's upset expression. "She failed to mention this little rendezvous to me yesterday."

"I can imagine why." Amanda snorted. "She has an argument with the guy, and he drops dead soon after? Not a great look."

I flinched at her blunt wording, but she had a point. "I wonder if we can track her through these videos." Would we find Janica following Kiefer around if we looked harder? I rubbed my eyes, already feeling the burn of staring too intently at a computer screen.

"It's possible." Amanda checked her sleek gold timepiece, which probably cost more than my car. "But I was planning on taking my client calls back home." Her cheeks colored slightly.

"Oh, gosh, it's almost eleven, isn't it?" The morning had flown by. "Please, head out." I assured her I was all set. "I'll text Gavin and Adrian with what we've uncovered. Maybe this cinematic confrontation will help them convince the DA that Charlotte wasn't the only one who was fed up with Kiefer."

"Sounds good." Amanda's smile glowed with hope. "But before I go, any idea what this dinner invite from Jasper is about? Why is the dress code white?"

"Dress code?" I giggled at my bestie's antics. "I missed that memo." I hadn't taken the time to read the email containing the details of tonight's dinner party, other than when it started. "Thanks for the heads-up."

Amanda eyed me suspiciously. "Avoiding the real question, huh? I take it you've been sworn to secrecy, then?"

I nodded sheepishly, although my resolve to keep his secret was waning. For one thing, I worried Jasper introducing Miranda as his "baby" might be triggering for our friend. "Can you feign surprise if I tell you the news?"

Amanda held a hand to her heart. "Of course."

"Jasper adopted a cat, and he wants to introduce her to everyone tonight." The words rushed from my lips.

"Omg. How adorable!" she gushed. "Aww, Jasper as a cat dad? I can't wait to see it."

I didn't miss how her expression grew a tad pinched, but she seemed genuinely happy to hear about Miranda's arrival. "He's kinda gone all *Dance Moms* on the poor thing."

"Good for him. I can't wait to meet her. Arthur and I have been talking about getting a dog or a cat, so maybe Deacon and Jasper can help sway us one way or the other." As she rose from her chair, she placed a hand on my shoulder. "I appreciate you telling me ahead of time. I know I said I didn't want to be treated with kid gloves, but...now I can go in, prepared and ready to celebrate Jasper's happy news." Her bright smile couldn't hide the sadness lingering in her eyes.

I nodded, my throat too tight to respond.

"Okay, I'll see you later." Amanda quickly gathered her things.

I escorted her to the door. "Let me know if anything pops up."

"And *you* let me know how Drew likes the website updates." She gave a fluttering wave of her fingers as she strolled toward the sleek Mercedes parked in my driveway.

Knowing I had several hours before Hudson got home, I buried myself in work, only pausing to celebrate when Charlotte texted that she was finally leaving the CSC.

Gavin and Adrian hated questioning me almost as much as I did. The lawyer Deacon hired is a total boss, though. She went toe to toe with the DA for a while. Whatever she said worked. I didn't think they'd let me go home, honestly.

My fingers trembled as I typed, **Glad to hear you're in the clear.**

Not totally. The DA was VERY adamant about that. But Gavin said they still had numerous leads to chase down. He and Adrian really wanted to know if I had anything for them about Kiefer's connections to the area, so I told them about Eric and Janica. I hope you don't mind.

I scoffed at the embarrassed emojis she sent. **Of course not. You and**

Deacon found that stuff on their socials. It's yours to share. But I have some new intel, too. Will fill you in at Jasper's dinner party tonight.

   Really?? That's great. Thanks, Cokes. See you there.

Relieved Charlotte had been released from questioning, I returned to my client work with renewed determination. If the DA had had enough to charge her, they wouldn't have let her walk out with just a warning. We still had time to make things right.

Chapter Twenty-Six

"Hey, babes, whatcha working on?" Hudson's lips pressed against my hair, stirring me from my concentrated reverie at my office desk.

I pointed at the graphic on my computer screen. "This client is dead set on the Papyrus font, and I'm trying to figure out how to diplomatically get through to them that it's not a good branding choice."

"Send them that classic Ryan Gosling *SNL* skit about the *Avatar* logo," he suggested with a boyish chuckle.

I furrowed my brow. "You know, you might be onto something."

Hudson raised a skeptical eyebrow in an *I was kidding* manner.

"That skit ironically showcases how Papyrus is normally associated with tea shops, stationery stores, and hookah bars." I snapped my fingers. "*Not* accounting firms." Using the examples highlighted by *Saturday Night Live*, I'd put together a brand association collage for my client in the hopes that seeing his accounting firm with the same branding as a smoke shop would kibosh the idea.

Hudson grinned. "Who knew bingeing *SNL* clips on YouTube would become such a valuable business strategy?"

I giggled as I rose from my desk chair to give him a proper welcome home. "How'd your studio time go?"

"Eh, all right." His demeanor grew stiff. "Millie asked Diamond to give us a run-down on everything concerning Kiefer Marsh."

My ears perked up. "Anything new?"

"Well, considering the police haven't officially released a cause of death or that they're investigating it as a tried-and-true homicide, Diamond didn't have much for us to go on, so Millie told us to shelve it for now."

I took a step back from him. "You didn't tell them that Kiefer's allergy was purposely triggered?"

He shook his head. "I only know that as Hudson, Coco Cline's fiancé, not Hudson, star investigative journalist."

While I had to laugh at his ever-so-humble flex, I threw my arms around him and squeezed him tightly. In today's sleazy media world, where clickbait was king, Hudson's integrity continued to impress me. He could have very well broken the story about Kiefer's death being a homicide, but instead, he chose to protect Charlotte and respect the police's ongoing investigation.

"Are you ready to head to Ocean Hollow?" he asked after I released him. "Did you eat lunch?"

A roaring grumble from my stomach reminded me that I had been so absorbed by captions, color schemes, and content creation that I'd forgotten to stop for food.

Hudson's warm brown eyes twinkled. "Guess that answers my question. Wanna grab something on the way?"

"Sure." I shut down my computer for the afternoon. "But nothing too filling. Jasper says he's having dinner *catered*."

"For a cat?"

We both laughed at Jasper's over-the-top shenanigans.

"Arthur texted me that he and Amanda were both excited for an evening out." Hudson's happy expression faltered. "I...was a bit worried it would remind them of their gender reveal party, so I told him what the surprise was."

"I clued Amanda in, too," I softly reassured him. "I thought the same thing."

A sigh of relief escaped Hudson. "Arthur still seemed pleased to be included, so I hope it won't be too painful for them."

I considered texting Jasper about possibly toning down his excitement, but then I remembered Amanda's comment. She wanted something to celebrate, and she probably wouldn't appreciate me meddling in such a way.

"I'm just glad they're coming," I admitted as I glided into the kitchen to collect my bag. "It'll be nice to have everyone together for an evening."

Hudson's forehead wrinkled. "Anything new from Charlotte and Deacon?"

"I'll tell you in the car."

We opted to take Hudson's sporty BMW and decided to grab a salad from Zaddick's on the strip. During the twelve-minute drive, I brought him up to speed on the intel we'd uncovered this morning.

"So, Janica very well *could* be our culprit," I concluded as we parked the coupe. "I can't believe I made such an amateur assumption, thinking she wasn't at the festival just because she didn't go with Eric and Kiefer."

"We all make mistakes, Coco." Hudson's supportive tone was full of genuine sympathy. "There's no need to dwell on it."

As someone who prided herself on being on top of everything, I couldn't help it. "And even though we saw him and Kiefer part ways, Eric isn't in the clear yet," I added in an effort to change the subject.

Hudson threaded his fingers through mine as we walked toward the town's most popular deli. "Smart move. Yes, you've got some video footage for reference, but those are all very finite moments in time. Who knows what happened beyond that?"

I nodded. "I'm eager to hear Eric explain his movements that day for myself." We only had Janica's word that he'd left the CSC event, and with her story now called into question, the waters were muddy at best. Maybe, if we had time, Hudson and I could stop by Janica's studio and speak with her again. I wanted to see how she reacted to the video I'd found capturing her and Kiefer's argument.

Inside Zaddick's, the combination of fresh-baked bread, cheeses, and deli meats nearly made me cave and get a salami-stuffed wrap. Resisting the urge, I left Hudson to place our salad order and grabbed a top seat by the windows.

"Hey, Coco!" Lacie Burbank waved from a table across the way. She was joined by Daniel Wu, the owner of Mystic's Cards and Games. Rosie and Thomas from Sweet Resolutions also sat with them. "You guys dining in?"

I popped down from my seat and greeted the group warmly. "Nah, Hudson and I are getting food to go." I pointed to my fiancé, who was waiting near the counter.

"Hang here with us then." Lacie pointed to an open seat at the table next to them. "We're almost done, anyway."

"Late lunch breaks?" I asked everyone as I dragged the chair over to join them.

Daniel grinned. "I'm on hour two of mine. It's painfully slow today. I'm honestly thinking about closing Mondays altogether." He'd taken over the family game shop more than two years ago.

"I've been telling you to do that since your dad handed you the keys." Lacie narrowed her pretty brown eyes. "Why the sudden change of heart?"

Daniel fiddled with his wheelchair, not quite meeting her gaze. "I don't know. I thought having a full day off to do things might be nice. Go on adventures and such."

"I think it's a great idea." Rosie smiled as she adjusted the brim of her Tar Heels baseball cap. "And since Squeezed is closed on Mondays, maybe you and Lacie can go on adventures together."

At her coy comment, Daniel's skin flushed, and Lacie's cheeks darkened.

I glanced between the couple. It was one of the town's worst-kept secrets that the two of them shared romantic feelings for each other, but they'd yet to go public with their declarations. I caught Rosie's eye, and she winked.

Lacie cleared her throat. "So," she began, her tone indicative that she wanted to change the subject, "are we really going to ignore the big elephant in the room?" She studied me with a raised eyebrow.

I gulped. I didn't like where this was going.

"I heard from Quincy this morning that Charlotte's latte caused that guy to die at the festival." Lacie folded her arms as she waited for my response. "Is it true?"

Quincy Novak owned a boutique clothing store on the strip, located next to Lacie's juice bar. Due to the overheard conversations of her clientele, she was a notorious gossip, and I was honestly surprised Quincy hadn't told Lacie before now.

I answered as diplomatically as I could. "I'm not involved in the police investigation, guys. But I know Charlotte had nothing to do with what happened."

"Duh." Lacie's expression twitched with sympathy. "As if Charlotte would ever serve something harmful." She sighed. "But her café was a ghost town when I went in this morning. Poor girl looked near tears while making my iced chai."

Rosie swatted her boss on the arm. "This is all your fault, Thomas. You just had to blab about your stupid yoga class."

Thomas had the decency to shrink with shame. "You know how I get when I have a secret. And I've already apologized to her." He shot me a pleading glance as if I would be the one to absolve him. "She even has carte blanche when it comes to anything she wants from Sweet Resolutions, free of charge."

A lifetime of free chocolates in exchange for sullying her sterling reputation? As delectable as Tom and Thomas's handmade treats were, I wasn't sure the deal was quite fair.

Rosie still glowered at the chocolatier.

"How would a drink from Charlotte have killed the guy, anyway?" Daniel tilted his head. "I mean, unless the police found poison—which I highly doubt." He shot a panicked glance my way. He clearly didn't want me to think he was siding with the town gossip.

Lacie propped her elbows on the table. "Quincy thinks the man was allergic to something in the latte."

I struggled to keep my expression neutral as I thought, *Score one, Quincy.*

"Don't people prone to severe reactions carry around epinephrine or something?" Daniel countered.

Thomas stroked his chin. "Yeah, if he was that allergic to something, shouldn't he have had an EpiPen with him?"

"H-He didn't have it on him." I glanced down at my lap, trying to push the memory from my mind. "I tried his pockets, but I couldn't find one to administer the injection."

A strained silence fell over the table.

"Oh, Coco." Rosie gasped as her eyes welled with tears. "I'm so sorry you had to go through that. I can't imagine how scared you must've been."

I sent her a sad smile, grateful for her empathetic kindness.

Lacie winced. "Yeah, I'm a jerk for bringing it up."

"It's fine." I brushed the topic to the side. "I just hope we get answers about what happened soon enough."

"Agreed," Thomas chimed in. "If there was a nefarious angle to this incident, I'm sure the police will get to the bottom of things."

"I don't know." Daniel rubbed his arms nervously. "Wasn't this guy from North Carolina or something? Seems bizarre for someone in Central Shores to target him."

"*I'm* the one from North Carolina, Dan," Rosie interjected, her tone slightly affronted as she pointed to her UNC baseball cap. "The police report said the victim was from *South* Carolina."

"Eh, same difference." Daniel shrugged, although only Lacie laughed at his joke.

Rosie sullenly swirled the leftover ice from her soft drink while Thomas studied her with fatherly concern. I realized Daniel's flippant comment, if overheard, might have people thinking Rosie had some tie to Kiefer due to their "Carolina" connection. Just what we needed: more innocent people getting tangled up in the gossip surrounding Kiefer's death.

Chapter Twenty-Seven

"Caruthers! Order up!" a gruff voice called Hudson's name at the counter.

"That'll be us." I rose from my chair to join my fiancé. "We've got some errands to run. It was nice seeing you guys."

I bid the group goodbye, and it wasn't until Hudson and I were out on the sidewalk that we heard, "Coco!"

I turned to find Thomas and Rosie rushing toward us.

"Look, I'm really, really sorry about Charlotte." Thomas wrung his hands together vigorously, and I half-worried he'd hurt himself. "I feel like a complete idiot. I have no excuse other than wanting to feel like the herald of juicy news." His shoulders sagged at his admission.

He seemed incredibly torn up, and I felt kinda bad for him. "I appreciate you telling us this," I motioned between Hudson and myself, "but if you already spoke and made peace with Charlotte, that's really all that counts."

"We're also encouraging our customers to visit Brewed to Perfection." Rosie looped her arm through Thomas's. "If they bring a receipt from Charlotte's, we're giving them a fifteen percent discount."

My mouth dropped open in astonishment. "Wow. That's really nice of you."

"It was Rosie's idea." Thomas patted the young woman's forearm. "She insisted we make things right. It's one of the many reasons why Tom and I decided to give her a well-earned raise."

She blushed at his obvious praise.

"That's awesome, Rosie!" I gave her a quick congratulatory hug. Not only did she deserve it, but the timing couldn't have been better for her, given her financial struggles.

"Thanks, Coco." Rosie tugged at her shirt, clearly uncomfortable with the attention. "Well, we better get back, or poor Tom will think we've gone AWOL. Bye, guys. See you around."

I almost said, "See you tomorrow," but I held my tongue. I wasn't sure if Rosie wanted her Sweet Resolutions bosses to know about her second job. So, instead, Hudson and I merely wished them good luck with the rest of their Monday and headed toward the resident parking lot behind the strip.

"Thomas is learning the hard way how quickly news travels in a small town," Hudson said through a grim sigh.

I shuddered. "I know I should be mad at him for sharing what he overheard, but he seems genuinely remorseful. Add to that the discount they're giving B2P customers. Rosie's such a sweetie to think of that."

"Yeah. It makes me glad we're helping her out. It's good to know people other than us have Charlotte's back." Hudson draped his arm around me as we walked.

I leaned my head against his shoulder. "Because they know she'd do the same for them if the tables were turned. Goodness, imagine if everyone thought Kiefer was from North Carolina? They'd all be coming for poor Rosie just because she used to live there."

Hudson stopped mid-step. "Have you checked to see if anyone in Central Shores has moved here recently from South Carolina? Other than Charlotte, I mean." His budding excitement didn't give me a chance to answer. "With all the new development popping up in the area, maybe someone else from Kiefer's past randomly ended up here."

I considered his theory. "How would we even begin to approach a task like that without police resources—" An idea struck me like lightning. "Omigosh, *The Central Shores Citizen*!"

My mom would throttle me if she knew I'd forgotten about her latest town council pet project. *The Central Shores Citizen* was a weekly town council newsletter intended to introduce new members of the community. Since our town population had grown by leaps and bounds over the past nine months, Mom launched this new campaign in an effort to make our new residents feel welcome. Of course, people had to opt in to the newsletter in accordance with privacy laws, but since she'd published the first issue in January, Mom had yet to run out of people to feature.

As Hudson ate his fill of salad in the car's AC, I tapped my way to the .gov website where *The Central Shores Citizen* was housed online. With roughly twenty-four digital issues to scroll through, I used the search feature to see if the phrase "South Carolina" was mentioned on the page.

The anticipation that had coursed through my veins moments ago vanished at the "0" return value. "Hashtags. No mention of South Carolina in any of these bios."

"Try 'SC'?" Hudson suggested.

I followed his recommendation, adding a comma after the initials to avoid getting any and all words that included 'sc' within them. "Good idea, but no dice."

"Bummer." He handed me the salad container so I could enjoy the crunchy, crisp snack while he drove to Ocean Hollow.

I skillfully shoveled the balsamic-coated leaves into my mouth while skimming each newsletter to double-check my search results. Perhaps the page was formatted in a funky manner so that the little bios paired with each resident entry didn't get scooped up by the browser's Find feature.

"Most of these are families with kids," I murmured through a mouthful of lettuce and tomato. "I would've thought Tom and Thomas signed up for this. It would be a great PR move for them. Rosie's not featured here, either." Although, given how private she tended to be, that wasn't exactly shocking.

Hudson drummed on the steering wheel. "Maybe parents are hoping their *Citizen* feature will help kickstart some play dates."

I snorted at his not-so-out-there theory. Every time we hung out with my sister, Thea, and her husband, they'd always bemoan how hard it was to set up playgroups for their five-year-old triplets. "What do you bet that's *really* why Mom launched this initiative?" I snickered.

Hudson barked out a full-bellied laugh. "Mimi on a mission."

My mom—or 'Mimi' to the triplets—helped Thea with childcare when she wasn't busy with her duties as town council chair. And now that Taran, Blake, and Parker were five, they were giving Mom a run for her money. It hadn't gone unnoticed that she hadn't pestered me in recent months to give her more grandchildren.

For the remainder of the drive, Hudson filled me in on recent *Crime Sweet Home* developments, including the news that someone had reached out to the local Crime Stopper's tipline this afternoon. They'd learned through a friend that Hudson's show was investigating the disappearance of Jermaine Norris and believed they had information relevant to the decade-old missing person case.

"We don't know what was revealed," Hudson admitted, "But the Lincoln PD detective assigned to Jermaine's case said that our recent interviews have likely made some people nervous."

"That's great!" I proudly patted his thigh. This wasn't the first time a *Crime Sweet Home* episode had reinvigorated a stalled investigation. "Do you think it was Ivy Chu?"

Hudson shrugged. "Perhaps our questions prodded at her conscience. I made sure to mention Jermaine's family needing answers, especially since his mom's illness is terminal."

My heart twinged in my chest. "I feel for her. It's so unfair Mrs. Norris has to go through all this pain." I'd met the entire Norris family when Hudson interviewed them at the WMTG studios a few weeks ago, and they were the sweetest people.

Minutes later, Hudson slowed the car to a stop in front of a cute, ranch-style home. "375 Grandview Ave. This is it."

"At least according to the Internet." I studied the vacant front porch. "We know how reliable it can be."

Hudson smirked. "The mailbox says 'Brady' on the side, so I think we're okay." He pointed to the decorated container, painted with every type of sports ball you could imagine.

I stuck my tongue out at him, and he laughed. "All right, let me do the talking," I said. The last thing we needed was for Eric to suspect Hudson was here, acting solely as my bodyguard.

We got out and scanned the street. Eric lived in a nice residential area overlooking the bay. His neighbors didn't appear to be outside enjoying the weather, so hopefully, we wouldn't be under too much scrutiny.

I hurried up the porch stairs and knocked on the door. As I waited, Hudson scoped out the property. "No car in the driveway," he muttered once he joined me on the porch. "No garage, either. But there is a shed tucked behind on this side." He gave a casual shrug of his shoulder, indicating the direction.

We waited a minute before I knocked again. "No cameras or anything." At least, not that I could see. Could Eric be avoiding us, or was he not at home?

After my third round of knocking went unanswered, I balled my fists in frustration. Gold Score wasn't open on Mondays, so where was this guy? "You said there was a shed in the back?" I shot a clarifying glance at Hudson.

He nodded. "Want to see if he's working in it?"

I answered by skipping down the porch steps.

Once we rounded the side of the house, the shed came into view. I'd been expecting a tiny shack, but this structure looked more like a detached garage—minus the massive door.

The long, narrow windows were too high for us to see inside, and the steel door offered no peek-hole, either.

I pressed my ear against the warm metal and strained to pick up any sign of activity inside. "Doesn't sound like he's in here, either." I knocked for safe measure.

Thunk.

The muffled noise groaned from within the shed.

I turned to Hudson, wide-eyed. "Did you hear that?"

His jaw clenched. "I did."

"It sounded like something falling." I chewed worriedly on my lip. "Or *someone.*"

We listened for the sound to repeat itself, but heard nothing.

"What should we do?" I wrung my hands. "Eric might've hurt himself in there."

In answer, Hudson reached for the doorknob and shot me a look of surprise when it swung open. "Just a quick peek," he cautioned.

I bobbed my head, motioning for him to hurry. Hudson stepped over the threshold, and I followed him, scanning the scene.

My nerves immediately quelled. The shed was empty. Well, empty of Eric or someone in trouble. It was filled top-to-bottom with sports memorabilia—jerseys, caps, trophies, gloves, bats, balls, you name it. Stuff hung from the walls and sat on shelves. There was even an extended workbench running the length of the back wall. A framed jersey with the name OGDEN hung over the bench, with more jerseys spread across the top.

"Who's Ogden?" I whispered.

"Jonathan Ogden." Hudson stared at me with mild disgust. "He anchored the Ravens' offensive line? The first Raven to be selected for the Pro Football Hall of Fame?"

His probing remarks forced a meek shrug. "So, he's kinda a big deal?"

"Just a bit." Hudson squinted as he stared at the framed jersey. "Dang. This one's signed." He pointed to the right shoulder.

I nodded, trying to look impressed, but my gaze caught the jerseys splayed out across the workbench. "These are all Ogden ones, too." I took a step closer, noting a black Sharpie pen resting on the shiny material. It took another moment to register what I was seeing. "Hey, wait. Some of these are signed…" I counted off three of the eight jerseys.

Hudson joined me and leaned closer to one of the signed items. He sniffed and broke into a coughing fit. "C-Cokes," he gasped once he could speak, "that ink is *fresh*."

My insides went cold as I did another sweep of the shed, taking in all the memorabilia. Amanda's earlier comment about the bleeding signature on Arthur's Ray Lewis jersey rang through my mind. "Do you think this is a *forgery* studio?" I whispered.

Hudson grabbed my arm and tugged me backward. "We need to leave. Now."

Scrambling toward the doorway, we crossed the threshold and stepped out into the afternoon sunlight just as a shiny aluminum baseball bat came swinging toward us.

Chapter Twenty-Eight

I felt Hudson's body curl around me as we braced for the pain, but a few seconds passed before I realized the impact hadn't occurred.

"Holy sh—aren't you Coco Cline?" a male voice squeaked.

I opened my eyes and met Eric Brady's confused gaze as he lowered the baseball bat to his side.

"H-Hi, Eric." With Hudson's aid, I straightened. "Your friend Janica asked me to check on you." I waved awkwardly as I laid the groundwork as to why we were there.

Eric still looked shaken. "She messaged me about you yesterday. I didn't know you were coming over, though." He ran a hand through his disheveled brown hair and eyed the shed behind us.

"My fiancé and I were doing errands in the area, and I thought I'd stop by to see how you were doing," I hurriedly explained, and Hudson gave a sheepish wave in introduction. "Janica was *really* worried about you when I was at her studio for a consultation." I made sure to exaggerate Janica's concern in the hopes it would endear Eric to us.

"She was worried about me?" The brightness in his voice made me feel somewhat sorry for him.

I nodded aggressively, scrambling to clarify what we were doing snooping around his property. "We heard some scary noises coming from your shed and thought you might be in distress." I smoothed back my hair, almost having regained my composure after nearly being clocked with a baseball bat. "What with the rumors that someone murdered Kiefer, we feared *you* might've been targeted, too."

"Me?" The color in Eric's face drained. "You think I'm in danger?"

"With a killer still on the loose," I said, hugging myself for effect, "who knows?"

"Sweet Baby Peas, I didn't even consider..." Eric spoke more to himself than to us. "Uh, well, as you can see, I'm fine." He wiggled the bat in his hands. "Sorry about that. I just got back from the post office and saw the shed door open. Thought a raccoon might have gotten inside or something."

"It's totally our fault," I reassured him. "We should've known better than to go inside, but we were just *sooo* worried something had happened to you."

Hudson's elbow connected lightly with my side. I could almost hear him telepathically saying, *Tone it down a bit, will ya?*

"When we saw it was empty, we turned right around, figuring we'd wait for you on your front porch." I prayed he believed we hadn't looked too closely at the jerseys lining his workbench. "Anyway, I know you and Janica are fans of mine, so I wanted to offer my help or advice." I hurriedly brushed past the fact he'd caught us trespassing. "Whatever you need. Janica said you were feeling a bit overwhelmed by the police attention?" My tone inched upward to coax him into speaking freely about the matter. When he didn't, I added, "I can *totally* relate."

Eric stared at us for a moment. "I'm not sure you can."

"Oh, please," I batted away his remark with a flighty laugh, "I've had the entire online world convinced I was a killer merely because I found a dead body."

His nostrils flared. "Yeah, well, that makes more sense than the police thinking *I* did something to Kiefer. He was one of my best pals. Heck, I wasn't even at the festival when he died."

Still mindful that he had a bat in his grip, I lifted my palms in surrender. "Well, with the truth on your side, you've got nothing to worry about, then."

I didn't miss how Eric's gaze darted to the shed before settling back on us. Did he believe our story about being concerned he'd been hurt? The last thing we needed was for him to figure out we'd seen his little forgery operation.

"I watch enough true crime shows to know how police can twist a narrative to fit the story they want," he finally said.

"What can they possibly twist?" I tilted my head to the side, doing my best to keep my voice light and airy. Perhaps if I gave off a ditzy vibe, Eric would loosen up.

"Nothing." A grunt whistled through his bared teeth. "Nothing. You should go." He used the bat to gesture toward the road.

"But I'm here to help." This interview was going further and further off the rails. "You said you weren't at the CSC festival when Kiefer collapsed. That alone should prove your innocence."

Eric scoffed. "I was at Harper's Pub, but because I paid with cash and have no receipt, that still hasn't gotten the police off my back."

Harper's? Hadn't Janica told me that Eric left because of a client issue? Had he lied to her, or was he lying now?

"Paid cash, huh?" I folded my arms. I considered everything I'd learned through various shows and podcasts about GPS tracking. "Oh, dear. I can see why they're still on your case."

Eric's gaze narrowed. "Why?"

"Did you have your phone with you?" I countered. When he nodded, I said, "Harper's Pub is close enough to the new CSC building that your phone probably shows you in the vicinity where the crime occurred." While I was totally pulling the explanation out of thin air, it sounded plausible enough, given the location Eric had mentioned. At this point, I wasn't even sure Gavin and Adrian had been able to obtain such data yet.

"Great." Eric chucked the bat onto the grass, his frustration evident. "Just great."

Hudson cleared his throat. "I'm sure once the police realize you had no reason to want Kiefer dead, this will all blow over, dude." He draped an arm around me, his stance casual and non-threatening.

Eric started massaging his hands. "Dunno about that," he muttered.

"Were things not good between you?" I asked softly.

He didn't immediately respond.

"Come on, Eric, let me help you." I smiled sweetly. "I've done it before, right?"

Thank goodness my reputation must've preceded me because Eric finally relaxed somewhat. "Things were fine. I mean, they *had* been a little rocky, but Kiefer and I talked it over. We got everything straightened out."

"Talked what over?" Hudson raised an eyebrow.

Eric shifted on the balls of his feet. "I hadn't been forthcoming about how I felt about Jan—a girl," he stammered, "and once I told Kiefer about it, he pledged bros before hoes."

It took all my strength not to roll my eyes at his gross comment. "So, you patched things up?"

He nodded vigorously. "Yeah. Totally. We even went to that Central Shores festival to hang, just the two of us."

Was that why Kiefer appeared to give Janica the cold shoulder in those Instagram videos? He was putting his friend first? But if that was true, a big part of Eric's story still didn't add up. "So why did you ditch him for Harper's?" Amanda and I had unearthed video of Eric leaving the event, looking annoyed. "Janica said something about a client thing?"

"That's just what I told her." His cheeks grew red.

Huh? Why did he feel that he had to lie to Janica? Unless...

"I didn't ditch Kiefer," Eric continued, staring at the ground while he shuffled his sneakered feet. "He told me he'd seen some blonde he used to date and wanted some time alone with her. See if they could 'rekindle' things. I joked he rebounded quicker than Jayson Tatum."

While Hudson chuckled at what I assumed was a sports joke, spasms of panic shot through my stomach. What the hashtags? Had Kiefer's ultimate goal been to seduce Charlotte?

"He couldn't believe how hot the girl had gotten," Eric continued, oblivious to my inner turmoil. "Kept mentioning how great she looked with long hair."

"He didn't tell you her name, did he?" I gulped, afraid to hear the answer.

Eric shook his head. "Nah. He just called her a cheerleader."

I flinched. Charlotte had been a cheerleader in college before she left.

Eric paused, and his eyes widened. "Jeez, you don't think this chick had something to do with his death, do you? I didn't even think to tell the police about Kiefer running off to find her." He palmed himself on the forehead.

"How stupid could I be? I swear, between losing Kief and panicking about the cops...I haven't been thinking straight." He began backing away from us. "I should call the detectives right now and let them know. Thanks for shaking some sense into me, Ms. Cline. Man, I'm an idiot."

I stared, speechless, as Eric waved hurriedly over his shoulder and jogged toward his front door. Never in all my investigations had I ever made matters worse than I had just now.

"Flaming hashtags!" I whisper-screeched the second Eric disappeared inside the house. "Omigosh, Hudson, we've royally messed things up."

His comforting arms were around me. "Shh. Take a breath, Cokes. It'll be fine."

"It will *not* be fine," I hissed. "Did you hear him? Eric is practically gift-wrapping Charlotte as the prime suspect."

Hudson tried to calm me down with a knowing stare. "He didn't get the woman's name, remember?"

"Oh, come on." This time, I couldn't suppress an eye roll. "How many of Kiefer's former cheerleader ex-girlfriends with amazing blonde hair are walking around Central Shores?"

At my biting words, Hudson's expression crumpled. "Even so, all Eric's statement proves is that Kiefer went to talk with Charlotte. Which the police already know."

"Yeah, but that part about wanting to *rekindle* things with her? That's new." I began to shiver, my anxiety getting the better of me. "I'm confident that Gavin and Adrian wouldn't manipulate the story, but what's to prevent the DA from thinking that Charlotte was provoked into murderous action if Kiefer suggested they get back together?"

"Okay, now you're just spiraling." Hudson pulled me toward the car, clearly eager to get me out of there. "Did Charlotte ever say that Kiefer talked about them getting back together?"

"Well, no, but—"

"I know you think we've messed things up," Hudson cut through my babbling, "but look at it this way. Now, we understand why Eric left the CSC festival and why his alibi is so tricky to prove."

His calm, stoic demeanor usually made me feel better. Not this time. Concern for Charlotte began to bubble over as I climbed into the front passenger seat, and my breathing started coming rapidly. "H-Hudson," I said through my gasps, "I think I'm having a panic attack."

"Okay. I'm right here." He knelt on the sidewalk beside the open car door, rubbing my back in a slow, rhythmic manner. It was one of the only things he could really do when I got like this. "Let's breathe together." We'd both learned long ago that him telling me to take deep breaths only exacerbated the matter.

Tears pricked at my eyes as I focused on the steady repetition of our in-sync inhale/exhale. I let my vision grow unfocused, trying to hone all my attention to relaxing the suffocating pinch in my heaving chest. I don't know how long we sat like that, me in the car with Hudson perched on the sidewalk, but eventually, the terrifying, invisible fist gripping my insides loosened.

"It's passed." I slumped against the seat in relief. "I'm fine."

Hudson's dark eyes pooled with worry, but he simply nodded. "Okay." He rose from his crouched position, and I could tell his limbs had gone stiff from the awkward angle. "Do you want to go straight home, or should we stop somewhere to get you a drink?"

I appreciated him giving me a choice when I knew his protective urges screamed for him to get me somewhere safe. "My throat is kinda dry," I admitted, my tongue feeling like sandpaper from all the heavy breathing. "Water, or maybe a lemonade, might be good."

"Got it. I'll drive through the center and see what's available," he said once he'd settled into the driver's seat.

Now that the worst had passed and my emotions were in order, I reviewed what had transpired at Eric's with a level head. By his own admission, he had no proof that he'd been at Harper's Pub, and with the busy foot traffic from the CSC event, it's possible that no one on staff would remember serving him. Add to that his phone location data, and a theory began to emerge. "Eric said he watches true crime shows. What if he purposely crafted a weak alibi to cover his tracks?"

"What would be the point of that?" Hudson turned onto the main road that led to Ocean Hollow's shopping center.

"If he decided to kill Kiefer while they were attending the festival, he would know his phone data would put him in the vicinity." I drummed my fingers on my lap. "So, what if Eric concocted an alibi that the police would have a hard time proving? Paying cash at a busy restaurant? If Harper's staff said they didn't remember him coming in, a good defense lawyer could easily plant a seed of doubt as to why."

"Fair. We only have his word that he and Kiefer patched things up." Hudson shot me a quick side glance. "But his version of events also explains why that video between Kiefer and Janica seemed heated. She must've cornered him before he made his way to Charlotte's booth, and Kiefer told her whatever was going on between them was over."

I wrinkled my nose. "You're right."

"And if Eric and Kiefer patched things up, what reason would Eric have for killing him?"

I rubbed my temples, trying to get my brain to work. "I know we played it off like we didn't see anything, but there is *clearly* something illegal going on in Eric's shed," I added a few extra syllables for emphasis. "Maybe Kiefer found out and wasn't cool about it."

"So, Eric kills Kiefer to cover up his fraudulent merchandise scam. Now we're cooking." Hudson gave me an encouraging grin.

I didn't feel as confident. "Maybe I'm biased because of how he treated Charlotte, but would Kiefer really *care* that Eric was breaking the law and selling forgeries?" I couldn't objectively arrive at an answer to my question.

Hudson frowned. "His criminal history suggests maybe not."

"Let's say Eric told us the truth about everything between him and Kiefer," I hedged. "That puts Janica in the hot seat, right? As the jilted lover?"

Hudson dipped his chin. "You know what they say? Poisoning is a woman's weapon."

I pressed my lips together. "I would've thought you'd be more woke than that."

He chuckled at my teasing.

Chapter Twenty-Nine

A few minutes later, we claimed a parking spot in front of The Center Deli, aptly located in the middle of Ocean Hollow's shopping area. As we got out of the car, I caught sight of The Twisted Candle Bookshop a few doors down. "Hey." I turned to Hudson. "Any chance you can grab the drinks while I sync with a client?" I pointed over my shoulder. "I want to run by some website updates with Drew Wilson."

Hudson paused, and I could see he was torn over leaving me on my own so soon after a panic attack episode.

"I'm fine, babe." I squeezed his forearm. "Really. And you're only a phone call away."

He debated a moment longer. "Okay. Lemonade?"

"Surprise me." I kissed him on the cheek and hurried down the sidewalk toward Drew's.

Dedicated to showcasing teenage detectives like Trixie Belden, Encyclopedia Brown, Jupiter Jones, and Drew's namesake, Nancy, The Twisted Candle was your quintessential new-and-used bookstore paired with an escape room challenge in the back. Amanda and I had done an Enola Holmes-themed session once (so CoA could authentically convey the experience to would-be customers), and I had to admit, it was my kind of fun.

Today, the shop was quiet, with only rows of tall bookshelves greeting me. "Hello?" I called softly, for the sales floor itself wasn't very big. Most of the store's space was allocated to the featured escape room.

"Welcome!" Drew burst out from behind a curtain partition, her curly red hair getting caught in the process. "Oh. Hey, Coco." A wide smile spread across her pale, freckled face as she tugged her hair free and pushed her dark green glasses up her nose. "What brings you by?"

"I was in the area doing some errands," I casually explained my unannounced drop-in, "and I thought I'd see if you had time to review the website updates Amanda and I made this morning."

"Ooh, yes, please!" She clapped with glee. "I'm so excited to announce the book club. It's been hard keeping it under wraps since the idea came to mind."

I pointed to the computer that also served as her register. "Can I pull up the page? We haven't enabled it yet, so we need to go through your admin profile."

Drew ushered me behind the counter. "Have at it."

With deft fingers, I pulled up her Squarespace domain and tapped on the book club's landing page.

Drew's squeals of delight had me rubbing my ears. "Omigosh, Coco. I love it! Oh, look what you did with the logo." She practically jumped up and down. "Approved. Totally approved. Could you send me a PNG of that logo so I can use it for other branding materials?"

I grinned at her enthusiasm. "You bet." When we'd first started working together, she'd been upfront that technology wasn't her strong suit, but Drew understood the importance of building an online brand and wasn't afraid to learn. I loved clients with her willingness. It amazed me how often people let fear of learning new technology hold them back from being successful in today's market.

As I navigated to the page's settings and enabled it to go live on Drew's site, I forged ahead with my real reason for coming by the bookshop. "So, have you heard the latest drama out of Central Shores?"

Drew raised an eyebrow. "You mean about the guy who died over the weekend?" She moved to a nearby bookshelf to straighten a few titles. "I saw that terrible video circulating online. With you." Her lips grew downturned. "I'm sorry you had to go through that."

I recoiled at the reminder that a video capturing Kiefer's final moments would forever haunt the Internet. "Thanks." I took a breath and asked, "I heard the man was staying in the Ocean Hollow area. That he was a friend of Eric Brady's."

"Gold Score Eric?" Drew looked surprised. "I didn't know that." She tapped her chin. "Guess that's why he closed early yesterday."

Her murmured comments burst the balloon of hope I'd been holding onto. She hadn't seen Kiefer and Eric palling around town.

Drew shook her curls. "I still can't believe Janica made it to work, given how close she seemed with the guy."

I glanced up from the computer screen. "Janica Rice?"

"Yeah. I saw her around town with him a *ton* these last few weeks. He was kinda hard to miss, being so tall and beefy." Drew shifted a few books, sliding them into different spots. "I thought they matched online or something, and he was in the area visiting her. But you're saying he was Eric's buddy?"

When I nodded, she shuddered. "Yeesh. Some friend."

"What do you mean?"

Drew snorted. "It's no secret that Eric is head over *huh-heels* for Janica." She added some sass to her words. "A few of the shops in the center even have a betting pool about when she'll finally acknowledge his feelings for her. Guy has been friend-zoned since day one."

I frowned. "Poor Eric."

"Yeah, I feel for him, too." Drew sighed. "Did he know about Janica hanging out with his pal?"

"According to Eric," I said as I closed out of the Squarespace admin window, "he and Kiefer—his friend—talked it over. Kiefer said he was going to bow out and tell Janica he wasn't into her."

Drew's eyes widened behind her glasses. "Good lord, did that guy have a death wish?" Her hand flew to her mouth once she realized what she'd said.

I arched a questioning brow. "What makes you say that?"

Her features contorted with guilt before she whispered, "Janica kinda has a reputation for being a little…uncooperative when it comes to being dumped."

"Uncooperative?" I leaned forward, perching my elbows on the countertop. "Come on, Drew. You gotta give me more than that."

She smirked. "I take it you *are* helping the police with their investigation, then?"

"I'm just interested, that's all." I motioned to the shelves filled with mysteries lining her store. "Surely you can understand the feeling."

"I understand it from the viewpoint of a *fictional* character," she countered, her gaze troubled. "But I'd be way too afraid to get tangled up in police business in real life." She hugged herself. "This means Eric's friend really was murdered, then, huh? So many rumors going around, from him dying of heatstroke to some type of accident..."

The sound of the front door opening interrupted our chat, and Hudson appeared, holding two large beverage containers.

"Hey there, Drew." He greeted her warmly as he handed me a drink. Hudson and I had done another one of her escape rooms for a fun date-night activity. The theme had been a tribute to the OG girl sleuth: Nancy Drew. "How are things since Coco and I escaped Shadow Ranch?"

"Well, they were just getting juicy." The bookshop owner's expression turned teasing. "Your fiancée is pumping me for information about Janica Rice."

Hudson shot me a somewhat reprimanding look, which I supposed I deserved. He probably wasn't happy to hear that I was back on the case, not even twenty minutes after a panic attack. "Oh? And anything to add?" He sounded resigned to his fate as my dutiful sidekick on this adventure.

"Is this on the record for *Crime Sweet Home?*" Drew grinned.

I held up my hand. "We're just trying to figure out if anyone had reason to want a guy dead who wasn't even from around here." *Other than one of my best friends, that is.*

Drew sobered at my truthfulness. "Like I was saying, Janica has a habit of getting into trouble with her exes."

"What kind of trouble?" Hudson probed.

"Oh, just blasting stuff on social media. Trying to cause issues with their employers. Letting air out of their tires. Harassing their new girlfriends through texts." In mock boredom, Drew counted the wild offenses on her fingers. "How the woman continues to do such good business is impressive, given her murky personal life."

I took a sip of the drink Hudson had chosen. It was a yummy peach-tea-type thing. "Impressive, indeed." Rand's off-handed comment about Janica being "obsessed" with Kiefer took on a troubling new light. Her problematic behavior was disturbing, but online harassment took a very different mindset compared to actively poisoning someone's drink with a substance deadly to them. Had Janica's dangerous behavior escalated when Kiefer broke things off at the festival?

Drew's cheeks lost their pinkish hue. "You don't think Janica had a hand in this, do you?"

"I'm not sure. I don't know her all that well." But what I had learned over the last few days alarmed me. Janica had gotten close to Kiefer and fast. It was very likely that she knew all about his allergy. We'd heard from multiple sources that she was aggressive and possessive, *and* we had proof that she'd been at the CSC grand opening, where she could have easily gotten hold of some peanuts to drop in his cup. Motive, means, and opportunity.

"Goodness." Drew shivered. "Tomorrow night's Chamber of Commerce meeting is gonna be awkward, knowing what I know now."

I swallowed. The last thing we needed was for Drew to give away to Janica that we suspected her.

She must have seen the panic on my face. "I can play it cool, though. Don't worry." She motioned to the books behind her. "I'll take a page from Nancy and Co."

I smiled my appreciation. "I'm sure this will all resolve itself." I made a mental note to call Gavin and Adrian on our drive back to Central Shores. It was time to fill our friends at the police department in.

We chatted a few more minutes about the book club launch before Hudson and I bid Drew goodbye. It wasn't until we were buckled back in the car that Hudson unleashed his disapproval.

"I thought you were going to fly under the radar." He rubbed his temples, unable to keep the disappointment from his tone. "Drew's super nice and all, but what's to say she doesn't mention to someone that you came by and were looking into Kiefer's case?" He jammed his iced drink into an open cup holder slot.

"All I said is that I was *interested* in it." I scowled, not in the mood to be lectured. "Come on. After solving three murders on my own, thank you very much, people would be suspicious if I *wasn't* asking questions."

"On your own, huh?" Hudson looked more hurt than upset over my snapping retort. "What happened to the dear old Sleuth Squad and all *our* efforts?"

I reached across the center console and grabbed his hand. It was slick with perspiration from holding his drink. "I'm sorry. I didn't mean it like that. I wouldn't have gotten anywhere without you guys." I sighed as I stared out the windshield. "But I can't help that folks are automatically assuming I'm wrapped up in this. And lying to people who I consider friends makes me feel so gross."

"Even if it keeps you safe?"

I struggled to meet his worried gaze. "I'm sorry. I messed up. Yet again." I leaned back against the headrest, my earlier fears resurfacing.

Hudson must have noted my change in mood, for he started the engine and didn't berate me further. "Why don't you give the detectives a ring and tell them what we've uncovered?"

I dialed Adrian's number. Because I knew I had to come clean about questioning Eric, I selected the cop who was least likely to yell at me.

"Hey, Coco, what's up?" Adrian's chipper voice bubbled from my speaker. "Solved the case yet?" he added with a coy chuckle.

"Maybe." Two could play at that game, after all.

The background noise faded on his end. "All right. I'm all ears. *Especially* if this helps explain why we received a call from Eric Brady not thirty minutes ago that ended with him pointing the finger at a woman who—from the sounds of it—suspiciously resembles Charlotte."

I gulped. So much for thinking Adrian wouldn't call me out for bad behavior. "About that…"

I ended up putting him on speakerphone so Hudson and I could share all the details from our entire Ocean Hollow outing.

"According to people we've spoken to, Janica has a history of lashing out at lovers who've scorned her," I offered in summary. "It's not out of the realm of possibility that she laced Kiefer's drink to make him sick. Or worse, if she took his EpiPen and tossed it."

"Hmm…" Adrian's voice trailed off on the other end. "I don't know, you guys. Yes, this could be a crime of passion, but I'm more inclined to think this boils down to the classic money being the root of evil."

"Money? How—" I cut myself off as the lightbulb dawned. "You think Eric silenced Kiefer to protect his little forgery scam?" In all honesty, my chat with Drew about Janica had sidelined the theory in my own mind.

"Or Kiefer wanted in on the scheme, and Eric didn't want to share the spoils," Adrian suggested.

By now, Hudson and I were home, seated at our kitchen countertop and enjoying the last of our fruity tea drinks. "But Eric didn't seem too concerned about *us* going to the cops with what we saw," I pointed out.

Hudson chuckled. "To be fair, I think you dazzled him a bit, Cokes. He totally bought that we were too worried about him being hurt to notice anything." He leaned closer to the phone mic. "Speaking of, are you gonna bring him in on selling fakes?" he asked Adrian.

Our detective friend sighed. "Yes, but I'd like to do it in a way that doesn't make Eric suspect *you* guys are the ones that narced on him."

"We could loop Arthur in," I suggested. "Amanda mentioned that his supposedly 'signed' jersey from Gold Score is already bleeding."

"I'd rather *not* involve more civilians if I can help it." There was a hint of exasperation in Adrian's tone.

I reached for my shoulder, massaging the knot growing there. Between nearly getting whacked with a baseball bat and my dad getting into a fight with a rusted pipe—

"Hold up!" I straightened in my seat. "Hashtags, why didn't I put the pieces together sooner?"

"What pieces?" Hudson tilted his head.

"Adrian," I said excitedly, "I don't think Eric's working alone." I quickly explained the scene Dad and I had stumbled into behind Saucy Sid's on Sunday. "Neither Dad nor I believed Sy was telling the truth about owing money to those guys. What if they found out their merch was fake, and Sy was the guy they bought it from?"

"Sy Ramone is, what, Eric's henchman? Partner? Seller?" Adrian sounded skeptical.

I shrugged before remembering he couldn't see me. "Maybe it's worth having a chat with Sy about his dealings with Eric. They're really tight." Charlotte had even told me that, out of their friend group, Eric and Sy appeared to be the closest. At least, according to their socials. "If anyone knew what Eric was up to, I'd be willing to bet it would be Sy."

"Jeez. Murder, back alley brawls, and forgery rings. Have we been dropped into a rerun of *The Sopranos?*" Incredulity dripped from Adrian's sarcastic reply.

I had to agree with him. This was not the Central Shores of my youth.

"All right. Well, you've given Gavin and me plenty to think about." His sigh reverberated through the phone. "I'm still waiting for a few Harper's Pub employees to call me. See if they can confirm Eric's presence. So far, nothing."

Hudson nudged me with his elbow as if to say, *You might've been right about his faux alibi, after all.*

"Gavin and I will also pay Janica Rice a visit tomorrow in person," Adrian added. "She couldn't—or *wouldn't* speak with us over the phone today, so we'll turn up the heat."

"No other results back on the EpiPen or B2P cup yet?" I hedged.

"Annnnd we're done." Adrian even laughed. "I can only put my neck out so far, Coco. I hope you understand that."

"I do." I truly did, although I couldn't suppress the disappointment wriggling within me.

Adrian stressed, "Gav and I are keeping Eric's comments about a blonde woman to ourselves for the time being. But if the DA hears of this tip…"

He didn't need to say aloud what I already feared: Charlotte would be in major trouble, all because of me.

Chapter Thirty

After signing off the phone with Adrian, Hudson reached for my hand. "You sure you're okay to go to Jasper's tonight?" His gaze darted to the wall clock. Jasper's dinner party was in an hour.

"Yes, please. I need to distract myself with some frivolity." My mind was so overstimulated with case theories. A night with my friends might help the dust settle. Or maybe they would inspire my next steps. Beyond nailing down Eric's alibi, I really had no idea what to do. Was there anyone else besides Janica and Eric who could've had a reason to want Kiefer dead?

Sage's cryptic tarot card reading about jilted husbands and unplanned pregnancies floated through my mind. *Oh, great.* It wasn't an encouraging sign for my investigation if I was seriously contemplating such abstract speculations.

I opted to ignore all the nagging case questions and focused on preparing for Jasper's party. White wasn't my best color, so adhering to the dress code would prove challenging.

"Think this will pass muster?" Hudson struck a flamboyant pose, showing off the ivory chinos and short-sleeved button-up he'd selected. While his shirt boasted little embroidered navy anchors, it was still in the realm of white.

I giggled. "Looks great." I turned my attention back to my dresses hanging in our walk-in closet. The closest thing I had to a white outfit was a silky robe I'd been given for being a bridesmaid for one of my college gal pals. I studied its loose, quarter-length sleeves with a fashion-forward eye, an idea percolating.

I rushed to my bedroom jewelry box and dug out a gaudy brooch my mom had gifted me for my twenty-first birthday. It was a sparkly moissanite starburst set against gold plating with a pearl in the middle. I don't think I'd worn it once in the near decade since.

Grabbing it, I returned to the closet and slipped the robe off its hanger. After some finagling with the belt and brooch, I assessed myself in the floor-length mirror. With the brooch positioned to make the neckline less plunging, the robe almost looked like a shimmering wraparound dress.

"That's pretty," Hudson murmured as he kissed my exposed collarbone.

I wiggled away from his seductive touch. We had to be at Jasper's soon, and my bestie would throttle me if we were late. "It's pajamas." Although I had to admit, I looked pretty chic. Perhaps this would inspire a *Trending Topic* post about necessity breeding an inventive wardrobe.

I mentally cringed at the materialistic idea. *Not exactly discovering the key to world peace, am I?* But I was good at what I did, even if it no longer left me feeling fulfilled like my CoA work or even my amateur sleuthing exploits.

Rae Livingston's offer to purchase *Trending Topic* and all its related IP poked enticingly at the back of my brain. Maybe it was time to give up my blog since it no longer brought me the joy it once had.

Eric Brady's dazed expression suddenly came to mind. Hudson and I had narrowly avoided getting beat up with a baseball bat, all because Eric was a fan of my work. Moments like that would dry up once I stepped away from the online platform I'd created. Did I really want to give up what little fame I had, especially if it helped me get out of scrapes like today?

Focus, Coco. One problem at a time. I wasn't in the right mindset to make decisions about my career, especially with Charlotte's freedom hanging in the balance.

Pushing my inner turmoil aside, I did my hair and makeup to top off tonight's look, and soon, we were ready to walk up the cul-de-sac. Thankfully, I had a bottle of sparkling wine in the fridge that I could bring as a gift, so we wouldn't arrive empty-handed.

The setting sun cast a peachy glow over our cozy little development, and the sight left me feeling somewhat more relaxed as I strolled hand-in-hand with Hudson, the effects of my panic attack forgotten.

A silver Tesla was parked in Jasper's driveway, meaning Arthur and Amanda must already be inside. I hoped they'd be able to enjoy the evening. After so much heartbreak, they deserved it.

I pressed the smart home doorbell to announce our arrival. Through the speakers, Jasper's voice chimed, "Enter," in a snooty butler tone.

Hudson chuckled as he reached for the handle and ushered me inside.

Seeing Amanda, Arthur, Charlotte, Deacon, and Eli all seated in Jasper's mid-century modern-style living room, I realized we were the last to arrive. Except our host, who appeared to be MIA.

"Hey, guys." I waved as everyone rose from their chairs to exchange hugs. "Where's the man of the hour?" I asked, checking to make sure I hadn't missed Jasper.

Eli used the beer bottle in his hand as a pointer. "He's been holed up in his bedroom since I got here."

As Amanda and Arthur nodded, "Same," Charlotte gnawed on her lower lip. "Is he all right? He's not sick, is he?"

I caught Amanda's attention, and I could tell she was suppressing a grin as we thought the same thing. Jasper was planning a grand entrance.

Before anyone could answer Charlotte's question, the sound system wired throughout the house blared to life. Elvis Costello's "She," made famous to our generation by the iconic *Notting Hill* movie montage, filled our ears and, thankfully, drowned out the gurgling laughter bursting from me.

The room went dark as the lights dimmed, all except for an overhead one in the hallway. A few measures into the crooning song, Jasper stepped out from the shadows wearing a white tuxedo and holding a large, plush purple pillow in his arms. Atop the frilly throne sat a cool and poised Miranda, completely unfazed by the pomp and circumstance as her unhinged owner slowly marched toward the living room.

Jasper's expression was so serious I don't think anyone else knew how to react. Charlotte, Hudson, and Deacon were all frozen in place. Eli's and Amanda's eyes looked like they might pop out of their heads, and Arthur's jaw was nearly on the floor. I tried my best to rein in my laughter, but it was physically making my stomach ache.

"Presenting Her Royal Felineness, Ms. Miranda Purriestly," Jasper boomed with authority as he lifted the pillow, the lights in his house automatically switching to illuminate his current position at the command. I was actually impressed by the thought he'd put into the scene design. It must have taken hours to choreograph and automate his smart home routines to get it just right.

Elvis Costello's voice faded, giving way to the stunned silence Jasper and Miranda's appearance had invoked.

After a beat, Jasper's head inched to the side so he could glare at us from behind Miranda's fluffy body, and I took that as our cue to applaud this stunning, artistic feat.

"Yay!" I clapped my palms together, nudging Hudson into action with my elbow.

Charlotte, Amanda, and their partners soon followed suit, leaving only Eli in an immobile state of shock. I prayed this theatrical stunt wouldn't spell the end of their budding romance.

"Omigosh! She's gorgeous!" Charlotte shimmied forward as Jasper lowered Miranda to pet-able level. "When did this happen? Where did you get her?"

"Just yesterday." Jasper beamed. "I saved her from the streets of Ocean Hollow."

"Wow!" Deacon looked impressed as he joined his girlfriend. "She must've really taken to you to let you parade her around like this."

"Our bond is very deep." Jasper swelled with pride. "Even the vet was impressed by how calm my mere presence makes her. Must be because Miranda sees me as her savior."

Or she's already suffering from Stockholm Syndrome. But I kept the snarky thought to myself.

Amanda slid forward and began scratching Miranda under the chin. "She's so soft. Oh, that fur. Those eyes! What a beauty."

"Please, do go on." Jasper was clearly enjoying the shower of compliments as if he'd made Miranda himself.

He finally relented and shared how he had rescued Miranda from the brink of death. I decided it was better to keep quiet throughout his animated retelling because I honestly lost track of the number of embellishments. Somehow, we'd gone from a three-and-a-half-foot-deep koi pond to a bottomless sea roaring with white caps.

"I didn't realize you knew how to perform CPR, let alone on a cat." Hudson, too, struggled with this version of events since he'd heard the original play-by-play from me.

Jasper stroked Miranda. "I guess it was my innate need to help people that guided me forward."

Oh, Sweet Baby Blue Ivy. "Can I get anyone a refill? I need a drink." I surveyed the empty cocktail glasses and bottles among my friends.

"Er, I do." Eli stood awkwardly away from the crowd gathered around Jasper and Miranda. "But I'll come with."

He didn't have to follow me far since Jasper's condo was open-concept.

As I navigated the fridge looking for mixers, I studied the handsome twenty-eight-year-old out of the corner of my eye. His expression had gone quite slack. "You okay? I realize that was a bit much."

"Huh? Oh, yeah. I'm fine."

Clearly, he was *not* fine.

"I promise, Jasper isn't normally this...deranged." I patted him on the shoulder in reassurance.

Eli chewed on his lower lip. "Honestly, it's not that. I appreciated the throwback to *Modern Family.*"

Impressed he knew the TV show reference that inspired Jasper's shenanigans, I asked, "Then what's got you bothered?"

"Uh, this is kind of embarrassing." Eli lowered his voice even more. "But I'm sorta terrified of cats."

"Wha—oh, dear." I said a quick mental prayer, thanking a higher power that I hadn't laughed or asked if he was joking. Eli, with his six-foot-plus frame and imposing muscles, appeared genuinely distressed.

He reached to rub his shaved head. "I got trapped in a closet with my granny's cat when I was four, and that thing was demon spawn, I swear.

I had so many cuts and scratches on me by the time someone found us, I needed fifteen stitches." He tugged up the leg of his white shorts, revealing a gnarly scar on his light brown skin.

"Yikes!" I murmured my sympathies. "I take it Jasper isn't aware?"

Eli shook his head. "Usually, I tell the guys I'm dating that I'm allergic to cats, but given Jasper's tendency to care only about himself…" he admitted half-jokingly, "I didn't think I'd need to worry about him wanting to take care of another living creature."

"I'm with you on that." I shot a sidelong glance at my bestie since second grade. He was currently kissing Miranda repetitively on her little pink nose. "The only thing I've ever seen him kiss this much is his reflection in the mirror."

Eli chuckled, his shoulders relaxing slightly. "I'm happy he's happy, though. It's a sweeter side of him."

I wrapped my arm around him. "You should tell him how you feel, Eli. Not just about cats, but everything. You mean a lot to him. I'm sure he'll find a way to make this all work."

"Thanks, Coco. I'm willing to make this work, too." He sucked in a deep breath. "I should go say hello to the feline of the hour."

I watched with pride as Eli inched his way across the condo, positioning himself an arm's length from Miranda. The poor guy's fingers were trembling as he reached out and lightly rubbed her head. With the deed done, he whipped his hand back and pocketed it safely in his shorts. Luckily, everyone else at the gathering was too preoccupied by Miranda's cuteness to notice Eli's skittish behavior.

After another round of celebratory drinks and more fawning, Jasper finally motioned for us to move outside to his back patio. As we spilled out of the condo, a home catering crew stood ready to serve at a yummy-looking buffet table.

"Dang. Jasper really went all out," Hudson whispered in my ear as we got behind Charlotte and Amanda in line. "Who knew such a nurturing side existed?" he teased.

I eyed Jasper carefully as he chatted with Eli. Miranda had been left inside to recuperate from "such taxing activity" (Jasper's words, not mine), so Eli seemed more relaxed and looked to be enjoying himself at last. I hoped they'd talk soon. I didn't expect Eli to ask Jasper to get rid of Miranda or anything drastic, but they definitely needed to figure out a way forward if their relationship was to grow.

Everyone was eventually seated around the outdoor dining table with their plates full of brisket, mashed sweet potatoes, baked beans, and buffalo cauliflower. Jasper spent a few more minutes chatting about Miranda's first vet visit this morning and how he'd been told the vet had never seen "a more intelligent and beautiful creature."

"When's her MENSA acceptance ceremony?" I asked, and everyone— except Jasper—laughed.

"Speaking of geniuses," Charlotte interjected as her gaze slid to me, "you said you uncovered some new deets in the case, Sherlock Hashtags?"

My insides writhed at how hopeful she looked. Goodness, I hoped I hadn't royally screwed things up for her. "Well, we *did* have an interesting trip over to Ocean Hollow." I turned my attention to our host, silently asking if I could steal his thunder.

Jasper flippantly flicked his wrist, gesturing me to continue.

Hudson and I took turns sharing the events of the afternoon. Even the fact that Eric had called the police to tell them about Kiefer wanting to rekindle a romance with Charlotte. The only thing we omitted was my panic attack. I didn't want my friends to feel sorry for me.

"Adrian says they're keeping Eric's 'tip' on the down low until they speak with Janica and confirm Eric's alibi," I concluded on a somewhat optimistic note.

"If there's an alibi to confirm. Who uses *cash* anymore?" Jasper shivered as if the word alone would give him cooties.

Charlotte frowned at his dramatics. "Well, I appreciate that Gavin and Adrian are willing to go to bat for me, but what if the DA finds out they're holding back?" Her forehead wrinkled with worry. "I wouldn't want them getting into hot water on my account."

Deacon wrapped an arm around her. "It's not like they're required to report every single minute of their progress. Gavin texted me that they're set to meet with her on Friday to give another update, so I imagine we have until then to make sense of the whole thing."

"From the sounds of it, Janica seems the most likely suspect," Arthur offered his two cents. "Woman scorned and all."

Amanda twirled a strand of her hair. "But isn't it odd that she arranged for Coco to help Eric with the police? Wouldn't she *want* suspicion to fall on someone else besides her?"

I stared down at the dish of delicious strawberry shortcake in front of me. Jasper had really gone all out with the catered menu. "This case is going in circles. Until we can either pinpoint Eric's and Janica's whereabouts or expand our search beyond their friend group, we're stuck."

"Who works at Harper's that we could question about Eric being there?" Jasper popped a plump strawberry into his mouth.

Hudson stroked his chin. "That might be hard to track down because of all the college kids back in town working summer jobs."

"And without straight up asking Janica if she poisoned Kiefer after their argument at the festival—" I cut myself off.

Charlotte winced. "I know that look. You are *not* going to confront her, Coco."

"Yeah." Jasper nodded. "Not only is that asking for trouble, but she could drag you online. Even superfans have their limits."

The sensible side of me knew they were right. The impatient, egotistical side, however, had different ideas. "I've already laid the groundwork with her about doing a collab with *Trending Topic.* What if I invite her out to get coffee and see where our conversation takes us?"

The unhappy glares staring back at me were answer enough. "Okay, fine. Scrap that." I raised my hands in defeat.

"Speaking of work," Amanda began, giving a sheepish glance at her watch, "we should probably head back. Arthur's heading out of town for business, and I've got a CoA meeting first thing tomorrow in Rockaway."

I checked the time. It was already past nine—which was basically midnight for us wizened millennials.

"Gosh, that evening flew by." Charlotte gathered her dinnerware from the table as she stood. "I need to get to bed, too. The café won't open itself." Her mood soured. "Although, what's the point if no one shows up?" she grumbled, more to herself than to us.

My heart went out to her. I knew she could survive a few bad days of business, but anything more than that had the potential to really harm my bestie. Brewed to Perfection was Charlotte's pride and joy, and I would do whatever I could to help restore its reputation within the community.

Even if it meant having a little sit-down with Janica.

Chapter Thirty-One

"Let it be known I am *not* happy with this," Hudson muttered the following morning as he pulled on a polo T-shirt over his bronzed abs. "But I'm glad you asked me for help instead of going rogue."

I blushed as I finished dusting my cheeks with shimmering powder. "Hey, I know better than to face a potential killer on my own." I cupped his chin and turned his focus away from the bathroom mirror. "I just want to ask what happened between her and Kiefer at the CSC festival. See if Janica goes on the defensive or anything." When I'd last chatted with her, Janica had given the impression that she hadn't even gone to the event. Now that I had proof she did, I wanted to hear her side of the story.

Hudson kissed the tip of my nose. "I wish Delaware wasn't an all-party consent state so I could record this little sting operation for *Crime Sweet Home.*"

A devilish grin spread across my face. "Ah, that's the beauty of our meet-up plan. Since I've framed this little sync as a collaboration initiative, it won't be too weird for me to suggest recording some video to use in our online campaign posts."

"So why are we meeting Janica at Sweet Resolutions and not at Charlotte's?" Hudson countered.

"I don't want Charlotte tangled up in this any more than she already is." I fluffed my hair one more time and called it good. "Besides, depending on what Kiefer shared with Janica about himself, she might already know Charlotte's his ex."

Hudson arched a skeptical eyebrow as we ambled into the kitchen. "You really think Kiefer would admit to being a domestic abuser?"

"Probably not. But who knows what kind of cringy spin he put on things?" I pointed out. "Better safe than sorry, right?" I gathered my tablet, which was lying on the counter, and stuffed it into my work tote. "We don't want Janica clamming up if she recognizes Charlotte."

"Are we eating there?" Hudson patted his stomach, looking longingly at the bag of bagels next to the toaster.

I grabbed his arm and tugged him toward the front door. "Yes. You have to try these new cinnamon chocolate croissants Tom started making last week."

My left leg bounced nervously as I drove toward the strip. Beyond yummy croissants and protecting Charlotte, I'd chosen Sweet Resolutions for a few other reasons. One, I needed to go over some sponsored ad ideas with Tom and Thomas for their socials, and two, I wanted to speak with Janica in a public, busy place. With all the rumors swirling about Charlotte's lattes, I figured Brewed to Perfection might still be a ghost town. Meanwhile, Sweet Resolutions would be buzzing with people who needed their chocolate and caffeine fixes.

By the time I pulled into the residential parking lot behind the strip, Jolly's dashboard read nine o'clock, meaning we had about forty-five minutes before Janica was scheduled to arrive. Plenty of time for Hudson and me to enjoy some breakfast pastries.

My phone buzzed with a notification just as I turned off the ignition. "Ugh, I hope she isn't bailing on me." Our meeting had been totally set up last minute, but Janica seemed excited when I DMed her on our walk home from Jasper's party to talk about a "collab."

Thankfully, it wasn't Janica. It was a link from Deacon that he'd posted into our group chat.

Seems like reality has finally hit Eric.

A reply from Jasper had already popped up. **Or he's realizing he needs to play the role of grieving bestie better instead of telling his friends to lie to the popo.**

Eager to see what lay on the other end of the link, I clicked it. I leaned over the console to share my screen with Hudson, but since he was in the group chat, too, he'd done the same.

The link prompted my Facebook app to open, and soon, I was staring at a photo that captured a group of friends on a sandy-white beach. The group consisted of six people in total. From the way arms were wrapped around each other, they were all couples. I spotted Eric with his arm around a cute redhead while Kiefer had a beautiful blonde woman pressed against him. For a second, my heart leaped into my throat, thinking it was Charlotte, before quickly realizing my error. The woman's hair was finer and lighter colored than Charlotte's thick, amber waves. She was more athletically built than Charlotte, too. Her eyes were hidden by massive sunglasses, but there was something about her...

"Why does this woman remind me of someone?" Hudson asked aloud what I was thinking. "I mean, at first I thought—"

"It was a picture of Charlotte? Yeah, me too." I studied the other people in the photo. The only ones I could identify were Eric and Kiefer. I then read the caption Eric posted.

Throwback to happier days. Miss you like crazy, bro. Can't believe you're gone. Rest in Power, Big Kief.

He'd also tagged the location of the photo. Seabrook Island, South Carolina.

"Throwback, huh? How long ago was this, you think?" Hudson asked.

I studied the clothing everyone wore. With the women wearing high-waisted jeans, it couldn't have been more than a few years old. "Not very. High-waisted jeans only made a comeback recently. Kiefer and Eric also look pretty much the same."

"Some throwback, then." Hudson snorted.

I typed into our group chat, **Does anyone else think the woman with Kiefer looks familiar?**

Jasper immediately replied, but he sent it to me privately rather than through our group chat. **She looks kinda like Charlotte. I almost had a heart attack when I first saw it. The last thing our girl needs right now is to be publicly linked to Kiefer's past. But I guess Kiefer had a**

type.

Yeah. Maybe that's why he had no issue bowing out so Eric could pursue Janica. He honestly wasn't interested. With her brown hair and petite build, she looked nothing like the tall, curvaceous babe in the photo or goddess-like Charlotte.

I wondered what Charlotte would think when she saw the pic. Maybe, if we were lucky, she'd know who the woman was. Someone from their college days, perhaps?

Refocusing on the mission, Hudson and I pocketed our phones and climbed out of Jolly. My stomach was rumbling like crazy. I needed food, stat.

I scanned the parking area as we walked, checking for any sign of Janica, only to then chide myself for being overtly paranoid. Janica wasn't a Central Shores resident, so she'd have to use the paid lot a few blocks down. *Get a grip, Coco. You've done this plenty of times before.* Granted, I hadn't really *known* who my killers were before coming face-to-face with them in the past, but in this instance, I felt confident that I had my bases covered when it came to protecting myself against Janica Rice. Hudson was here for backup. We were meeting in a public place. And we planned to capture everything on video.

Hand in hand, Hudson and I took the alley between Harper's Pub and Jewel's Ice Cream, the blue waters of the Atlantic sparkling across the road. It was shaping up to be a beautiful day.

Readying myself for what came next, I stepped out from the shadows of the alley and onto the sidewalk, Hudson right by my side.

BAM!

Hudson's arm encircled my waist and yanked me back, preventing me from tumbling to the pavement as a large figure smacked into me.

Chapter Thirty-Two

"Jeez, what the—" I swallowed my annoyance as I registered my assailant. "Thomas? Everything all right?"

The German chocolatier hadn't been as lucky as me. Since he didn't have a Hudson to catch him, Thomas Neumann collided with the side of the building. Luckily, though, he didn't look too badly banged up.

"Thomas?" I repeated, for the man leaned against the brick siding, his jaw a bit slack. "You didn't hit your head, did you?"

He blinked, his hazel eyes wide with confusion and panic. "N-No. I'm fine." He pushed himself upright and brushed off his chocolate-smeared apron. "Sorry," he mumbled before taking off down the alleyway.

We stared after the fleeing man. "What's gotten into him?" Hudson did not look amused by the strange situation.

"I have no idea." Once Thomas disappeared into the resident parking lot, I turned to my fiancé. "He seemed rather anxious. I hope things are okay at Sweet Resolutions."

Hudson pressed his lips together. "Let's find out."

We half-expected to find the chocolate shop in a state of chaos, but to our surprise, only a few patrons milled about. Rosie was behind the counter filling orders, and Tom didn't seem to be anywhere in sight.

"Hi, guys." Rosie waved in greeting as we made our way to the counter. "I'll be with you in a second."

"I'll grab a table." Hudson kissed my cheek and darted to one in the corner.

I waited while Rosie bagged some chocolate-covered caramels and handed them to an awaiting customer. I nervously eyed the two remaining cinnamon chocolate croissants, hoping the woman in front of me wouldn't snatch them up.

To my relief, she ordered two dozen chocolate-covered apricots in a gift box, which Rosie promptly packaged and wrapped.

"Sorry about the wait. I'm on my own out here for the moment." Rosie puffed out a burst of air when she got to me. "Tom's at a craft fair today, and Thomas is taking care of payroll stuff in the back." She frowned slightly as she glanced over her shoulder toward the admin office. "Not sure why it's taking *that* long. I hope my raise stuff went through all right."

That's odd. She didn't seem to know her boss had made a mad dash toward the parking lot. But perhaps he'd left something related to the shop in his car.

Rosie interrupted my reverie. "What can I get you?"

With my stomach taking priority, I ordered the last croissants and two coffees.

She paused before typing the request into her tablet register. "I would've thought you'd already gotten your coffee." Rosie pointed to the Brewed to Perfection cup sitting next to her workspace, her name scrawled in Charlotte's looping script.

I appreciated her show of support and was glad people in the community were willing to stick up for Charlotte. "I planned to, but I'm meeting a potential client here this morning and am running a bit behind," I fibbed. I didn't want Janica to even see me with a B2P coffee cup in case it triggered something within her.

"I get that." Carefully using her forearm, Rosie wiped a thin line of sweat away from her forehead. She already looked tired, and the shop had only been open for a little more than half an hour.

"How are you doing?" My gaze flicked to her still-present roots as I tapped my credit card against the reader. I hadn't noticed them when I'd run into her yesterday at Zaddick's because she'd been wearing her Tar Heels hat. "Did you end up treating yourself to a salon day?"

"No." Her cheeks grew pink. "I realized blowing one hundred bucks on a hair appointment wasn't the smartest money-saving move." She handed me my receipt. "I'll just pick up a boxed dye instead."

"You know, I have some great recipes on *Trending Topic* for homemade face masks. Add some cucumber slices, and you've got yourself a ready-made spa day." I'd never tell a woman to her face that she looked tired, but Rosie needed to prioritize her own needs above others. She worked hard for her employers and deserved to pamper herself every now and then.

She brightened as she plated our pastries on a candy-themed plastic tray. "Thanks for the tip."

"Do you know when Thomas will be free?" I switched to business mode, knowing my time was limited before Janica's arrival. "I've got some marketing stuff for him and Tom to review."

"Oh, you can go on back now if you want to." Rosie motioned down the short corridor with her shoulder as she poured our two coffees. "Tell him to hurry up and get back out here while you're at it," she joked as she moved to help the next customer.

I carried the tray to the table Hudson had claimed. "BRB. I'm gonna go have a quick chat with Thomas," I said as I placed our order in front of him.

"Didn't we just see him book it toward the parking lot?" Hudson arched an eyebrow.

I shrugged. "Maybe he came back in through the side door." I pointed to the unmarked exit adjacent to the business office.

"All right. But I'm not waiting." Hudson motioned to a gooey, drool-inducing pastry and licked his lips.

I laughed. "I'll be right out."

I gave Rosie a wave to indicate I was going to speak with her boss and hurried down the short hallway. "Hey, Thomas?" I called as I rapped my knuckles against the door.

To my surprise, it swung inward under the light force of my knock.

I stuck my head inside, momentarily shocked by the clutter. Given their Type-A personalities—takes one to know one, after all—I would have expected Tom and Thomas's workspace to be as spotless as their shop.

Boxes towered along the walls, and shelves were stacked with an array of cookbooks, baking ingredients, and Sweet Resolutions-branded paper products. In the center sat a desk covered in half-filled coffee cups, discarded plastic gloves, files, three-ring binders, and a laptop. "Looks like someone left in a hurry." I guessed Thomas hadn't returned from whatever errand he'd been in a panic to complete.

I searched for a place to sit and wait for him, but the only available seating was a patched-up leather desk chair. I needed to move away from the door to prevent Thomas from hitting me with it on his way back, so I scooted to an uncluttered spot in the corner.

I glanced at my watch. If he wasn't back in five, I'd write a message on a Post-It note and join Hudson. We still had to prep ourselves to question Janica.

I jumped at every little sound from the corridor, hoping it was Thomas returning, but five minutes passed with no sign of the German chocolatier. Maybe he'd had to run out and grab more ingredients, but I just couldn't shake the look of apprehension in his eyes.

With time against me, I searched the messy desk and found a scrap of paper. I hastily scrawled a note, hoping Thomas would be able to read my terrible handwriting. "I should just text him," I muttered as I placed the message on the laptop keyboard. I figured it would be the one place in this office where Thomas might actually see the note. But as I did so, my gaze drifted absently to the computer screen, and my mind zipped into focus at the words **Employee Record** next to a portrait of Rosie Miller.

Interesting. What was Thomas doing looking at Rosie's employment records? She'd mentioned he was doing payroll, so perhaps it had to do with her recent raise. I inched a bit closer to the laptop, trying not to knock over boxes of candy cup wrappers stacked beside the chair.

I skimmed the information despite its confidential nature. I couldn't help myself.

Cara Rosemary Miller, "Rosie," 33, Female, She/Her, Single, Current Residence: 235 Dunesberry Lane, 302-555-2093, Former Employer: CandiWorks, SC, References: MaryAnne Cuthbert—

"Hold up." Something squirmed to the forefront of my mind. *CandiWorks, SC?* "That can't be right." Rosie had moved here from North Carolina, not its southern neighbor.

Hadn't she?

I extracted my phone and typed in the business name. My stomach flipped when the Google info loaded.

CandiWorks. Location: Seabrook Island, South Carolina. There were no other businesses with that name, much less one in North Carolina.

And wait… Seabrook Island? As in, the place mentioned in Eric's throwback photo tribute?

My eyes widening, I returned my attention to Rosie's employment record photo. Could it be? With shaking fingers, I pulled up the old pic Eric had shared on his socials and zoomed in on the blonde woman's face.

"Hashtags!" I hissed as I compared them side by side. No wonder this woman had looked so familiar! Yeah, their hair colors might have been different, but those were totally blonde roots I'd seen peeking out from Rosie's head. Add a couple of years and a few pounds, and the beautiful mystery woman under Kiefer's arm was Rosie Miller.

"Or should I say Cara?" I studied the photos, my skin humming with triumph.

"I'm sorry?"

Her confusion caught me so off guard that I dropped my phone, and it landed with a *thud* on the desk.

"What are you doing, Coco?" Rosie's voice inched upward, her expression wary. "Where's Thomas?"

"I-I don't know. He wasn't back here when I arrived." I waved a nonchalant hand toward the laptop, trying to play off my snooping as low-key as possible. "I figured I'd pull the campaign numbers up for him to review when he gets back."

"Why did you call me Cara?" Her brown eyes bulged. "N-No one calls me that anymore."

"Um…" I couldn't explain away that one.

She moved forward, shoving a few towering boxes to get to the desk. "What are you—are those my employment records?" she cried through a muffled shriek.

231

"I'm sorry. They were already on the screen." I thought back to our strange encounter with Thomas. How he was running toward the parking lot in a panic. Had he put the pieces together, too? Had he examined her records while doing payroll and realized that Rosie had been lying about her North Carolina background this whole time? A background that tied her to a murder victim? And if that was the case, where was he?

I grabbed my phone and inched away from the desk, trying to put as much distance between us as possible. The cluttered office didn't allow for much breathing room, but I was certain I could make it to the door if I timed things right.

"So, you've figured it out." As Rosie glanced my way, I debated whether I should call for help or throw something at her while I attempted to make a run for it. I supposed I could do both. Hudson was only thirty feet away, after all.

But before I could make a move, Rosie's trembling hand went to her mouth to stifle a sob. "I'm so sorry, Coco. I swear, I didn't mean for it to happen." Tears ran down her cheeks, her makeup smearing. She hugged herself and sank to the floor, weeping quietly while she rocked on her heels.

Her regretful reaction was a first for me. The killers I'd met in the past had never shown the slightest bit of remorse.

"I-I just…when I saw him, standing there at Charlotte's booth, I-I went into full-on panic mode." Rosie held my gaze, her eyes red and watery. "I thought he'd f-found me, and I was p-petrified of what would happen."

A lump formed in my throat at the terror radiating from her. "Why?" I feared I knew the answer, but I wanted to hear confirmation for myself.

Rosie started shaking uncontrollably, and I found myself kneeling to wrap an arm around her. "He—Kiefer was a brute. I tried leaving him so many times, but somehow, he always convinced me to take him back." She wiped vigorously at her nose.

"About six months ago, I realized I had to disappear so he couldn't find me. I left my family, my friends, and my job behind to get away from him. I promised myself a new start." She shook her head, as if ridiculing her naive actions. "I dyed my hair, gained a little weight, deleted my social media, and even started going by Rosie." She tugged at her brunette ponytail for emphasis. "I found a UNC hat in the lost and found bin at the women's shelter I first stayed at. It g-gave me an idea for a believable backstory. I thought I'd done a good job leaving my life in Seabrook behind, but somehow...Kiefer still caught up to me." She leaned into my supportive hug, collapsing into another fit of sobs.

"Everything okay back here?" Hudson's head poked in through the doorway, his expression going from curiosity to alarm in an instant.

Call Gavin, I mouthed.

Rosie stiffened in my arms at Hudson's arrival. "No, it's not." She wiggled away from me, and for a moment, I thought she was going to book it. "I need to turn myself in. I can't let poor Charlotte be raked over the coals any longer than I already have."

Hudson's investigative instincts seemed to have evaporated on the spot, for he just stared at Rosie, speechless.

"I swear, Coco. I didn't mean for him to die." Rosie gripped my arm, her fingers like ice. "He was supposed to use his EpiPen. Kiefer *always* had his EpiPen on him." Tears again spilled from her sorrowful eyes. "I-I just wanted him to get sick and leave, so I could slip away without him seeing me."

I didn't like feeling sympathetic toward a killer, but I couldn't help it. I believed her. "Then let's go down to the CSC and have a chat with the police, Rosie." I patted her hand as tenderly as I could manage, despite my innate fear that she'd snap and do something to hurt Hudson or me.

"No need."

Rosie and I both jumped as Hudson stepped aside. Gavin and Adrian appeared in the doorway, their expressions full of grim sorrow.

"Now, Rosie," Gavin said as he took a tentative step into the office. He knocked over a stack of cookbooks in the process. "I must remind you that anything you say can and will be used against you in a court—"

"I did it. I'm the one who put peanuts in Kiefer Marsh's coffee." Rosie dropped her face into her hands. "But I swear, I didn't mean for him to die. H-He should've had his EpiPen on him."

Together, the four of us coaxed Rosie out of the office and into the corridor, where we could all move more freely. It was then I spotted a nerve-wracked Thomas wringing his hands as he watched the scene from behind the chocolate counter.

"Thomas came into the station to share his suspicions about Rosie," Gavin murmured in my ear. "While updating Rosie's profile in their payroll system this morning, he stumbled across something troubling. When confirming her employment details, he noticed her previous job was actually in South Carolina, not North Carolina, like she's always claimed. Thomas then realized Rosie's references were never checked—she interviewed so well that neither he nor Tom gave them more than a cursory glance. Normally, he wouldn't give such discrepancies a second thought; people are allowed to reinvent themselves. But for the last few days, Thomas told us that Rosie has appeared anxious and withdrawn at work, with her change in attitude curiously matching the timing of Kiefer's death. Since she wasn't being truthful about her past, he feared what else she might be hiding, so he came down to the station and suggested we question her."

I nodded, understanding why Thomas had been so alarmed when we'd run into him earlier. He believed he'd hired a killer. And he'd been right.

Chapter Thirty-Three

"Usually, when we crack a case, I feel happy." Jasper woefully sighed as he stroked Miranda's white fur. "This time, though, I just feel really sad."

"Me, too." Charlotte hugged a warm mug of hot cocoa to her chest. "Even if it does mean I'm free and in the clear."

As the core members of the Sleuth Squad, Hudson, Charlotte, Jasper, and I sat around Jasper's living room, still processing everything that had transpired over the last few hours. Not long after Gavin and Adrian had taken Rosie into police custody, Deacon had been summoned to the CSC to help the forensic team analyze the remaining crime scene evidence; while he wasn't "officially" on the case, Chief McInnis wanted him there to review the team's conclusions.

"That's quite charitable of you." Hudson raised a mug to Charlotte. "Considering Rosie was the reason you were under suspicion in the first place."

I knocked his arm, although I was careful not to make him spill his drink on Jasper's white furniture.

"Sorry," he admitted with a grimace. "I guess I'm still trying to reconcile with myself why *I* feel bad for a killer."

"Because Rosie didn't *mean* for him to die. She was scared about coming face-to-face with her abuser, and she reacted out of fear." I stared at the drink in my hands, wishing it would warm the chilliness that clutched my heart.

Rosie had gone willingly to the CSC, and when I'd asked to come along, neither Gavin nor Adrian had said no. So, I texted my apologies to Janica, and Hudson dropped me off at the station. Under the guise of helping Bernie with her press release to announce the results of Kiefer's death investigation, I was able to listen in on Rosie's confession from the viewing room through a two-way mirror.

As soon as Adrian and Gavin had her situated in the interrogation room, the truth spilled from her. She told them about her past and how her toxic relationship with Kiefer caused her to flee South Carolina and reinvent herself. How she'd panicked when the very man she'd been running from appeared at a booth near hers at the CSC festival. Once she'd gotten over her initial shock, Rosie told Thomas she was going on break. She wanted to put as much distance between her and Kiefer as possible.

But to her horror, after Kiefer collected his drink from Charlotte, he spotted her in the crowd and started heading her way. Rosie didn't think she could outrun him, and she panicked that if she made a scene, Kiefer would find a way to punish her. So, she distracted the teens scooping ice cream at Jewel's booth and grabbed a spoonful of peanut bits used for sundae toppings, covertly dumping them into her hand. Once Kiefer caught up to her, Rosie figured she could sneak the peanuts into the drink he'd gotten at Charlotte's and trigger his allergy. Since she knew he always carried an EpiPen, she assumed he'd medicate himself, and all would be well, but she'd at least buy herself some time to leave the festival and text her bosses that she'd gone home.

"I remember his grip on my right arm when he caught up to me," Rosie admitted, her voice faint and far away. Her tears had ceased, but sorrow still clung to her in the interrogation room. "He turned me around with a bone-chilling smile and said, 'I'd know that—*butt* anywhere.'"

It was clear from her hesitation that Kiefer's language had been more lewd.

Another mournful sob escaped her. "I contemplated just throwing the peanuts at him, but then he set the cup on a picnic table next to us so he could pull me into a tight hug. He then whispered," Rosie gulped, terror flickering in her eyes. "'Now that I've found you, I'm never letting you go.' At first, I was so scared, I couldn't move, but then I realized, from this position, I could drop the peanuts into his drink without him noticing." She straightened her shoulders as if to summon her courage. "Once I'd done so, I told him how surprised I was to see him and that we should talk in private. I asked him to meet me around the back of the CSC in five minutes. Based on his leering expression, I think he thought I was extending the invite for a hook-up. But whatever the case, it was enough for him to release me and let me head off on my own." Rosie closed her eyes and massaged her temples. "I was nearly at the parking lot when I started hearing shouts and screaming. Poor Coco yelling for an ambulance." She hung her head. "By the time I ran back to see what was going on, the paramedics had already left. At first, I honestly thought a festivalgoer had a heart attack from the heat or something. It didn't even cross my mind that it could've been Kiefer. I mean, he *always* had his EpiPen with him." Whatever strength she'd been holding onto dissolved, and Rosie collapsed into wailing cries. The interview ended there.

Too disturbed by what I'd learned, I wasn't much help to Bernie as we tried to compose a statement about the police having a suspect in custody. In the end, she shooed me away and said she'd send me what needed posting online. I didn't argue with her. I texted Hudson to pick me up at the CSC; I needed to get away from all the tragic sadness and be among my friends.

"What are the odds? I can't believe Rosie and Kiefer knew each other." Charlotte shook her head, bringing me out of my grim thoughts. "I always sensed she was a kindred soul, but because we both love chocolate and coffee...not this."

I reached for Charlotte's hand and squeezed. "I'm just glad we have answers and that you're all right."

"What will happen to her?" My bestie's eyes welled with tears. As I expected, she was taking the news about Rosie hard.

I sighed. "It all depends on whether or not the DA believes Rosie's telling the truth about the missing EpiPen."

A rapid knock at Jasper's front door jolted us upright in our chairs, preceding the appearance of an excited Deacon.

"Do come in," Jasper greeted him dryly as Deacon sat down on the couch next to Charlotte.

"Sorry to interrupt," he said breathlessly, "but I thought you guys might want an update."

"Did you run here?" Hudson eyed Deacon up and down. He *was* breathing quite heavily.

"Nah, just listen." Deacon's gaze glittered with intrigue. "We were able to match the partial print on the EpiPen."

We all braced ourselves, sharing worried looks with one another.

Deacon chuckled. Apparently, our collective response was not what he expected. "This is a good thing, guys. At least, it is for Rosie."

"What do you mean?" I scooted to the edge of my seat.

"The prints didn't match anyone in IAFIS," Deacon explained, "but they didn't match Rosie's either."

My brow inched upward in surprise. "Really?"

"So, whose are they?" Hudson asked on everyone's behalf.

"Janica Rice's."

"What?" we all burst out, with me adding, "How did you figure that out?" If I remembered my true crime podcasts correctly, you couldn't just randomly get someone's fingerprints without due process.

"I had a hunch," Deacon said with a sly grin. "Many interior designers hold real estate licenses so they can negotiate selling renovated properties on behalf of their clients. And in order to hold a real estate license..."

"You have to be fingerprinted!" I snapped my fingers in triumph. "That didn't even cross my mind. Good work, Deacon."

"Well, it is *my* job, after all." He tipped the brim of an imaginary hat. "I ran the partial print against their database, and bingo!"

"Did Gavin and Adrian bring Janica in?" Charlotte tugged his arm for more deets.

Deacon nodded. "At first, she swore up and down that she never touched an EpiPen at the festival. Adrian even gave her a way out, asking if she *could* have picked it up, thinking it was trash."

Jasper rolled his eyes. "How gentlemanly of him."

"Well, when she denied it and said it wasn't possible, they threw the fingerprint evidence at her. That got her talking." Deacon snorted. "She claims she found Kiefer's EpiPen on the ground as she was leaving the festival. Since he'd just dumped her, Janica thought she'd get back at him by throwing it away. She knew he'd flip out once he discovered it missing and that it would be a total headache to get the 'script refilled. She said she never considered the possibility he might actually *need* it. He'd always been careful about his allergy whenever they hung out."

I shivered. Given what we knew about Janica's tumultuous dating history, I could totally see her doing something foolishly awful in retaliation simply to inconvenience Kiefer. Being without his EpiPen would certainly cause high levels of stress for him until he replaced the prescription. "Do you believe her? Did she really not think he'd need it?"

Deacon's expression grew stormy. "She certainly won't be getting any Citizen of the Year awards for her actions, but at this point, it's hard to prove malicious forethought without her confessing to it."

I folded my arms. I didn't like this outcome.

Deacon must have seen my dismay, for he reached out and patted my knee. "I know it's not the concrete justice you're used to delivering, but it at least proves Rosie's story to some degree."

His words renewed a conflicting spark of hope. "That's true."

"What will happen to her?" Charlotte's eyes watered with compassion.

Deacon kissed her temple. "The DA will charge Rosie with manslaughter. Where that's a class B felony in Delaware, she could see as little time as two years. Her lawyers could even make a case for self-defense, given the circumstances, so time will tell."

"Time will tell." I nodded, relief unfurling within me. The last few days had been a whirlwind, and to top it off, we'd ridden an emotional roller coaster with this case. I warred with the conflict in my heart. My previous investigations had been so straightforward: killer = bad guy. But Rosie's story would give me nightmares for the foreseeable future. She'd been scared of Kiefer, and she'd reacted in fear. While he hadn't deserved to die, she also hadn't meant for it to happen. I hoped the DA and Rosie's defense team would reach an agreement so that justice could be served both ways.

Chapter Thirty-Four

Ten Days Later

Rae Livingston's flawlessly youthful beauty was slightly overshadowed by her scowling expression. "You won't get another offer this good, Coco." Her snide tone vibrated through my computer speakers.

I bowed my chin in acknowledgment, my webcam capturing the demure reaction. "I understand that, Rae. But *Trending Topic* is my baby, and I just can't give it up. Not even for your generous offer."

Rae studied her nails a moment before sighing. "What if I doubled it?"

Her words packed a punch. With *that* kind of money, I could retire before thirty and ride off into the sunset in glamorous style. Maybe spend my days doing charity work. But then I thought about my platform, my new vision for *Trending Topic's* future, and all the people I could reach.

"Again, your generosity is humbling, Rae, but I have to decline." I stared at her through our Zoom call. "*Trending Topic* is not for sale."

"Fine." Her response was clipped. This was clearly a woman used to getting her way. "Then we'll see how long you can last in the influencer space once I get my own brand up and running."

"Good luck." I summoned a sweet smile, doing my best to take the high road. I didn't appreciate the socialite model throwing threats in my face, but I doubted we'd be competing for the same online demographic much longer.

Rae didn't even say goodbye before she ended the call. The Zoom window went dark, and my stoic strength crumbled. I collapsed against the back of my desk chair, relieved to be done with delivering the tough news.

I closed out of Zoom and stared at the browser window that filled my computer screen. The draft of *Trending Topic's* new homepage stared anxiously back at me. Gone were the bright pinks, yellows, and oranges that my subscribers were familiar with. Its new teal-violet-and-lavender color scheme bathed the page, setting an entirely new tone for my blog. Had I made the right decision, passing on over six *million* dollars for what I'd spent years building? I hoped so.

Hudson certainly supported my choice. We'd spent the past week discussing Rae's offer and what it meant for my work with *Trending Topic*. Much of our discussion had revolved around the media attention Rosie's arrest had brought to our front doorstep. While the case had been wrapped up with much less fanfare than my previous forays into solving crimes, my name had inevitably trended to the top once the news broke. It seemed whenever wrongdoing surfaced in Central Shores, the online world expected Coco Cline to get involved.

So, why fight it?

And why limit my scope to Central Shores?

I had the platform, influence, and reach to make a difference when it came to unsolved mysteries, and it was time I embraced the change that I had been fighting against for so long. My passions and interests over the years had evolved, and I was no longer fulfilled by blogging about beauty, lifestyle, and entertainment. Someone happy with such things wouldn't be asking herself whether she should give it all up. She wouldn't be contemplating selling the brand she'd spent years building. No. It meant it was time for her to change course.

And change course, I would. I smiled proudly at my website's redesigned homepage showcasing the new name: *Trending Topic Mysteries*. I'd spent the last few days readying the site for launch, declaring my new mission:

There are thousands of unsolved and active cases worldwide.

Together, we just might help close them. Let's get these victims the justice they deserve. Welcome to the Sleuth Squad.

Yes, *Trending Topic* was getting a major content overhaul. No longer would I dedicate the space to beauty tutorials and décor recommendations. I'd leave that to the Rae Livingstons of the world. My new purpose was to feature active and unsolved cases each week, detailing how the public could help. Hudson's *Crime Sweet Home* had definitely served as inspiration. I could use my high-profile platform to shine the Internet spotlight on victims needing attention.

If I lost followers and subscribers along the way, so be it, but I could no longer deny where my passions lay: I was ready to embrace the title "crime-solving influencer."

The first case I planned to highlight was an unsolved kidnapping from the Wilmington area. A seven-year-old girl had gone missing during her walk to the school bus, and little had been uncovered about her whereabouts in the ten years since. Given that no ransom had ever been asked, the Wilmington police were hopeful she was still alive, perhaps abducted by someone aching for a daughter of their own. Whatever the case, her family deserved answers, and I hoped, by reigniting public interest in her story, we had a chance of getting them.

I double-checked the go-live settings for the page, the butterflies in my stomach fluttering at my internal countdown. My followers expected a new *Trending Topic* post every Saturday, and tomorrow morning, they'd be getting way more than they bargained for. But my mind was set.

I was ready.

I closed the browser, the anxious butterflies turning into tingling excitement. The next chapter was almost here.

And to celebrate, the OG Sleuth Squad would be arriving shortly. I couldn't wait to share the news. Everyone but Hudson was in the dark about my decision. My wonderfully supportive fiancé was already down at the beach setting up the coolers and our portable grill for the Friday evening festivities.

Jasper arrived first, with Miranda tucked securely under his arm in her sparkly, bright pink harness. It clashed terribly with his brown-and-blue swim trunks, but he didn't seem to care. I'd witnessed him walking her around the neighborhood in her harness over the last few days to prepare her for tonight's gathering—well, more like dragging her around. Miranda hadn't quite taken to the contraption as quickly as Jasper had hoped, but he also hadn't given up.

"Will Eli be joining us?" I raised a curious eyebrow as I scratched Miranda's chin.

Jasper didn't seem to notice my underlying intrigue. "Of course. He's on his way. He's coming directly from the gym."

I glanced at Miranda, wondering whether Eli had spoken with Jasper about his uneasiness around cats. While I *could* insert myself into the situation, I decided it was better for Eli to take the lead.

Amanda and Arthur arrived minutes later in their designer swimwear, followed by Charlotte, Deacon, and Maisie.

"What are we celebrating tonight?" Arthur asked once everyone had exchanged hugs. He gave Miranda the side eye in Jasper's arms. "She's not announcing her candidacy for president, is she?"

As we all chuckled, Jasper lifted his nose. "Miranda would have DC eating out of the palm of her...paw."

Maisie was already going wild sniffing Miranda's little feetsies, her tongue lolling out to the side in a happy-dog smile. Luckily, the two seemed to get along with one another.

Jasper nodded toward me. "This was Coco's summons, not mine."

I zipped my lips, indicating that everyone would have to be in suspense a little while longer. "Why don't you guys head down to the beach and get started on drinks?" I waved everyone through the condo and out to the back deck. "I'll wait for Eli."

I watched until my friends disappeared amongst the sand dunes before pulling out my phone to check the time. Six o'clock. Gavin and Adrian should be free by now.

I dialed Gavin's number, and he picked up on the first ring. "We've been expecting you, mademoiselle."

I laughed at his terrible French accent impersonation. "You said six, so... how did it go?"

Adrian's voice joined the line. "Our sting op was a total home run."

"Shouldn't the metaphor be a touchdown?" Gavin joked. "Since we did bust them with Lamar Jackson jerseys."

"Them?" I needed to know the details.

After Hudson and I had tipped the police off about Eric's potential forgery ring, the detectives had set up a small undercover operation with Bernie's help. Since Bernie was relatively new to the area, they'd sent her to Saucy Sid's to ask Sy about getting her husband a signed Lamar Jackson jersey. Sy was more than happy to assist her in the matter; he said his buddy sold sports memorabilia and had *just* been talking about a Jackson jersey he'd received. He gave her Eric's information and said he'd be in touch. As soon as Bernie left, Sy excused himself to take a call out back—which Adrian witnessed because he'd been assigned to tail Sy once Bernie vacated the pizza parlor. Adrian heard Sy tell Eric they needed a jersey done up by tomorrow, and with those condemning words, Adrian broke his cover to confront him.

"Sy crumbled like an oatmeal raisin cookie." Adrian scoffed as he finished recounting the tale. "It was kinda pathetic."

"But it sure made it easy to bring Eric in for questioning while we raided his little forgery factory." Gavin chuckled. "It's gonna take a while to figure out all the people he defrauded unless he and his lawyers decide to play ball."

"Maybe Coco could write a blog about it and ask people to come forward."

I rolled my eyes at Adrian's teasing. "Just say the word, and I'll whip up a feature," I shot right back.

Gavin's cheerfulness vanished. "You know that's not allowed, Cokes."

"I know, I know." Due to my consulting gig with the Central Shores PD, I'd come clean with them about my upcoming plans to rebrand my blog and turn my focus to featuring true crime stories. Chief McInnis hadn't been thrilled by my course correction, but even he admitted the attention I could bring to cold cases might end up being a good thing. As long as I didn't post about ongoing Central Shores investigations. "It's a conflict of interest," he'd grumbled. "We can't have you featuring cases from the department you *work* for. Defense attorneys would have a field day." It was a stipulation I was willing to uphold if it meant keeping my consulting contract with them.

"Well, I'm glad Eric's little enterprise is closing its doors."

"Thanks to you, Coco," Gavin added. "We appreciate you coming to us with this instead of trying to take Eric and Sy down yourself."

"No problem. You guys know sports aren't my thing."

The detectives laughed before telling me to enjoy my weekend, and we said goodbye. "See you on Monday." I smiled enthusiastically as I hit the End Call button.

The timing coincided with a knock on the door, and I found Eli standing there in his gym clothes.

"Hope your dress code for the evening isn't too formal." He blushed as he motioned to his tank top and shorts.

"Oh, this outfit was for a client call." I motioned to the A-line sundress I'd worn to impress Rae Livingston. "My swimsuit's underneath. Everybody else is already down at the beach. You actually might be overdressed," I teased as I welcomed him inside.

He cleared his throat, my joke not even fazing him. "Uh, so Jasper's here?"

I nodded. "With Miranda." I studied his nervous demeanor. "Are you gonna be okay? Did you tell him yet?"

Eli sighed. "I've tried, like, eight times this week." He rubbed his neck, his cheeks growing darker by the minute. "I just can't bring myself to burst his bubble. That cat has made him so blissfully happy. And she's a nice cat. I think, over time, I can get used to her. Conquer my fears and all."

I patted his shoulder, feeling sympathy for his conundrum. "You're a good guy, Eli. It warms my heart to hear how much you care about Jasper. But remember, you also deserve your own happiness."

"He *does* make me happy." Eli's brow furrowed with determination. "Didn't I read on your blog recently that you've partnered with some online therapy service? MindSet?"

"MindMatters," I clarified. "It's been a great outlet for me. Dr. Ashawari and I covered a *lot* of ground during yesterday's session." From lingering concerns about Kiefer's case to Rae's offer to going in a new career direction, we'd blown through our thirty-minute session in the blink of an eye.

Eli snorted. "I bet." His expression turned serious. "But maybe it's time for me to actually get the help I need rather than living with this phobia."

I gave him a one-armed hug, which was a bit hard since I could barely reach around his muscular back. "I can't believe you read my blog."

And I hope you're not getting used to it...

Eli helped me carry a few six-packs of beer and hard seltzers down to the beach, and soon, we joined our friends. Hudson and Arthur chatted at the grill while Amanda lounged on a beach chair with Miranda snoozing on her lap. Deacon and Jasper were playing a netless game of badminton, and Charlotte was taking pictures of Maisie rolling around in the sand.

"Hey! You made it!" Jasper's entire face lit up at Eli's arrival, and he ran over to kiss him on the cheek in greeting.

Eli squeezed his hand. "I'm here and ready for anything."

"You've gotta be with this crowd." Jasper gestured his racket toward the fun, carefree scene.

Once drinks were flowing and burgers came off the grill, I couldn't help but marvel at the warm, jovial sight around me. I was so incredibly grateful to have such wonderful friends in my life. Friends who didn't hesitate to help whenever one of us was in trouble. Friends who, without a doubt, would support my decision to relaunch my blog as *Trending Topic Mysteries* (although Jasper would undoubtedly make a fuss). The Sleuth Squad had my back, and I had theirs. Whatever challenges came our way, we'd tackle them like the ultimate social media collab—together, with style.

Acknowledgments

Every book is a journey, and I'm beyond grateful for those who have walked this path with me.

First, my thanks to Shawn Reilly Simmons and the dedicated team at Level Best Books. Your belief in this series has meant everything, and I'm so fortunate to have you in my corner.

To J.C. Kenney, Leah Dobrinska, Lori Robbins, Melissa Green, and Carol Ayer, your friendship and encouragement keep me going in this rollercoaster industry. I'm very lucky to have such talented artists in my life.

To my *Bookish Time* community, your enthusiasm and encouragement make every step of this adventure even more rewarding.

A big shout-out to readers Deborah Almada and Paula Charles. Their suggestions of Elizabeth Taylor and Queen Meryl Hashtag sparked the PURRFECT moniker for Jasper's new, fierce feline friend, Miranda.

And finally, to my beloved readers, thank you for taking a chance on my writing, for spending time with these pages, and for making this journey possible. Your support is everything.

About the Author

Sarah E. Burr lives near New York City. Hailing from the small town of Appleton, Maine, she has been dreaming of being Nancy Drew since she was a little girl. After not finding any mysteries in corporate America, Sarah began writing some of her own. She is the author of the Book Blogger Mysteries and the Court of Mystery series. Sarah is also the author of the award-winning Trending Topic Mysteries and Glenmyre Whim Mysteries. *You Can't Candle the Truth* was a 2022 NGIBA Best Mystery Finalist, a 2022 Silver Falchion Best Supernatural Mystery Finalist, and was accepted into the Indie Author Project Select collection. *Too Much to Candle* was a 2023 NGIBA Best Paranormal Finalist. Most recently, *#TagMe for Murder* was named a 2024 NGIBA Best Click Lit Fiction Finalist.

Sarah is a member of Sisters in Crime. She is also the creative mind behind BookstaBundles, a content creation service for authors. Sarah is the producer and co-host of *It's Bookish Time TV*, a web channel featuring live-streamed author interviews and book discussions. She writes as a member of the Writers Who Kill blogging team. When she's not spinning up stories, Sarah sings Broadway show tunes, plays video gaming, and enjoys walks with her dog, Eevee. Stay connected with Sarah and receive free short stories via her newsletter: https://bit.ly/saraheburrbookssignup.

SOCIAL MEDIA HANDLES:

Instagram: @authorsaraheburr

Facebook: https://www.facebook.com/authorsaraheburr

AUTHOR WEBSITE:

https://www.saraheburr.com

Also by Sarah E. Burr

Trending Topic Mysteries:
#FollowMe for Murder
#TagMe for Murder
DM Me for Murder

Glenmyre Whim Mysteries:
You Can't Candle the Truth
Too Much to Candle
Flying Off the Candle

Book Blogger Mysteries:
Over My Dead Blog
Dearly Deleted

Court of Mystery:
The Ducal Detective
A Feast Most Foul
A Voyage of Vengeance
A Summit in Shadow
Throne of Threats
Paradise Plagued
Burdened Bloodline
Sovereign Sieged
Crown of Chaos
Harrowed Heir
Ravaged Reign
Innocence Imprisoned
Ardent Ascension
Eternal Empire

www.ingramcontent.com/pod-product-compliance
Lightning Source LLC
Chambersburg PA
CBHW020615110726
47899CB00002B/521